An Eternal Flame

Seven Hills Two

by

Sue Campbell

www.fast-print.net/store.php

An Eternal Flame
Copyright © Sue Campbell 2012

ISBN 978-178035-243-5

First published 2012 by
FASTPRINT PUBLISHING
Peterborough, England.

Dedication

To Those Whom I Love
and
To Those Who Love Me.

ONE

The young woman threw herself onto the sofa on the far side of the kitchen. "She's dead, my Mum's dead!" Veronica Montgomery cried out.

Maggie, her adopted mother was abruptly tugged out of her daydreaming and she stared at the forlorn creature, now curled into a fetal ball and moaning pitifully to herself. She gripped the edge of the granite worktop and the full impact of her daughter's words suddenly hit her like a tsunami.

"Has something happened to Caroline?" she uttered in a low voice, her heart beating like a kettle drum in her chest.

Veronica looked dazed and confused for a moment and then realised, with a lump in her throat that her emotional entrance had been misinterpreted. The woman who had been part of her life for the last twelve years now had tears in her eyes. She looked like she was about to collapse with shock.

Veronica suddenly felt guilty and selfish. She propelled herself off the sofa and launched herself into Maggie's arms, wrapping her own upper limbs tightly around her. "I am so sorry, Mummy. I didn't mean to scare you. I wasn't referring to *Mum*. When I was out in town this morning someone from Birthlink rang me on my mobile-"

Maggie disentangled herself and perched on one of the stools at the breakfast bar, relief flooding through her. Just for a moment she had thought that something awful had befallen her darling wife, Caroline. The two of them had been married for sixteen years now and the very thought of life without her soul mate by her side frightened Maggie so much, that for her own sanity she deliberately never gave it a moment's contemplation. She actually felt quite nauseous for a second or two, but the gravity of her beloved daughter's words hit her and it was now her turn to do the comforting.

"Birthlink, that's the charity that's been conducting a search for your *real* mother, right?"

Veronica nodded, leaning back against the sink. "They have been really thorough. They found her name on the Adoption Contact Register for Scotland, but she was marked as-."

She gulped, squeezing her eyelids tightly closed in a vain attempt to fight back the fresh tears. "It said she had died when I was four years old. They had even researched the archives at the Glasgow Gazette. Apparently, her body was found floating in the Clyde."

Maggie had dreaded this moment ever since her and Caroline had welcomed the bubbly toddler into their home thirteen years ago. She was an intelligent child, and had always had a clear idea of who and what she was. She adored both her adopted mothers, but from a very young age Veronica had had a strong desire to find out who her birth parents were. Now she was over the age of sixteen she had a legal right to make enquires, and it seemed like she had stumbled on the truth.

All Caroline and Maggie had ever known was the mother's name, date of birth and occupation. It never seemed to bother Veronica that she was the daughter of a prostitute. She was more concerned that her father had been listed as *unknown*.

On that winter afternoon, gazing out of the window onto the two cherry trees in their back garden, their bare branches still wearing their frosty coats, Maggie took Veronica into her arms and held her tightly. The seventeen year old girl, even in her distressed state was breathtakingly beautiful. She had the same mesmerising green eyes as Maggie, and her hair was the colour of freshly made straw.

Maggie, now fifty-five years of age also cut an impressive figure. True be told, her hair had lost some of its former lustre and her skin, despite careful moisturising had been robbed of its youthful clasticity, but all-in-all married life and being a mother suited her very well.

She still worked for Eaglesham Properties, albeit only part-time in the heart of Stirling and although she continued to enjoy her job as their longest-serving estate agent she was secretly counting the years to her retirement. Caroline was due to retire later that year, so in another five years' time both of them would be enjoying the fruits of a lifetime's hard labour.

****

Maggie's estranged husband, Andrew had died suddenly almost twenty years ago, leaving her free to marry her first and only girlfriend. In his will, he had left her his entire estate although she had magnanimously given away his beloved Mercedes to his then boyfriend, Steve. The three of them still stayed in the former marital home in Stirling and his luxury flat in Milngavie, a small town west of Glasgow continued to provide them with a substantial monthly income. For fifteen years it had seen a swift succession of tenants, but for the last five a middle-aged gay chap had stayed there. He seemed really settled and in a funny kind of way it was a fitting tribute to her late husband.

At the time, discovering that her spouse fancied men rather more than her had been terribly difficult for Maggie to cope with, but it had all worked out for the best, really. According to Steve, Andrew had started seeing a counsellor to *cure him of his queerness* but, in reality there was little that could be done. He had harbored a lot of self-loathing and his death, although tragic was in a way a blessing for him, rather like someone who was inflicted with an interminable illness.

After all these years Maggie still had no idea of how he had actually met his Maker. His body had been found in an underground car park in the Anderston area of Glasgow, and the Procurator Fiscal had deemed that he had died by natural causes, a massive heart attack in fact. Whatever the circumstances, his passing had enabled her to marry again, and adopt little Veronica.

Strangely enough, some of her daughter's mannerisms were uncannily like Andrew's had been. She would still flick rebel strands of hair out of her eyes as she did when she had been a youngster, and although she did her best to control her sudden flare-ups in mood her fiery temper had transformed itself over the years from mere toddler tantrums into bloody-minded assertiveness, often tinged with genuine malice. Andrew had had a similar cruel ruthless streak.

Veronica was currently studying for her Highers, and had her heart set on becoming a successful businesswoman, running her own hotel chain. Maggie had no doubt that she would achieve her ambitions.

Despite the difficulties of bringing up a child not genetically linked to either of them, both Maggie and Caroline never regretted their decision. In a way, they mirrored a more traditional family. Maggie only worked mornings at the estate agency. In the afternoons she cracked on with the housework, and by the time Caroline's key could be heard in the front door, it was not long before three steaming plates of delicious food were placed on their dining room table.

As the main proverbial breadwinner, Caroline had taken on the male role, both as provider and parent. She was more able to control their daughter, and even to her surprise had become rather a strict disciplinarian.

Maggie was Veronica's best friend, but she treated Caroline with due respect and deference. She did not quite call her, *Madam,* but at times the thought had crossed her mind. Veronica was certainly a very self-assured young woman and outside of the home was a force to be reckoned with but, inside their own four walls it was Caroline who was the boss.

****

Twelve years ago tragedy had hit the family, and the whole experience had transformed them into a very close unit. They all subconsciously knew the pecking order, but the love which bound them together was almost palpable. The Montgomery's were a proud bunch who revelled in, rather than shied away from their unconventionality.

It had been Veronica's first day at Stirling Primary School. The little girl had chatted non-stop on the twenty minute walk back home. She had gripped her mother's hand in excitement at both seeing her again, this was the first time they had ever been parted, and at the thought of telling her all her news.

As soon as she had tore off her coat, she had rushed upstairs and thrown her arms around their four year old cat who was dozing as usual on her bed. Old age had claimed the lives of both Archie and Olivia, the two felines who had shared their lives previously, but Lucky had since claimed Veronica's heart. In her enthusiasm she inadvertently frightened him and he leapt off the bed, bounding out of the door and down the stairs. Veronica, eager to tell her usually docile friend all her news had chased after him.

Maggie, most uncharacteristically had failed to close their front door properly. Veronica followed Lucky across the main road running parallel to their house. She was hit by a passing motorist speeding on his way back to work, after a particularly long and alcohol-fueled lunch. Lucky made it across safely, but the little girl somersaulted off the car's bonnet and lay crumpled on the tarmac. Maggie heard her scream and as she cradled her limp body in her arms, tears had streamed down her cheeks.

The proceeding events were but a blur to her now. Both she and Caroline had kept up a constant vigil between them at Veronica's bedside. The little girl had sustained a broken leg, but it was her head injuries that were of more concern. She had remained in a coma for a month but, miraculously had regained full consciousness.

After six months convalescing at home she had

returned to school as if nothing had befallen her. It took a great deal longer for Maggie to forgive herself. Caroline had fussed about the two of them like an old mother hen. The whole tragic incident bound them even tighter together.

****

By the time Caroline returned home from work that evening Maggie and Veronica had their supper prepared and were sat down together on the sofa, both sipping a dram of their favourite whiskey liqueur. Maggie knew that her daughter would need a lot support from them both to grief over the death of her mother.

As they were chopping up the vegetables Veronica had related a dream to her that she had experienced, just as she was coming out of her coma after the accident all those years ago. She had never mentioned it before to either her or Caroline in fear that it would upset them in some way.

She had seen a woman with blonde hair and green eyes standing at the end of a tunnel, gazing fondly at her. She had known immediately that it was her birth mother. Veronica had greeted and beckoned to her, but the vision had faded before the woman could reach her.

"I knew then, Mummy that I would never see her again, but I had to be sure. After all, it was only a dream, and they don't always come true, do they? I so wish this one hadn't!"

Maggie had held her close and the two of them had wept together, lamenting how cruel life could be sometimes.

Wiping her eyes, Veronica had stated with steely determination, "I am going to find out how she ended up in her watery grave. Somebody must have put her there. I don't care what she was or, or what she did. She was my mother, that's all that matters. Somebody will pay for this!"

Maggie had felt, just for a moment quite scared of her daughter. Memories of Andrew's behaviour the year or so before his untimely demise had flashed into her mind. He had been determined to wreak his revenge on those he deemed had done him a disservice, she concluded, and it now felt as if history was repeating itself. Knowing her daughter, she would discover how her birth mother had met her premature death and, no doubt who her father had been too.

A shiver passed through her as she stood up and threw her arms around her darling wife.

TWO

Thirty miles away, later that same day Lyn clinked her champagne flute against Clare's, and leant over the table to plant a kiss on her wife's full lips. "Happy Anniversary, darling!"

Both women were fifty years of age. Clare was as dark-haired as Lyn was blonde. Although neither could be described as particularly vain, they both assisted Mother Nature to keep the signs of maturity at bay by dyeing their locks as required, to conceal any traces of grey.

They had been married almost as long as Maggie and Caroline, and now that it was December it was time once again for the annual celebration of their love and commitment to each other.

****

Lyn's divorce had been incredibly messy, both in regards to the division of property and in an emotional sense. Her husband, Stefan had refused to either leave or sell their house in Stirling. There was no way he could raise the cash to buy his wife out.

Eventually, after much negotiation with the bank she and Clare had taken out a joint loan, and bought Stefan's share. It was fortuitous at the time that Clare was raking in decent sums from the royalties of her now bestselling books, and that the marital home was on a modest scale.

Once everything was settled and Stefan had found a new home for himself and their two boys Clare and Lyn had decided to sell the two-bedroomed terraced house, and move away from Stirling. Just the thought of accidentally bumping into her husband again brought tears to Lyn's eyes.

He had forced her to choose between him and Clare, and although she knew that she had made the only choice that her heart would permit the loss of her marriage still grieved her deeply. She would always love Stefan, and to have caused so much pain to someone whom she cared for was both out of character, and very painful. She was not *in love* with him anymore, but she was pretty certain that his feelings for her had never changed.

Despite her best efforts of persuasion, Lyn's sons never accepted that their mother had forsaken her marriage to set up home with a woman. For ten years both of them had refused to even talk to her on the telephone, let alone meet up, but eventually after they had both moved into their own flats a relationship was re-established between the three of them.

It transpired that unsurprisingly Stefan had been feeding them falsehoods about their mother and her new lover. Lyn felt that things would never be quite as good as they had been before she had started her affair with Clare, but they had all certainly become much closer recently.

As for Stefan well, he never fully recovered from the destruction of his marriage, and vowed to never trust a woman again. He would date occasionally, but every time there was a hint of something blossoming between him and his lady friend-of-the-moment he broke off the relationship. He enjoyed being physically close to another person, but he knew that he would never allow himself to fall in love again.

****

Lyn and Clare now stayed together in Morningside, just a five minute walk away from where Clare's brother Grant and his husband resided. The four of them spent a lot of time in each other's company, both socially and professionally.

Duncan was now the editor-in-chief at his publishing company *Adonis,* and their workload was such that they currently employed five administrative assistants who doubled up as acquisition readers. Essentially, they scanned all the new submissions and passed them onto Duncan if they felt that they would fit nicely onto their list. It was quite a responsible job, deciding the fate of an aspiring author and Lyn, as one of the employees took her role very seriously. Even after all these years she still felt proud to be married to one of their highest earning writers.

It was so much more fun there than in the Stirling library where she used to work. At Adonis her duties were often challenging, and she loved her colleagues. For most of her days at the library she had been the only member of staff on duty, and not all of her customers had been as friendly as Clare!

She was good at her job, and when the two couples went out together Grant found it rather difficult to steer the conversation away from the subject of publishing, and all things literal.

He still worked at the private clinic in the genteel suburb of Morningside south-west of Edinburgh. He was fond of remarking that if Adonis moved its premises into the area then they could all rise just half an hour before the start of their respective working days and, still be at their desks or, in Grant's case the operating table, perfectly turned out and, on time!

****

It was thanks to the two men that Clare and Lyn's wedding reception, and subsequent honeymoon had been so memorable. Grant and Duncan had used a gay couple to plan their civil partnership, and they had recommended them to the two women.

Scottish Wedding Consultants had arranged the whole

thing with effortless perfection, as well as sorting out the legal paperwork. Edinburgh Castle was the obvious choice for the venue, and the subsequent photographs were dramatically stunning.

Created 340 million years BC the castle was proudly perched on a volcanic rock, overlooking the city. King David had built the fortress in the year 1130. Within the walls a chapel was constructed, and dedicated to his mother Queen Margaret. In 1250 she had been canonised as St. Margaret of Scotland for her numerous acts of piety and charity. For many years she would personally serve the local orphans and the poor before she sat down for her meal. It was in this esteemed place of worship that Clare and Lyn's union had been blessed.

The Civil Partnership Act did not allow any form of religious activity to occur during the process of actually registering the union, so that was held in the Queen Anne Building in the heart of the castle. It had been a small intimate affair. Both of Clare's parents were long deceased, and Lyn's mother although very much still alive just could not accept the fact that her only daughter now described herself as a lesbian. The public declaration of their love for each other was therefore only witnessed by a handful of friends, and of course Clare's beloved brother, but that had made it all the more special really.

Following the reception back in the Queen Anne Building the wedding breakfast was served. It was

naturally authentic Scottish. There was a choice of
starters including wild smoked salmon served on a bed
of free-range scrambled egg, and for the main course
one could select either Kirkcaldy Stovies made of
onions with minced and corned beef, or a Tipsy Grouse
Casserole. The latter was liberally laced with a blended
whiskey, the label on the bottle complementing the
game bird.

Their marriage had taken place in early December so
Lyn had suggested some hearty fare to warm their
guests. A slice of Clootie Dumpling served with custard,
or a generous piece of whiskey cake was on offer to
complete the feast.

Much later that unforgettable day the newly weds had
taken leave of their friends and family, and settled
themselves into the Heriot Suite at The Witchery Hotel,
just along the road from the castle. Clare had swept Lyn
onto the sumptuous four-poster bed with its antique
gothic oak headboard. It was lavishly draped with
embroidered gold and green velvet hangings. For that
first evening at least, they had barely noticed much else
for the consummation of their marriage was the
dominating thought in both their minds. They had been
lovers for almost a year previously, but that night Clare
made love to her new wife with a renewed tenderness
and passion. They both delighted in many orgasms
before the winter sunshine had streamed into their
opulent *lust den*.

****

Clare gazed lovingly at her wife. "I love you with all my heart, darling. Thank-you for this gorgeous ring too."

She proudly displayed the ruby and diamond eternity ring. The light from the candelabrum reflected romantically off the precious stones. "Guess this means I've got you for ever, eh," she laughed, returning Lyn's kiss.

For a change, it was Clare who had prepared their supper that evening. Usually, Lyn returned from work in the early evening, and more often than not she would find their breakfast things still cluttering up the kitchen sink. Generally speaking, both women were pretty tidy around the house, but if an idea for some storyline flashed into her mind of a morning then all thoughts of domesticity slipped from Clare's thoughts.

Shortly after they had moved into their Morningside house, and Lyn had started working at Adonis Clare did prepare their evening meal every day, but she was not a terribly good cook, and in a funny kind of way Lyn felt more comfortable running the household. Before long they had settled into a routine.

Lyn did most of the cooking and the general household chores whilst Clare, who had been taught the rudiments of mechanics by her late father many years before would tinkle with their car, if needs be. To take a break from writing she would fervently grab the mower, or do some simple maintenance tasks that required attention. Lyn would often joke that they were more stereotypical than the average heterosexual couple, but they were both extremely happy in their roles, and within their marriage. They still fancied each other something rotten. Lyn could see the now very familiar build up of lust dulling Clare's exquisite green eyes.

All of a sudden, Lyn found herself being shoved up against their ceramic hob cooker with Clare's hands hungrily roving across her body.

"I want you so badly," Clare gasped, sliding her hands up under Lyn's skirt, and gripping each of her buttocks under her cotton panties.

Lyn could feel own urgency as her clitoris demanded attention, and an intense moist heat emanated from her groin. "My God, you're on fire this evening. If this is what cooking does for you, perhaps you should take over completely!" she exclaimed.

"No, I'll leave all that domestic stuff to the expert, but you must admit I do make a *mean* prawn curry," Clare boasted as she deftly removed her wife's panties, and tossed them theatrically across the kitchen. They landed on Toby's head, their two year old cat who grabbed them with his paws, and started purring loudly.

"Would you look at him! He gets as turned on by your

delicious fragrance as I do."

Lyn giggled, "That sounds just slightly *too* weird!"

As Clare's fingers were feverishly exploring the area between her legs, she in turn was tugging off her wife's jumper, and releasing her breasts from their snowy white bra. Her generous nipples were already erect, and Lyn sucked gently on each one in turn, eliciting a deep moan from their owner.

Clare by now was thrusting two fingers in and out of Lyn's vagina, as she pushed her own still clothed lower body against her. Lyn could feel her orgasm building and she momentarily stopped what she was doing, and kissed Clare with heartfelt urgency and love. Their bodies were now pressed tightly together, just allowing room for Clare's hand to bring her wife's passion to a climax.

Just as she was about to come Clare lifted Lyn's bottom up onto the flat surface of the cooker, and gently pushed her backwards. She bent her own knees and buried her head in Lyn's crotch. She had only to lick her clitoris once or twice before Lyn bucked convulsively. Clare lapped up her copious ejaculate, and then took her once more into her arms.

"Bloody hell, Clare if I had known sex would be that good with a woman I would never have bothered with men at all. That has got to be one of the most *satisfying* orgasms that I have ever had," she gasped, holding her wife in a tight embrace.

Clare laughed, "You always say that. Perhaps like a decent Cheddar my technique improves with age. Like you, I was a lesbian virgin when we met, and trust me I *haven't* been practising during the day here on my own!"

Lyn reluctantly broke away, and started loading their plates into the dishwasher. "You might not have a daytime playmate, but I've seen those novels of yours. Some of the scenes are so sexy that even I blush when I read them. Sometimes I feel a bit like the proverbial guinea pig. Your imagination concocts some steamy fantasy whilst I am out at work, and then you try it out on me to see if it works." She had her back to Clare as she wiped the surfaces and stretched up to put the cruet back into the cupboard.

Clare lit up a cigarette and took a deep drag from it, blowing smoke rings seductively. She confessed, blushing, "Well, you may have a point there, but one could hardly call it *vivisection.* We might be getting on a bit, but our sex life sizzles like newly weds."

Lyn gazed around the now tidy kitchen and pulled Clare up from her chair. "Sweetheart, I'm most definitely *not* complaining. Marrying an author, especially one who writes erotica so superbly, and profitably was the best move that I ever made. I would be delighted to be your *lab rat* any day of the week!"

Clare laughed and turned off the light. "Goodnight, Toby," she called out to their cat who was now fast asleep, Lyn's panties tucked beneath his paws.

She turned to Clare who was locking the front door, yawning noisily. "Come on, Sleepy Head! I've a few fantasies of my own to try out on you."

Clare looked at her greedily, raising her eyebrows in a quizzical fashion.

"The first one involves two ladies and a tubful of hot water, so get up those stairs!" Lyn ordered. She flicked an used tea towel at Clare's ascending bottom.

The local kirk chimed its hourly peal as the two women collapsed in a heap onto the bathroom floor.

Suffice to say, that it was another hour before they were finally soaking themselves in the foamy water, one at either end of the bath tub. Clare rubbed soap onto a flannel and kneeling, being careful not to drown the carpet, she gently washed her wife's breasts. Playfully dabbing her nose with a spot of foam, she whispered, "Happy Anniversary, sweetheart."

THREE

Detective Chief Inspector Peter MacDuff was snuggled up to his wife one morning the following week. His mobile rang and sleepily pressing it to his ear, he mumbled, "MacDuff here." He recognised the caller as his Sergeant, Jimmy Jack.

"I'm so sorry to disturb you, sir," he stated apologetically, "but another body has been found."

DCI MacDuff glanced at his clock radio. It was just eight o'clock. On rising from his bed and pulling aside the heavy velvet curtains he groaned at the snow flakes falling silently onto his lawn.

"I'm on holiday, man. What happened to McGovern? I handed everything over to him yesterday."

Detective Sergeant Jack explained to him that the gentleman in question had telephoned in sick with a nasty bout of influenza the previous night. Detective Chief Superintendent Lennox had been most insistent that despite his scheduled leave MacDuff was to handle the case.

DCS Lennox was the same age as his inferior, and it was a cause of persistent irritation to MacDuff that he had successfully secured the top spot, rather than himself. Lennox's boss was one Commander Banquo, a woman of all things.

Apparently, the body had been found at the Hermitage

of Braid and Blackford Hill, a local nature reserve situated to the south of Edinburgh. The popular haunt laid under the Braid Hills between the suburbs of Morningside and Liberton. The ancient woodland nestled in the bottom of the glen along the course of the Braid Burn. A much loved area of natural beauty, it was a haven for wildlife including woodpeckers, owls, shrews and bats. It was amongst the broad-leaved trees that the unfortunate soul had been discovered by a local walker.

This was the third body found in the vicinity of one, or other of the seven hills of the city. The first one, a young woman in her early twenties had laid undiscovered for three days, according to her post mortem results. Her last resting place was on Calton Hill in some thick undergrowth, and the second on Corstophine, the wood-covered ridge within the prosperous district of the same name, three miles west of the city centre.

This was the area that the understandably irate Inspector MacDuff resided with his good lady wife of ten years standing. Resigned to his fate, he informed his sergeant that he would meet him at the crime scene.

Peter had been with the Lothian and Borders Police Force for thirty years, and was one of their longest-serving officers. Now in his late fifties, he was not far off retirement, and his wife made it all too clear to him on an almost daily basis that *tomorrow would not be soon enough*. Why she ever married a serving police officer still puzzled him.

It was standard policy that wives accompanied their senior ranking husbands to formal functions, but Mrs MacDuff always made such a fuss. Truth be told, she and Commander Banquo had *hit it off* rather badly from the onset.

Perhaps they *both* admire the way I wear my moustache, Peter mused darkly as he drew on his silk thermals, and prepared himself for the extreme weather waiting to greet him on that supposedly first day of his long-awaited for vacation.

****

In Glasgow four days previously, a stocky man was addressing a young woman. She was knelt at the feet of a youth a few years younger than herself. "Come on, sweetheart," he urged, "you're supposed to be enjoying it!"

Enjoying it? That's really funny, Melanie thought sarcastically. The guy stunk of BO, and she had seen better cocks on the male geriatric ward where she worked as a care assistant. The government hospital payed poorly, and with personal debts starting to overwhelm her Melanie had leapt at the chance of earning some extra cash to ease her, and her elderly mother's lives. She tried desperately to act her part as requested, and moaned theatrically as she moved her mouth up and down the man's shaft.

She had been *moonlighting* for just over a month now, but only at the weekends. Her neighbour, Joan had recommended her to the film company. They both stayed on a housing estate by the name of *Easterhouse*. It laid six miles east of the city centre. Infamously, it had been the destination of choice for the former Conservative Party leader Iain Duncan Smith in 2002. He had wandered around the run-down grey concrete blocks, his camera crew recording every hand gesture and verbal utterance which he made. The honorable Member of Parliament did his best not to step in the dog mess, or crush the hypodermic syringes carelessly discarded by the local heroin addicts. Easterhouse had been used as a showcase example of a broken Britain.

Now twenty-five years later it was the epitome of good taste thanks to the government currently in power, the British Traditionalist Party.

****

Formerly a mere splinter group of the infamous British National Party or *BNP* as they were more commonly known, the BTP had gained more public support than their parent party had ever acquired. They had been elected to govern the country ten years ago, and although their policies angered many people a change in the voting system had allowed them to acquire a working majority and for their leader, one David Campbell to find himself accepting the keys of Number

Ten Downing Street. The BTP's manifesto had one primary goal. They wished to restore public and self-discipline to the United Kingdom.

The education system was reverted back to as it had been in the 1980s and before, with the emphasis on core subjects rather than abstract teaching methods. Capital punishment was reintroduced for murder, sexual crimes and drug trafficking, and corporal punishment was now widely used in both the public and private schools. Classes were compulsory for all prospective parents to encourage them to raise their children to respect them, and their fellow citizens. Politeness and good manners were promoted throughout society.

Other countries of the world started to respect the UK again, but although trading relations with many of them were at their all-time best their inhabitants were only permitted to gaze at the island. There was now no immigration whatsoever. Great Britain had morals and a sense of purpose again.

It had become a society akin to the 1950s, with one major difference. Homosexuality was now positively encouraged, and any incidents of homophobia were severely dealt with. Public displays of affection other than mere hand holding were discouraged though, whatever one's sexuality. Self-discipline was of the utmost importance, after all. Any couple of whatever mix of genders could marry. Civil partnerships were now *old hat*.

No longer was Scotland's largest city overrun with dusky-skinned people, or even any one with a slightly foreign accent. Many of its previous Asian residents had taken up the Party's voluntary repatriation scheme and the rest had slowly disappeared, so that the only accents that one heard on the streets were either Celtic or English.

The Ministry for Building Works had razed the old tenements to the ground, cleared the land of all of its detritus, and in their place had constructed blocks of apartments. They had all been put up for rent by the housing association who bought them, but very few of Easterhouse's original tenants were welcomed back.

Unemployment was not a bar to signing a new contract. A greater percentage of the population of Great Britain were now gainfully employed especially since the jobs previously filled by migrant workers had become vacant, but the situation was far from perfect. The phrase, *the best government is always in opposition*, rang true yet again. It was the alcoholics, drug addicts, unmarried mothers and of course, the foreigners who were turned away.

Considering that Melanie and Joan were none of these they were offered shorthold tenancies. The rents were of course higher than before with the government means-testing each prospective tenant.

If it was not for the fact that Melanie was the main carer of her mother who was now in her mid-eighties she could have managed on the wages that the hospital gave her. She was a loyal supporter of the government, and believed their propaganda in regards to increasing the hourly rate of its public servants. She would have been much better off working for the private sector, but health jobs there were highly sought-after and the employee turnover was very low.

The Party was loathe to tax its citizens too highly to pay for all the restoration works. It constantly strived to maintain a realistic budget. The new occupier of Number Ten had promised to create better paid jobs, but they were still struggling with the debts left by generations of shoddy governments.

Like Melanie, Mr. Campbell was proud of his country and its people. He urged his electorate to bear with him and his Party. In a recent MORI poll, the market research company claimed that eighty per cent of those questioned believed the UK to be a better place to stay than ten years previously. The crime rate was low, people were polite to each other, there was no racism seeing as there were no foreigners, and the streets were clean.

****

The man whose penis Melanie was currently paying attention to was, in turn massaging the erect member of another actor. The sex industry had welcomed the relaxation of the previously strict rules and regulations which had governed it. Pornography was no longer looked upon as shameful, and the demand for it had subsequently increased dramatically over the last ten years.

Christopher, the owner of *Naughty But Nice* had taken over the firm from his father, Mike, and due to his sound business acumen it had become a very profitable concern. Unfortunately, Christopher was too greedy, and on returning from a recent trip to the United States he had added a new element of frisson to some of his films.

Already his company produced hard-core movies catering to every sexual variant and age range. The bisexual market in particular was very buoyant at that moment. People were now less keen on sado-masochism and cross-dressing films for some reason, but Christopher had unearthed an even more perverse taste.

The only downside to his latest venture was that they could not use the actress or actor again, and disposing of the inevitable waste at the end of the shoot was decidedly tricky. Despite that, the movies sold for ten times as much as their tamer bed fellows, and Christopher now had a loyal fan base.

A *black market* had developed uncannily similar to the underworld dealings during the two World Wars, but of course these beauties fed one's imagination rather than filling one's belly, or sheathing the legs of young ladies in silk stockings. If the police ever found out about *this* new lucrative sideline Christopher would without doubt find himself swinging from a rope.

The two men ejaculated simultaneously and left the set, each casually wiping their members with a tissue which they had ripped from a box conveniently placed on a table near the exit.

As per the script Melanie grinned at the camera and wriggled back onto the bed which dominated the room. The next part of the film intrigued her. She was to be made love to by a woman, something which she had never done before. She just prayed that this lover would smell somewhat sweeter than the last.

She took advantage of the pause in the proceedings to gaze around at her surroundings. The whole place looked like some huge film star's bedroom. It reeked of money. Gone were the days of sex films being made in dingy apartments. Pornography was big business now.

Once upon a time it was the single man or woman who, needing some material to aid their masturbation sessions would flick a DVD into their machine at home, but now it tended to be couples who used it to enhance their lovemaking. It was particularly popular with older people who perhaps required additional visual stimulation to arouse them.

Consequently, porn actors in their fifties and sixties were now starting to enter the business. A gentlemen in his twilight years preferred to see someone of a similar age to himself up on the screen whilst making love to his wife or husband, rather than some nubile youth.

Melanie luxuriated in the fake fur beneath her, and let her thoughts drift back to the holiday which she had shared with her Mum last year. Truth be told, it was that expenditure which had caused her finances to soar out of control, but it had been worth it to see her mother so relaxed and happy, soaking up the sun's rays on that beach in Spain.

Suddenly, Melanie's reverie was interrupted as she felt an unaccustomed tongue licking her down below. The sensation was quite incredible, both cooling and hot at the same time.

This is certainly better than sucking some guy's cock, she thought. The sensation abruptly stopped though as the woman who had a rather attractive face stretched over her body so that her full weight rested on top of her. Melanie lifted her head slightly to kiss the proffered mouth as she recalled the film's directions stating, and the two women kissed deeply. Melanie felt both aroused and excited.

This is not such a bad way to earn a week in the sun, she mused. Then she felt her neck being squeezed tightly. As her life seeped from her she saw her mother smiling in the distance, and wracked with pain she grasped her outstretched hands.

FOUR

Three hundred and fifty miles south in the City of Westminster Buckingham Palace was still the official home of the sovereign. It had become the principal royal residence back in 1837 on the accession of Queen Victoria, the present King's great-great grandmother.

The political system now hovered somewhere between a constitutional and an absolute monarchy. Although the present government had been elected by the populace, they were in reality simply advisors to King Rupert the First. There was no struggle between the monarch and the BTP. Indeed restoring full power to the House of Windsor had been at the core of the party's election manifesto. They decided though for practical reasons to wait until a new monarch had succeeded to the throne before enacting the Bill.

In the past Great Britain had been virtually destroyed both morally, and in the financial sense by a succession of incompetent governments. The general public as a whole had become depressed and despairing. The majority were in agreement with the BTP that a King or Queen would be a far better figure to enforce a new ethical code.

Rupert had succeeded to the throne five years previously following the death of his dear father King William the Fifth. He was the first monarch since the sixteenth century to wield so much power over his country, and its citizens.

The parliaments of Wales and Scotland had been dissolved. Four very distinct countries still nestled under the United Kingdom umbrella. They had retained their individuality, but their regional councils were answerable only to the King. There were now no laws or legally organised opposition dictating to the monarch.

King Rupert was in his early thirties, and he was considered to be a fair and just man. He had a slim figure with defined muscles, although since being crowned finding the time to work out in his private gymnasium was becoming increasingly difficult.

He had a healthy appetite which was satisfied by his personal chef who lived-in at the Palace. Being a pescetarian, his diet was naturally low in fat and high in fibre. The inclusion of omega-3 fatty acids and high density lipoproteins found in the fish reduced the probability of the monarch succumbing to cardiovascular disease. He had inherited his fine bone structure from his grandmother, but he was blessed with brown hair from his father's side. Indeed it was so dark that from a distance it appeared black.

Rupert was not a vain man, but his mother had drilled into him as a youth how much one's personal appearance really mattered. She was still fond of telling him that one could tell a lot about a man from the *state of his shoes*. Thanks to Nigel, his valet the King's always gleamed like patent leather.

Rupert's style of dress was also admired, and often copied. More often than not, in public he would appear in a handmade three-piece suit. His material of choice was Harris Tweed which was dyed, spun and handwoven in the Outer Hebrides. In warmer weather his dress was perhaps a little more casual, but in public he was never seen without a tie. He had these specially made for him in London's Saville Row. Ducks and pigs had both decorated the royal neck wear.

The King was greatly loved both by his people and his family. He was a very contented man. Despite this, he was mindful of his country's history, and he took great care not to abuse the power which had been bestowed upon him. The last thing he needed was a Civil War to contend with. He left the day-to-day running of the country to his government, but all their policies were discussed and agreed with him first. David Campbell had a formal audience with him on a daily basis which ensured that no new laws were passed without the King's express agreement.

Rupert's formative years under the watchful gaze of his parents, William and Catherine had been strict, but full of love. His Nannie was terribly proud of her former charge and truth be told, she often influenced his decision making. She still stayed in the Palace and was a particular favourite of the King's husband.

Fifteen years younger than the monarch, Stephen had fallen in love with the then Prince of Wales five years ago, and their marriage had marked a precedent. Prince Rupert had been the first member of the royal family to publicly declare himself as gay, although there had been rumours in the past that one of his second cousins may have been a closet lesbian.

His mother had two concerns in regards to her son's domestic arrangements. The first was that he would not be producing any heirs to succeed him. Rupert had assured her in regards to this point that his brother Neil more than made up for his own lack of fecundity. He was happily married with three healthy children. The two brothers enjoyed a close relationship, and indeed Rupert often sought his sibling's advice on matters of State.

The second was in his choice of spouse. Although Queen Catherine was very fond of Stephen she had always seriously doubted whether he had the necessary maturity to make him a fit royal consort. After all, he was only twenty-three years of age, and although she felt sure that his love for Rupert was true she feared that the pressures of being the King's companion would take a toil on their marriage.

Her husband, William had died prematurely in a freak accident. He had been obliged to wait until he was in his mid-fifties before the old King had passed away, and just as he was settling into the new role his life had been cruelly snatched from him. Nobody really knew what happened on that fateful day.

William had developed a passion for powerboat racing whilst playing the waiting game. As per royal protocol he had been accompanied by his bodyguard whilst out on the Thames. One minute they had been speeding through the water, cheered on by the usual crowd of tourists, then in an instant the boat was flipped up in the air and the two men disappeared beneath the surface. What was most strange was the fact that neither of them were wearing life jackets that day. The King was both very experienced and well qualified, having received personal tuition to enable him to acquire his *Royal Yachting Association Powerboat Advanced* certificate. Despite a speedy response from the lifeboat service, both men were dead on being fished out of the chilly water.

Perhaps Catherine's still raw grief was clouding her judgement. Rupert was besotted by Stephen, so what right did she have to question his obvious contentment?

Prince Stephen was always full of life. He was boyishly good-looking with a mop of dirty blond tousled hair, and he too loved his clothes. He preferred cravats over ties though. The royal couple certainly made a handsome pair.

The chef would cook him separate dishes to Rupert as

he loved his meat, and although he was happy enough to take the corgis around the grounds he avoided the gym like the proverbial plague. In reality, his preferred form of exercise was passionate lovemaking with his husband.

He found Rupert even more sexually attractive since he had succeeded to the throne. He had always had a penchant for powerful dominant men. Bedding the King of Great Britain, especially one who was in total control of the country's affairs still gave him an all mighty thrill.

The problem was that the frequency of their physical relations had decreased. Rupert was often burdened with worries, and overcome with exhaustion. Somehow, despite still fancying each other rotten, the fun element was dissipating from their marriage. Nowadays it was only Rupert's comic ties that reminded Stephen that his lover used to be a *bundle of laughs.*

The consort could never be described as a political animal. He would take his place alongside his husband in the Throne Room, as custom dictated for the King's daily audience with his Prime Minister, and for the receiving of the head of states from overseas, but in reality he took little interest in the running of the country. He did enjoy accompanying Rupert on his royal duties such as his monthly meetings to the regional councils and the state visits overseas, but he took it all rather lightly. He merely played at being a prince. It was all a great lark to him, but he was most diligent that his public image remained impeccable. He loved his husband unconditionally, but sometimes he yearned for the simple lifestyle that he had had before becoming a member of the royal family.

FIVE

"Happy Birthday, sweetheart," Duncan whispered into his husband's ear as he cuddled up to him later that week.

Grant mumbled in his sleep, dreaming as he was of taking one of his current patients over his consulting room desk. Subsequently, when Duncan reached over his curved body to grasp his penis it was already standing proud. "Someone's been having naughty dreams again," Duncan chuckled. "I trust it was *me* pervading your senses, and not some *hot* young registrar at the Clinic."

Grant was in that heavenly state, halfway between being fast asleep and fully awake. As he recalled his fantasy his rugged features reddened. *Fancy him having sexual thoughts about one of his clients!* Mind you, hernia or no hernia, Mr. Jack was very *fit,* as his niece was apt to say.

Veronica was not actually Clare's daughter, and seeing as his beloved sister was both post-menopausal and a lesbian there was not much chance that she would reproduce any time soon. His *niece* was in fact the adopted child of their closest friends, Maggie and Caroline.

Duncan had been Maggie's best friend long before he had fallen in love with the man destined to become his spouse. Over the years an emotional unbreakable bond had formed between the four of them. Veronica had instinctively gravitated towards her two mothers' friends, and almost immediately she had regarded them as her *uncles*.

Her family would perhaps have been regarded as rather unconventional ten years ago, but now gay adoption and surrogacy was as prevalent as the heterosexual variety. One or two of the religious factions were not too happy about the current situation, but at least there were far fewer wee mites languishing in children's homes now than there used to be. *As long as the child felt loved and cherished, what did it matter?* Grant was well aware that even some people without a particular faith would strongly disagree with his point of view. An example of this could be found in his very own bed.

Five years ago he had suggested to Duncan that the two of them could perhaps adopt a baby, or pay a woman in the United States to carry one for them. Several celebrities advocated the latter practice. His or Duncan's semen could have been mixed with the lady's donor egg, and then the zygote planted artificially into her uterus. After much heated discussion within which both had put forward an equally forceful but opposing case a truce had been called. Duncan believed, similarly to his sister-in-law that a child needed a mother *and* a father to provide him or her with a balanced stable environment.

So, Grant had become a fatherly figure to the young Veronica. Even now that she had almost reached the age of majority he liked to think that she looked upon him rather more as a paternal role model, than as an uncle.

By now, somehow Duncan was on Grant's side of the bed, under the sheets. He had his husband's member in his mouth, and was gently massaging it with his lips and tongue. Grant, a stone heavier than him reached under the bedclothes. He placed his paw-like hands under both of Duncan's axillae, and pulled him up into his loving arms. It still astonished many of the surgeon's patients that his clumsy looking extremities could perform such delicate life-saving work.

No words were exchanged between the two men. Grant just wrapped his muscular arms around Duncan's slim body and kissed him with such tenderness that, as they broke apart Duncan had tears in his eyes.

"Well, for a fifty year old you aren't 'alf bad," Duncan remarked in an feeble attempt at wit. "I reckon I love you more now than when we first met."

Grant looked intently at the man in his arms, and a great surge of love threatened to overwhelm him. Sure, sometimes Duncan did irritate the hell out of him, especially when he droned on about his work. It was even worse when they met up with Clare and Lyn.

After such an evening of incessant chat about the world of publishing the relief of greeting his colleagues at the Clinic the next morning, and scrubbing up for his first operation of the day was almost palpable. Not that Grant did not enjoy reading a good book on occasions, Alan Hollinghurst was one of his particular favourites, but he much preferred watching a story being enacted on the stage or a television adaptation of some novel.

After he had left the Royal Infirmary too many years ago now to remember, to become a consultant at the Edinburgh Clinic which at the time was a small privately managed concern a short walk away from where they stayed, the two of them had become regular theatregoers. Since then the Clinic had been tastefully developed and expanded. Both in its appearance and reputation it could stand proud alongside any private hospital or consulting room in London. Indeed only last month it had been referred to in *The Lancet* as *The Harley Street of the North*.

Every six months or so they could be found in the best seats in one or other of the city's art venues. They had become devoted, if infrequent patrons of the Royal Lyceum in Grindlay Street. On one such occasion the cast of *The Little Dog Laughed* transferred for just a week from the Garrick Theatre in London's West End. Both of them had loved the production, and they had vowed to take a break down in England's capital city sooner rather than later.

Once upon a time a deep streak of homophobia had run through Scotland's cultural life, and it was hard to find a decent gay play to watch. Of course now there were as many of that genre as the so-called *straight* variety. The Little Dog Laughed had been incredibly funny with lots of sharp one-liners. Essentially, the plot revolved around a up-and-coming actor who so wanted to become a star, but inconveniently he fell in love with a bright, but directionless rent boy.

****

Five years ago a change of circumstances at Adonis had brought mixed fortunes to the couple. The then director of the prestigious publishing company died most unexpectedly whilst out running in Princes Street Gardens, leaving an uncomfortable chasm in the hierarchical chain. Duncan had hauled himself up to editor-in-chief status many years before and had taken charge of the entire editing system, but his ambitions were still not fully realised. He was all too aware that he should have side-stepped into a larger more commercial House, but that would have meant relocating *down south*.

The very thought of living in London filled him with an illogical sense of foreboding, and Grant was reluctant to move away from the only family that he had left and start afresh in a new country. So, loyal to his current employer if only for personal reasons he stayed put.

Duncan had of course been devastated by John's

demise, but it felt so good to step into his still warm shoes and chair the firm's meetings, rather than to be a mere contributor. It was him that now felt obliged to work long hours, but he was blinded by ambition and failed to notice the effect that his workaholism was having on his personal relationship. Apart from their bi-annual trips to the theatre, Grant and Duncan's social life was practically non-existent.

Grant was not too keen on cooking, and more often than not it seemed pretty pointless to him to go to all that bother just for himself. Adonis usually ordered in a take-away if their staff were to toil well into the night, so Duncan never needed feeding when he eventually crawled home.

After work Grant would shower and change out of his suit, and then head his Rolls Royce in the direction of one of his favourite restaurants. Sometimes he drove into Edinburgh, left the car in its private parking space and strode into the heart of the city. Other times, especially if he did not have an afternoon theatre list or an outpatients clinic he would shoot up the motorway and sample the often hidden delights of Glasgow.

As Society became more tolerant of alternative lifestyles the gay bars had become less populated, and one by one they had closed their doors. No doubt the odd one or two would survive, like relics of a bygone age, to cater for those who bordered on the heterophobic. Thanks to the BTP, homosexuality was now widely accepted, and there was no need for gay men and lesbians to form themselves into ghettos. This did not make much difference to Grant though as he had never made an issue out of his sexuality, or been a fan of *queer* establishments. He was *straight acting,* and although he was often recognised when he was dining out on some exquisite fare, this was due to his reputation and success as a general surgeon both from his National Health Service days, and now as a private consultant, rather than because of his personal life.

The two of them were now comfortably wealthy, they loved their villa in Morningside, and were adored by their friends. Unfortunately, Grant's acquaintances who on the whole worked with, or for him at the Clinic had never met Duncan's. Sometimes it seemed to Grant that they lived parallel lives, only bumping into each other at the weekends when both of them were too exhausted to do much more than lounge around the house, catching up on the week's news in the Sunday papers. They now had a most efficient cleaning lady so Duncan was rarely seen sporting his frilly apron anymore.

****

Sometimes Grant would yearn for the old days when they did have time for each other. As he wearily turned his key in the front door Grant had always known that

Duncan would be there to greet him. The smell of their evening's supper would gently waft up his nostrils. His tiredness seemed to magically dissipate once his gastronomic appetite was sated, and at the anticipation of what was to follow. Sometimes they only managed the main course, and never made it upstairs to their bedroom. Duncan would only have to gaze lustfully at him over the table for Grant to feel his sleeping member stirring in his groin.

He would hastily wipe his mouth on his napkin, and then with a deep groan sweep Duncan from his chair into his arms. He would kiss him with all the pent up emotion of his day, and bodily carry him up the stairs, or to the sofa in the lounge adjacent to the kitchen. There was no time to undress.

Duncan would sink to his knees and run his smooth hands over Grant's belly, curling his pubic hair around his fingers teasingly. Erect, Grant could proudly boast a full eight inches of throbbing stiffness, and as Duncan had nuzzled his testicles his penis would begin to bob about as if it had been a wee creature in its own right.

Grant would watch as its entire length disappeared into his husband's mouth, and then as it slid with agonising slowness back into the fresh air. Duncan would then centre his attentions on its head, massaging it with his lips, but every so often gripping its shaft firmly in his right hand and stimulating that part too. Duncan would of course by that time have his own fine member

45

released from its lair, and he would masturbate whilst performing oral on the man he loved so dearly.

At some point their minds used to lock, and Duncan's urgent need to feel his lover deep inside him used to coincide perfectly with Grant's passion. With his trousers and underpants hastily pushed down to his ankles and holding onto the back of the sofa or the bed's headboard, he would sigh deeply as he felt Grant's penis pushing into his welcoming anus. On occasions a little *rimming* would be necessary to relax his sphincter sufficiently to allow pain-free access, but mere lubrication was usually enough.

Duncan had known he was gay since his adolescence if not before, and to him his rectum was his sex organ as a woman's vagina was hers. Unlike Grant, he had done his fair share of cruising in his formative years. Sex had always been an essential part of his life, but he had never associated it with love before. Grant had been his first real boyfriend, the other men had just taken him to satisfy their lust. *Not that he had complained at the time!*

Grant would thrust into Duncan, revelling in the waves of pleasure coursing through his own body. He had been a pretty adventurous lover back then, and they both liked to change their position once or twice during the act of lovemaking.

Duncan used to roll off the sofa onto the floor, hastily removing the entanglement of clothing around his ankles, and lay on his back. Grant would then strategically place himself over his husband, and as he inserted his penis once more Duncan's lithe limbs would naturally encircle his neck. This classic *missionary* position was the one that Grant currently preferred because it ensured lots of body and eye contact.

If Duncan was feeling particularly lustful it would be Grant lying on the floor with Duncan riding his penis. At such times the younger of the two men would achieve a double orgasm.

The imminent arrival of his own climax was to Grant, both now and back then, a bittersweet moment. He enjoyed anal intercourse so much that he never wanted it to end, although the sheer joy and freeing of tension as he did ejaculate was pure bliss. Sometimes he would stay inside Duncan and deposit his semen deep within him. He loved the feel of the muscles clenching him as if squeezing every drop from the meatus.

If the mood took him he would reach round and bat away Duncan's hand. Using his own meaty paw he fervently massaged his lover's shaft. If they ejaculated simultaneously they would smile at each other afterwards, and Duncan would kiss the end of his nose affectionately.

They would laugh then and their thoughts would turn to the no doubt delicious dessert which would be waiting for them in the kitchen. Duncan was a superb cook and his puddings were always divine. *Cranachan* was Grant's favourite, a simple but moreish combination of whiskey, oatmeal and cream. Raspberries added a sharp but fruity diversional flavouring.

****

Grant was roused from his reverie by Duncan's high pitched squeal. He was back under the bedclothes again with an ardent desire to feel the *birthday boy's* penis deep inside him. It was Saturday today and he had arranged a surprise party for Grant that evening.

As far as Grant was concerned it would just be the two of them going out for supper in Edinburgh, but Duncan had invited Clare, Lyn, Maggie, Caroline and Veronica to join them, along with some of the folks from both the Clinic and Adonis. Grant was always moaning about how they did not have any mutual friends, people that knew them as a couple, so Duncan hoped that tonight would go some way to rectify that. In fact he was really looking forward to meeting Grant's colleagues. He liked to hear from other people just how wonderful his husband really was.

"You've already come," he stated indignantly, pulling down the sheets to expose Grant's wilting penis and the telltale damp patch.

"I'm sorry. I was only half awake, daydreaming

48

really." Grant paused, remembering Duncan's comment about his registrar. "I *was* thinking about us though." He reached down and grabbed his husband's already stirring member.

"You'll soon be disappearing up my *Khyber* before you can ask, *Who's the sexiest fifty year old in the whole of Scotland?* I love you, wee man," Duncan laughed.

He set to work. Grant pushed all his worries aside, and thirty minutes later splattered his semen all over Duncan's back. He rubbed it into his skin and remarked, "That's better than any body cream you'll find in the shops!"

SIX

DS Jack pulled his duffle coat tightly around his slim body and shivered with the cold. He signed with relief as he spotted the bulky, slightly stooping figure of his governor making his way towards him through the scrub.

The area where the body had been found was now hidden from prying eyes by tarpaulin and orange marking tape. It had been partly concealed on discovery by the leaves shed by the oak tree in whose shadow it lay. The sergeant supposed that the hard ground had deterred the perpetrators from digging a shallow grave. There was only a week to go before Christmas.

Jimmy knew that the heart-wrenching task of breaking the news of this unfortunate person's demise would be left to him. He had been tasked with informing the relatives of the previous two women who had been found in similar circumstances. If the three murders were related, and it was certainly beginning to look that way, then another corpse would turn up in about four weeks.

The pathologist, a stocky man in his early forties came over to join the two detectives. He had completed the preliminary examination of the body, and had just finished pointing out to the Scene of Crime Officer the injuries which had been inflicted on the victim. The

SOCO chap had duly made a photographic record of them for forensic purposes, as well as taking general pictures of the body and the surrounding area.

"So, what do you reckon, Alex?" asked the DCI. "Has she been throttled as well?"

"Looks like, sir. There are scratches on the neck and some bruising. A closer look in the morgue will tell me for sure. I know legally we have got to carry out a full autopsy but to be honest, an external examination would suffice in this case."

Jimmy nodded his head and enquired, "Did she have ID on her, like the last two?"

"She did. We found her handbag just yards from the body." He handed a plastic bag containing the item to him.

"At least you won't have to DNA trace her, but whoever is murdering these poor girls certainly has a peculiar way of doing things. Perhaps next time he'll slip a calling card into his victim's purse and make life easier for us all!"

DCI MacDuff chuckled darkly and stamped his feet. *Just think, I could be tucking into a large plate of clootie dumpling and white pudding right now*, he mused, *rather than checking out another body*. He absent-mindedly rubbed his abdomen. My wife might be a bit of an old moaner, he thought, but she certainly knows how to line a man's stomach!

He waved his appreciation at the pathologist as he

carefully wound his way over to the crime scene. Inside the tent the woman was laid on her back, fully clothed. She appeared to be somewhat older than the previous victims. Peter guessed she was in her mid-fifties. She had dark permed hair, her age indicating that the luxuriant colour had come from a bottle. Pulling on a pair of latex gloves, he deftly lifted the hem of her blue skirt. There, emblazoned upon her thigh was indeed the murderer's calling card.

****

Jimmy Jack rapped on the door of the Easterhouse flat and waited. He was both surprised, and somewhat relieved to see the face of a middle-aged lady peering out of the entrance. He flashed her his identification card. "Hello, I'm Detective Sergeant Jack. I'm so sorry to disturb you. Does a *Mrs. Gordon* stay here please?"

The woman stuck out her hand in greeting and shook the sergeant's with a grim expression on her face. With a voice husky from too many years of chain smoking she explained to him that the person in question did indeed live there, and that they were expecting someone from the police to come round.

"I'm Joan, the next-door neighbour. It was me who reported Melanie missing three days ago. Mrs Gordon's her mother, but she is in her mid-eighties and was too distressed to do it herself."

"Do you mind if I come in for a few minutes? If Mrs Gordon has no objections it would be grand if I could talk to the two of you together."

Joan turned to re-enter the flat and indicated that he should follow. Jimmy admired her receding figure covertly.

****

DS Jack liked both men and women, but nobody except his own reflection knew about his same-sex attraction. Although the constabulary was now, at least in its public perception, tolerant of bisexuality his wife was most certainly not!

Mrs Jack would probably collapse with horror and disbelief if she ever found out that her husband of just two years took pleasure in being *the receiver of swollen goods* on occasions. That would be after she had screeched like a wild banshee, and slapped him across the face a few times. She had only revealed her violent side after they were wed, and sometimes Jimmy would genuinely fear for his safety. Another favourite of hers was to clap one hand either side of his head as if she wished to burst his eardrums. She had not attempted to kick him in the testicles yet, but he was always wary that one day she might try.

Jimmy also found it incredibly difficult to have any sort of rational discussion with his wife. She was always in the right, or she thought she was, and if he tried to disagree with her it just made matters worse. He had asked more than once why she felt the need to physically abuse him. She usually had the good grace to look a wee bit sheepish. She would explain airily that his *mere presence* irritated her, and that she felt frustrated when he could not grasp some idea or concept of hers. He usually questioned her further, and would enquire tentatively whether it would better if he moved out.

Her response to that one would differ. Sometimes she gave him a wry smile, told him not to be *so silly,* and then she just threw her arms around him. Even at such highly charged moments she always knew how to arouse him, and more often than not they would end up having sex, right there and then. It satisfied him in a physical way, but emotionally it simply felt like she was rewarding him for putting up with her bad behaviour.

At other times her response was completely opposing. She would shout at him until he was a cowering mess, and in tears he would traipse up the stairs and start to pack his clothes and toiletries into a holdall. She would stand there for a few minutes with her arms crossed and an unpleasant smile on her face, and then all of a sudden she would grab his bag and empty it onto the bed, laughing in a sadistic kind of way.

There's no need for you to leave, this time. Just be a good boy, she would state, making him feel more like a pet dog than a human being. She would trot back off downstairs, and then he would hear her singing to herself as she prepared their next meal, or she would just carry on with whatever she had been doing before their debacle, as if it had never happened.

Twice he did make it out of the front door, but she had raced up to him as he was about to turn out of their driveway. She had begged him then, in full view of the neighbours for him to forgive her.

Jimmy could never leave his wife, even if he did want to. She refused to seek professional help to deal with her problems, and to manage her usually illogical rage. She did go out to work, but she earned much less than he did. Jimmy dreaded to think what what happen if he ever did leave her. He could not imagine another man putting up with her violent moods. His wife might be a *domestic terrorist,* but he did feel sorry for her.

According to his mother-in-law, she had always been *difficult*. He could no more walk out on his wife than abandon a sick animal. In a way, the two scenarios were not dissimilar.

Anyway, what it really boiled down to was his love for her. He worshiped the ground she walked, or often stamped upon. He loved her with all his heart. When things were good between them he was the happiest man alive. He supposed that *behind closed doors* every marriage had its problems. Perhaps the day she did finally kick him in the groin he might feel differently, but he would probably just sigh deeply and take that latest development on board, like that fellow in the bible!

****

The white-haired lady tried to stand up as Jimmy walked into the living room. The place was crammed with furniture of the traditional type that the detective preferred himself. One could tell from a distance if a display cabinet, for example was made from solid wood like oak rather than constructed out of medium density fibreboard, or *mdf* as it was commonly known. He breathed in deeply, and relished just for a moment the aroma of polish and potpourri which he spotted gracing one of the occasional tables. The deceased was both the lady's carer and daughter, and indicating that she should remain seated, he took the chair which Joan suggested. He braced himself to break the sad news to them both.

Mrs Gordon was inconsolable, and between sobs she agreed to Jimmy's suggestion that their neighbour accompany him to the mortuary to identify Melanie's body. Thankfully, the force's Family Liaison Officer was free for an hour. The arrangements were made for her to come out to Easterhouse, and sit with the grieving mother.

Whilst they were waiting for her arrival Joan took the detective aside, and confided in him about Melanie's moonlighting with the pornography firm. She informed him that she had had a booking there the day she went missing. Joan liked and trusted the director of the company, and assured DS Jack that she was certain that *Naughty But Nice* had absolutely nothing to do with her friend's untimely demise. She was also most insistent that the details of both her and Melanie's employment as *actresses* there be kept confidential. The last thing Joan wanted was for Mrs Gordon to find out what type of film her daughter had been making, or that her neighbour's occupation was a little on the seamy side. To the older generation the pornographic business was still rather unpalatable.

Jimmy made a note of the details and thanked her just as another rap on the door indicated the arrival of his colleague.

****

That evening after Joan had settled the old lady she returned to her own flat, and sitting down on her sofa with a reviving cup of tea she reflected on the day's events.

The Family Liaison Officer had told her before she had taken her leave that she had had quite a blather with Mrs Gordon about her future care. The old lady had been most adamant that she did not want to go into a Home. Personal domiciliary care was still free of charge in

Scotland, and a social worker was to visit the pair of
them early the following week to set up a care package.

Joan had reassured the officer that she would be happy
to continue looking after all the old lady's needs as she
had been doing since her daughter's disappearance.
After all, she only stayed next door. The two of them
had already adapted to Melanie's absence. If Mrs
Gordon required assistance in the night she would bang
on their adjoining wall with her walking stick, and Joan
would then slip on her dressing gown and let herself in,
using the spare key. Usually, the old lady slept from ten
o'clock of an evening through to about six the following
morning, but since Melanie had failed to return that
fateful night Mrs Gordon had been plagued by
nightmares. They were so vivid that she would wake up
unable to differentiate between reality and her
dreamworld for a minute or two. Her daughter would be
screaming in all of them.

Mrs Gordon's husband had been murdered ten years
previously, and she feared that a similar fate had
befallen her beloved daughter. Mr. Gordon had been his
killer's final victim before the police had eventually
discovered the murderer's identity and whereabouts. His
trial had been front page news for months in the
newspapers. Mrs Gordon had been one of the five
relatives who had sat by the gallows. She had cheered
grimly as the noose had tightened around the prisoner's
neck.

Joan was not quite sure why she had divulged that snippet of personal information about Melanie to the police, but something had been niggling away in the back of her mind.

Gazing upon her best friend's body laying there on its lead bed had scared Joan something rotten. Melanie had looked so pretty, and as she had stooped to kiss her cheek Joan had whispered in her ear, *I will find the bastards that have done this to you, my love.*

Just for a second Joan could have sworn that she saw Melanie's chest rise and fall as if respiration was still a function permitted to her, but one look at her pale wax-like face had dispelled that thought firmly from her mind. She had kissed her once more, this time on the centre of her forehead, and tearing her eyes from the deathly visage she signaled to the police officer waiting patiently by the door that she was ready to go.

****

As Joan was taking comfort from her warm beverage, ten miles away Jimmy was unwinding from the stresses of the day in rather a different fashion. He too was safely cocooned in a wee flat, but he was not on his own.

He had checked into the station in the centre of the city after his drive back from Easterhouse, and was informed that the pathologist was waiting for him. He accepted the news with a resigned shrug of his shoulders, and grabbing a sandwich from the canteen on his way he attended Melanie Gordon's post mortem.

Alex Fraser was rather an eccentric fellow, and he pointed out the telltale cutaneous bruises on the deceased's neck with an almost childlike glee.

"Look at those faint oval bruises clustered over the carotid arteries," he remarked excitedly, pointing to the sides of her neck. "You can see where the assailant's fingernails dug into her skin," Alex added, indicating the comma-like marks.

Jimmy nodded sagely, feeling slightly nauseous. *Perhaps I shouldn't have eaten that tuna sandwich after all*, he thought, but he had been roused early from his bed that morning, and there had been no time to tuck into his usual oatmeal porridge for breakfast.

Despite watching countless dissections, he still regarded them as the worse part of his job. It was not because there was a cadaver lying there in front of him. That did not particularly bother him. It was all the *slicing and dicing* that he found difficult to handle. He supposed that he would feel similarly in an operating theatre. *As far as Jimmy was concerned a person's insides should remain hidden, as Nature intended!*

After performing the standard toxicology tests and taking swabs from the deceased's vagina, the pathologist proceeded to the next stage of the autopsy.

He placed a rubber brick under the deceased. Her arms and neck fell backwards. With the skin of her chest now stretched tight, Alex made a deep Y-shaped incision, starting at the tip of each shoulder and running his scalpel down the front of the woman's chest. He picked up a pair of shears from his tray of instruments, and began to saw through Melanie's ribs.

At precisely that moment Jimmy felt his mouth fill with bile, and he knew that if he did not make it out of the room *pretty damn quick* his lunch would soon be swimming inside the poor woman, as it had once in the ocean! He slapped his hand over his mouth, and made a frantic dash to the lavatory conveniently situated just outside.

Alex shook his head in despair at the feebleness of it all, and lifted out the chest plate. He peered inside the body, adjusting the overhead light. As he suspected, the lungs indicated that the victim had been a heavy smoker.

****

Jimmy shuddered at the memory and focused on the job-in-hand. He was sat astride a man whom he had never met before. He had the telephone number of a gay chat line discreetly stored on his mobile.

Rather than returning to police duties he had just popped his head around the rubber door and made his excuses to the pathologist. Alex, by then was carefully removing the deceased's organs in a dedicated fashion, revelling as usual in the wonders of the human body, so Jimmy had just waved cheerfully to them both.

The detective had set up a meeting with a local man in his thirties who conveniently stayed just up the road from the morgue. He wanted to block out all the unpleasant images from his day, and feeling a nice fat penis up his bottom would be an ideal way to relax before he had to steel himself, for whatever mood his dear wife might be in.

His *date* proved not to be the friendliest of fellows, but he was clean and well-endowed so Jimmy was more than happy. Even before the detective had had time to remove his coat, the well-built man had exposed himself, and had casually started playing with his own genitals. Jimmy had gratefully sunk to his knees, and paid homage to them.

Now here he was riding the big fellow, delighting in the sensations building up inside himself as each thrust pummeled his prostate into submission. His inguinal hernia was giving him a wee bit of jip though.

He was under a private consultant at the Edinburgh Clinic to sort that one out. Thinking about it, his surgeon had large hands too, like the fellow beneath him, but Jimmy could not imagine *him* thrusting wildly into another man.

All thoughts of dead bodies and difficult spouses were, for a few minutes at least firmly pushed into the background. As he climaxed, he thanked Mother Nature for homosexuals!

SEVEN

"Kathy, it's Christopher," the managing director and owner of Naughty But Nice stated hesitantly two days later. "I know it's your day off, but the police have been sniffing around and I think we should collaborate our stories."

The buxom brunette took a drag from her cigarette, and flicked ash into a saucer conveniently placed on the breakfast bar for just that purpose. Her usual chirpy expression slipped from her face like thawing snow did from a window ledge, and her features and general demeanour became creased with worry.

She had anticipated this development after the first body had been found three months ago, but once again had allowed herself a tentative sigh of relief when it became clear that the crime squad had failed to link the woman's death with her, or her employer. Now it seemed like they had, and she was scared witless by her inevitable death sentence.

****

Like Christopher, Kathy was a greedy person. She already made a lot of money as Naughty But Nice's top earning actress. One day her boss had called her into the office after filming had finished for the day. She had been rather anxious as an invitation into the plush lair was a rare, and an usually unpleasant experience.

Kathy knew that if her neighbours in the up-market suburb of Liberton which lay just three miles south of the city centre where she had stayed for the last twelve years, ever found out what she did for a living her eight year old daughter would no longer be welcomed at the local riding school from where she went pony trekking every week. She knew it would break her little's girl's heart to have to say goodbye to Molly, her beloved Shetland pony. Five years of age, she was a good tempered dappled grey mare, full of vitality and robustness.

The majority of the people who housed their equines at the stables were of upper middle-class stock, and the owner would fear the damage of its reputation if it became known that one of its client's mothers was a sex worker. Kathy suspected that hypocritically several of them probably used pornography regularly to spice up their own love lives, but not dissimilarly to refuse collectors or *the bin men* as her late father used to refer to them as, it was acceptable to use their services, but not to actually be one of their ike.

Kathy had researched the area just after she had moved there with her then-husband, David and she had discovered that its name was derived from *Leper Town*. Apparently, a small colony of people infected with that dreadful disease had been exiled there from the city centuries before. If Kathy was not *very* careful, a similar fate could befall her and her daughter, but this time they would be obliged to scurry back to the relative anonymity afforded by the heart of Edinburgh.

Christopher had a lucrative but dangerous proposition for his employee to contemplate. He wanted to diversify the business as his father had done years before. Essentially, its day-to-day running would stay the same. Indeed as far as their two cameramen, the administrator, her assistant and the rest of the current actors were concerned there would be no changes, but on Saturdays overtime would become available to a selected few.

"Have you heard of the term, *snuff movie?*" Christopher asked Kathy after he had most uncharacteristically poured them both a large dram of Talisker whiskey, the fine peaty single malt made on the beautiful Isle of Skye.

"No, sir. I don't think so," Kathy replied.

He explained to her that in all senses it was just your usual porn film, but with *one* major difference.

The forty year old sat in front of him raised her eyebrows expectantly, and then she realised what her boss was referring to. "Would somebody have to *urinate* on me, sir?" she asked with a slight grimace crossing her attractive face.

Kathy had no objections to having sex with either a man or a woman, and had only mildly batted her eyelashes at her first transgendered colleague, but she did not fancy getting drenched in someone's *pee*!

One script had directed a transvestite to take her in the missionary position. The slim fellow had made quite a convincing woman from a distance but up close one could see where he had shaved that morning, and it had freaked her out a wee bit when he had climbed on top of her in a Laura Ashley dress. Even now, she could remember feeling the sheerness of his stockings rubbing against her legs, and after the scene was finished he had wobbled something chronic on those high heels!

As far as Kathy was aware *vanilla sex* was their most popular film genre. Like herself most people steered away from any form of sado-masochism now, whether that simply involved mild spanking, or something altogether more painful.

They already made films within which the actor, whether male or female was required to urinate in front of the camera, but that was usually into the mocked-up lavatory bowl set up at the side of the set, or occasionally a chamber pot would be whisked out from under the bed and the actor relieved him or herself into that receptacle.

Christopher looked bemused. "Not *slash*, snuff. No, you wouldn't get wet in a *snuff* film. Well, not with urine, anyway."

"OK, so what would I have to do then?" Kathy enquired, still none the wiser.

"Well, for one thing you would not be required to work with the same actor more than once. Considering some of the squabbles that you have had with our regular crew that might not be such a bad thing," he replied.

"You're teasing me, sir. Just tell me what I have to do." She glanced at the expensive timepiece adorning her wrist. "I need to pick up my daughter from her pony club in half an hour."

"With the extra cash you'll make from this little venture you'll be able to buy her a *whole herd* of ponies." He paused, took a deep breath and explained that a snuff movie involved the deliberate death of one of the actors without the use of special effects.

"If you did agree to help me out the two of you would have sex as usual, but as a finale you would *snuff* out the other person," he informed with ironic calmness.

Kathy realised that she had drastically misunderstood her employer. It suddenly dawned on her what he was actually asking her to do, and she felt terribly nauseous.

"You want me to actually *kill* someone? To take their life?" she stuttered, the colour draining from her usually rosy cheeks.

He had nodded and reassured her that he would advertise for some new girls, that it wouldn't involve any of their existing team.

"But that's murder, sir. I could swing for that!"

She had hurried from the room then in a state of shock, but not before picking up the sheet of paper which

Christopher had pushed across the desk to her. *Terms and Conditions*, it was headed.

He grabbed her hand and pleaded with her. "Read those and come back to me on Monday if you are interested. If not, we'll both forgot this conversation ever happened."

He shoved the half empty bottle of whiskey at her as well. "Just something for your troubles. It goes without saying that I expect you to keep our wee chat to yourself. Be brave and come on board with me, Kathy. I have enough contacts to keep us both out of trouble, and there is already a burgeoning market out there for this type of film. I know you enjoy the pleasures of a comfortable lifestyle as much as I do."

She had stared at him but something made her listen to his words. He let go of her hand.

"This will make us both *very* rich indeed," Christopher finished confidently.

It was that phrase which had whizzed around in her mind for the whole weekend, and on Monday she had simply knocked on his door, pushed it open and nodded at him.

The following day she was sat on his side of the desk primed to begin interviewing the gaggle of prostitutes lined up outside.

****

An hour before Christopher had picked up his office telephone to inform Kathy of the sudden police interest in their covert business operations, DCI MacDuff had arrived unannounced at Naughty But Nice.

Peter had summoned his team in the incident room earlier that morning, and suggested to DS Jack that he go and interview the third victim's neighbour again. He assigned one of the clerks to research the pornography firm where she worked. He took it upon himself to visit the premises.

The second Mrs MacDuff was a very passionate woman, and she still enjoyed a physical relationship with her husband. Peter's first wife had been rather a prude, and had had no idea what a healthy sex life consisted of. She had been killed by a hit-and-run driver four years after they had wed. The perpetrator had turned out to be some lad out joy-riding with his mates.

Lonely but with his sex-drive still firmly intact Peter had experimented with pornography before he had re-married five years later. Sometimes his imagination had required some visual stimulation. He therefore felt well placed to check out Naughty But Nice. He really did not think that they had had anything to do with Melanie Gordon's demise, but according to what his DS had gleaned from the neighbour she had been slated to do some overtime there on the Saturday on which she had disappeared. After thirty years with the Force, Peter tended to rely heavily on his own instincts and intuition. They usually saw him right.

The first two victims had both been sex workers, plying their trade in the Anderston district of Glasgow. From the post mortem results it was clear that they were also both heroin users. They had been disowned by their families.

Taking illegal drugs was now regarded as *the lowest of the low* by much of the population, indeed a trafficking conviction meant a certain death sentence. There were certainly a lot less users now, and those that had the misfortune to become addicted were shunned by Society.

Despite extensive media publicity about the two cases, nobody had come forward to identify the bodies which had been found a month apart. Consequently, they had both been buried in an unmarked communal grave paid for by the State. If it was not for their respective photographs being pinned to the station's operation board, it would be like they had never existed.

****

"Good morning, sir. My name is DSI MacDuff. I am here to investigate the murder of a Miss Melanie Gordon," Peter addressed the slightly worried-looking director who had stood up in front of his desk as he had entered the well-appointed office.

Christopher felt his stomach give a nasty flip, and the hand which he extended to the detective was decidedly clammy. He swallowed hard, and fought with a degree of success to control his emotions.

How the hell had the police traced her back to him, he thought grimly, already seeing the hangman's noose swinging in front of his eyes.

"How can I help you, Officer?" he asked politely.

"We believe that the victim worked here. Is that correct?"

Christopher could literally feel his adrenaline pumping around his body. His heart was racing and he felt quite faint. *Should he deny that Melanie was ever an employee of his, or would that just make matters worse?*

For the police to be here at all somebody must have seen her entering, or leaving the premises on a Saturday. For the *special* shoots there were usually between three and five people present. Christopher doubled up as a director and a cameraman. Kathy was always the principal actress. He had just taken on two more actors so that they could expand further into the black market.

He *laundered* the films through the Netherlands, rather like the practices employed by criminals in the financial world. Rather than concealing the identity and source of illegally gained money, Christopher posted his DVDs abroad *dirty* and they came back *clean*, all nicely presented as any regular porn film would be.

It was true that where as once most adult films were made and distributed by mainland European companies, nowadays many British firms were producing their own. Pornography was not exactly encouraged by the government, but it was seen in a less distasteful light by the general public. There was never any mention in the blurb on the back of the box that someone had died in the story, but the consumers who sought out their particular brand knew what it contained.

Of course until their most recent production they could only cater for the lesbian market, or for men who liked to watch two women having sex. *There were thousands of them.* Kathy felt that she did not have the physical strength to manually strangulate a man, and she was reluctant to use a garrote.

The morning after Kathy had agreed to take part in the shoots she had mentioned to Christopher about just applying the technique of *erotic asphyxiation* in their films rather than literally killing the actress, but he had insisted that their clients wanted to see someone actually die rather than just become giddy and lightheaded which a temporary restriction of blood to the brain would result in. Furthermore, to make it work the actress would have to consent to having her brain deprived of oxygen. Although the state of hypoxia combined with an orgasm was said to create a rush no less powerful than cocaine, Christopher thought that it would be highly unlikely than any of the prostitutes that they had seen would agree to that one.

Better to let them think that they were just taking part in a standard lesbian film. They were all used to having sex with strange men and being paid for it. Who could resist the lure of making even more money for just simply lying on your back whilst a busty brunette nuzzled you down below?

It was well known that many sex workers took female lovers rather than finding themselves a boyfriend. Men usually disliked the idea of the woman they loved having sex with other men, even if it was her job. A girlfriend tended to be more understanding, and lovemaking was less like a working holiday.

Kathy's decision to take part at all had been purely financial at the onset, but much as it shamed her to admit even to herself, after she had taken her first life her motives began to border on the hedonistic. As she had applied pressure to that first woman's carotid arteries and counted slowly to fifteen an overwhelming feeling of sexual power had swamped her mind and body.

She then continued to perform cunnilingus on her lover, tracing slow circles around the base of her clitoris with the tip of her tongue. After a few minutes she felt for a pulse and indicated to Christopher who was filming all her actions that the actress was indeed dead.

In her euphoric state she had casually kissed the top of the woman's thigh, leaving an imprint of her lips on her still warm skin.

"Something for her to remember me by," she had quipped, as she had tugged her victim's skirt back down, and helped her boss to load the body into the back of his Land Rover. It was fortunate that there was a garage annexed to the studio.

Whilst Christopher was driving across Edinburgh to Calton Hill Kathy was on her way home to Liberton. Her daughter was thankfully not due back from her friend's for another two hours.

Still in an elevated mood she had stripped off her clothes, and thrown them into a black bin liner. There were some municipal bins on her way to work, so she would dispose of them on Monday morning. She ran a hot bath and lay back in the scented foam.

She was aware of one or two negative feelings beginning to encroach her mind. They were mainly ones of fear, and perhaps a little guilt. She thought back to her conversation with Christopher earlier in the week.

He had seemed full of confidence that their plans would be foolproof. She sipped the red wine from her glass perched on the edge of the bath and took several deep breaths, trying to relax. In her mind she ran over the day's events in detail, rather like playing back a DVD that one had recorded.

****

She had explored her sexuality after her husband had left her, and much to her surprise had discovered that having sex with a woman was rather pleasant. Kathy was unsure whether she could actually fall in love with someone of the same gender as herself, but she had covertly picked up the odd lady or two, and they had had a wee bit of fun. Obviously, she never brought them home. Her daughter was just beginning to cope with the sudden departure of her father, and Kathy thought it would be grossly unfair of her to reveal that her mother now preferred other woman.

She suspected that her estranged spouse had emigrated to France. There had been a note waiting for her on the kitchen table one evening after she had returned home from work. *Sorry*, was all it had said. He had always been a man of few words.

Kathy knew that the only reason that he had married her in the first place was because he had made her pregnant. He was like one of those hippies in the 1960s, a restless spirit. He had merely played at being a father, and a spouse. Kathy had loved him though, especially when he used to strum his guitar of an evening and sing folk ballads to her.

He used to talk about the three of them selling up and relocating to France in a dreamy kind of way, as if is was some sort of paradise here on earth. The only memories Kathy had of the country was their lack of modern toilet facilities. She had spent a holiday there once as a child, and more often than not the convenience would consist of a hole in the ground over which one was supposed to squat, rather than the usual lavatory bowl.

She had never bothered trying to track her husband down. What was the point? They were better off without him.

****

Relaxing at last in her bath, having refreshed it with even more hot water Kathy played the scene over in her mind from the time she had first kissed the young woman, right through to the point when she placed her lips on her thigh. The sensations she had experienced then once more aroused her, and she ran her hands over her slippery body, squeezing her nipples, and then slipping her fingers between her legs. She masturbated lazily, bringing herself to a powerful orgasm.

****

Meanwhile Christopher afforded himself a backward glance at his victim's last resting place. There had been heavy rainfall the day before, and it had been easier enough to dig a shallow grave within the undergrowth at the base of the hill. Thankfully, there were few people around. The promise of further inclement weather had kept the tourists in their hotels, or they had opted to meander around the tempting array of shops scattered along the Royal Mile. It was too early for the local gay men to make their way up onto the well-known cruising spot.

He wiped his muddy hands on a tissue, and strode back to his Land Rover. Christopher could almost smell the wads of cash which his new venture would generate. He had plenty of eager women on his books now who were keen to participate.

As he drove towards home he had an idea as to how to make his project even more profitable. Instead of the next woman dying on her first assignment he would keep her for a while. She could make two or three standard films, but only on a Saturday of course.

Also Christopher reckoned he could expand his market, without Kathy having to finish off a man. One of his contacts was a pimp in Glasgow who kept a nice stable of rent boys.

He could produce some rather interesting scenes involving four people, two men and two women. One of these would obviously be Kathy. Of course there would be no sexual intercourse seeing as the *boys* would be gay, but there would be plenty of oral shenanigans, and then his ever loyal Kathy could squeeze the life force out of her female lover after the two men had ejaculated.

Christopher rubbed his crotch thoughtfully. *Now wouldn't that make a thrilling movie!*

EIGHT

"Let *me* take care of that for you, sir," Veronica suggested to the man standing by the reception desk.

DS Jack swiveled on the balls of his feet to find himself locking eyes with the most beautiful woman he had ever seen. He guessed that she was in her late teens, but the fierce intelligence radiating from her twinkling green eyes suggested someone much older. Her lustrous blonde hair was cut into a fashionable bob, framing her elfin-like features.

Jimmy Jack was not known for his sense of romance, three years of marriage to his *control freak* of a wife had squashed all that, but for just a second he fell *head over heels* in love with the young lady, who was at this very moment grabbing his suitcase.

She had a slim boyish figure, but from the way she carried his luggage up the grand staircase leading from the foyer it was obvious to Jimmy that she was made of sturdy stuff. He was mesmerised and all he could do was smile his appreciation, and follow meekly behind her.

Veronica Montgomery grinned to herself. *If all the policemen attending the conference are as tasty as this one, then my working week will be a doodle*, she thought to herself.

She had only been employed at the Royal Highland for six months on a new scheme designed to create future managers for the hotel.

She had done well at her Highers, achieving one *A* and five *B* grades. Veronica had particularly enjoyed studying *Macbeth* for her English qualification, and in Business Management she had acquired vital decision-making and analytical skills. Her parents, or *my two Mums*, as she usually referred to them as, had encouraged her to apply for University, but by that time Veronica had had enough of sitting in a classroom. Her burning ambition was to run her own hotel chain, and it made much more sense to enter the world of hospitality sooner rather than later. Many young people of her age would take a *gap year*, a break between school and the rigours of higher education. Veronica took just six months off. For half of that time she back-packed around the Far East, inspired by her parents' recollections of their honeymoon.

It was made clear to her at the interview that she would be expected to work for six months in each area of the hotel before she was taken under the wing of the assistant manager. It was too far to travel from Stirling to Inverness every day so she accepted the offer of staff accommodation.

Her room was comfortable and spacious, with en-suite facilities. There were no communal areas, but she enjoyed taking her meals with the other employees in a room just off the hotel kitchens.

Sometimes whilst they were all relaxing after supper one of her colleagues would suggest that working at Inverness's oldest hostelry was like being *in service*. They were the domestic servants living *below stairs* at the beck and call of the gentry residing above them. Veronica would always chuckle to herself at that point. All being well, one day she would be more powerful than any of their wealthy guests.

She planned to remain in the service industry but had ambitions to become a successful businesswoman, running an international chain of five-star hotels. She would be worth far more than any of their current *masters*.

This was her last week as a porter. Next Monday she would take her place behind reception, and next year she was expected to perform the full range of chamber maid duties. Veronica was not really looking forward to clearing up after the guests, but no doubt she would tackle her chores with her usual quirkiness. She was just thankful that the scheme did not include a spell working in the kitchens.

She reached the guest's allocated bedroom, and with a flourish turned the key in the lock and pushed the door wide open. Jimmy walked past her into the room.

It was pleasantly old-fashioned in its decor with a very

high ceiling. In the brochure the guest accommodation had been described as *unobtrusively modern but with a classic ambiance,* and Jimmy thought that summed up his home for the next three days to perfection.

He still could not quite understand why this year's Police Federation of Scotland Annual Conference was being held in the Highland city of Inverness rather than down in the Lowlands, but if the rest of the staff were half as stunning as the creature who was now carefully laying his case on the luggage rack, then he would not be complaining!

This would be his first conference. According to the paperwork which his governor had thrust at him last week they were all here to *ensure that policing in the twenty-first century was able to meet the increasing challenges and expectations that it faced by the sharing of good practice.*

The maintenance of law and order was one of King Rupert's priorities. He was particularly keen to increase the number of capital offences to include all violent crime and treason. Jimmy was a strong advocate of the death sentence. It made no sense to him to lock up persistent criminals at the taxpayers' expense when on release there was a high probability that they would offend again.

No doubt there would be plenty of opportunities for discussion and debate with the representatives from the other Scottish constabularies over the next three days. DCI MacDuff usually did the honour on such occasions, but he had acquired a nasty dose of swine influenza last weekend, and so had suggested that his second-in-command attend instead. Someone from the uniformed side was slated to be there too from the Lothian and Borders force, but the plain-clothed chaps had little to do with them.

Jimmy had a feeling that the three days would drag somewhat, although he was looking forward to the National Detective Forum. It was the evenings that he was anticipating the most.

He had heard that gay men in the Highlands tended to rather shy, but *very* well-endowed. That was the reputation once held by men of colour, but seeing as one never saw a black or brown face anywhere in the United Kingdom nowadays it was unlikely that Jimmy would ever have the chance to test out that theory, if he had the desire to.

Veronica showed him the en-suite bathroom. It had a marble floor, and boasted both a walk-in shower cubicle and an freestanding bath with clawed feet. Fluffy navy towels complemented the Victorian style. The windows were decorated with pretty gathered curtains, and wood surrounded the hand basin which had brass taps. Jimmy felt as if he had stepped into some sort of bygone age. Maybe one day he would bring Mrs Jack up here and show her what interior design was all about.

His wife's tastes were uncomfortably modern. Their house was very metallic from the stainless steel kitchen to the chrome bedstead. Jimmy preferred warm wood, but he dared not make any suggestions for fear of invoking her violent temper.

She had punched in the face two weeks ago, and he had been concerned that he would be sporting a black eye for the conference. In their three years of marriage this was the worst she had been, and to be frank he was beginning to fear for his life. Of course professionally, he could usually tackle an aggressive suspect to the ground using his unarmed combat techniques, but to try that on his wife would only exacerbate the situation.

In his private thoughts he often reflected on how tragic his personal life really was, and he knew that with another woman, or simply on his own, he would be much happier. He felt trapped, that was the problem. She would never let him go, and nobody in the outside world would believe that a tough-looking police officer such as himself could be a victim of domestic abuse. Perhaps somebody would take him seriously, but to even contemplate the fallout from reporting the situation scared him. As a perpetrator of grievous bodily harm Mrs Jack could be swinging from a rope once the King had passed his new Bill!

"Is there anything else that I can do for you, sir?"

asked Veronica, disturbing Jimmy's daydreaming and making him start. She was hovering by the door, expectantly.

"No, that's fine," he stuttered, his face reddening as if he had been caught in an embarrassing situation. He reached round to the back pocket of his trousers, and pulled a crisp five pound note out of his wallet.

It was the porter's turn to feel uncomfortable for even in a four-star hotel such as the Royal Highland that represented an extraordinarily generous tip. Veronica warmed even more to the remarkably shy detective. She smiled her appreciation, too tongue-tied to utter the expected words of thanks, and hurriedly left the room. Once there was a physical barrier between the two of them she luxuriated in a moment of reflection.

Veronica was a pretty good judge of character and despite her youth, she was often able to read other people's emotions in an uncanny way. Her *two Mums* were quite in awe of their adopted daughter. There had definitely been *some* kind of chemistry between her and the Detective Sergeant, or perhaps this time her intuition had failed her.

Jimmy stared at the closed door and shook his head in bewilderment. Despite the few words exchanged between them he too had felt a frisson. He had been sorely tempted to ask the young porter out for a drink, but he had lost his nerve after thoughts of his wife hanging from a noose had invaded his consciousness.

"You're a married man, Jimmy," he sternly addressed his reflection in the mirror above the chest of drawers. "You need to get a grip of yourself. She's twenty years younger than you. She could be your daughter for God's sake!"

In an effort to claw his way back to reality, he started unpacking his case, carefully hanging up his two suits and placing his underwear neatly in the drawers. There was to be a formal dinner on the last night. Although as an employee of the Criminal Investigation Department he would not be required to wear a police uniform DSI MacDuff had stressed to him that it was *a black tie* affair. Covertly, Jimmy rather relished the opportunity to don his little worn dinner suit, with its starched white shirt and black bow tie.

His wife, seeing him for the first time in such attire just after they were married had remarked that he looked the spitting image of *James Bond*, the fictional British Secret Intelligence Officer created by the late Ian Fleming. Despite being Scottish, Jimmy had quipped that he trusted he resembled the suave Roger Moore rather more than the unrefined Sean Connery.

He decided to try out the en-suite facilities to freshen himself up for the evening ahead. He was really looking forward to sampling the delights of Inverness, but was rather more interested in its carnal pleasures than in its famous architecture.

He stripped off and walked into the bathroom. Lifting up the lid of the lavatory, he grasped his penis in his right hand and felt the familiar sense of relief as the stream of urine splashed into the bowl. Flushing it all away, he stepped into the shower cubicle and luxuriated in the sensation of the warm water pummeling his skin. They only had a bath at home so he delighted in this rare treat.

He let his thoughts verge on the homoerotic, but instead of muscular male bodies filling his mind images of his porter flashed in front of his eyes. The young woman was naked and dripping with water. She reached down to to his groin and grasped his by now erect member as he had held it similarly whilst urinating. Concentrating on this delicious image, Jimmy began to masturbate, holding his penis in a loose fist and moving his hand up and down the shaft. As he orgasmed, spraying the wall with droplets of semen he shouted out, "I love you, honey!"

Ten minutes later, feeling rather disorientated he stepped out onto the bath mat and toweled himself dry. He no longer had any urge to sample the delights of Inverness, not tonight anyway, and decided instead just to relax in his room. He checked his watch. It was seven o'clock. Suddenly he had an idea.

He picked up the receiver of the telephone next to his

double bed, and ordered his supper from the room service menu. He remembered reading in the Radio Times back home that there was a film on Sky which he had wanted to watch for ages. He had been so relieved to realise that it would be broadcast on one of evenings that he would be away at the conference.

It was called *Making Love*. Released back in 1982, it was about a married man coming to terms with his homosexuality, and the love triangle that develops around him, his wife and another man. It would certainly not be to *his wife's* tastes and anyway, he would feel uncomfortable watching it with her. Jimmy knew that his attraction to men would be with him for life, but he had no intention of destroying his marriage, however flawed it might be, because of it.

Half an hour later, he was sat in an armchair with a plate of steaming haggis, neeps and tatties on the small table in front of him. BBC2 was showing the first in a new series of *Queer as Folk*, another programme that he could not have viewed at home. The first two series had been set in the 1990s, but this latest one had all brand new characters, and reflected Society's changing attitude to homosexuality. *Manchester 2025* flashed up on the screen just after the credits had rolled, so that meant just last year.

The former gay village around Canal Street had definitely become more cosmopolitan. From what

Jimmy could ascertain, the clubs and public houses were just as vibrant as they had been thirty-five years previously, but their clientele was no longer solely *queer*.

The opening scene began with a panoramic sweep of a nightclub interior. Men were kissing women, as well as their own sex. Of course, some heterosexuals still disapproved of gay relationships, but rather like the so-called racists years before they usually kept their opinions to themselves in fear of prosecution. After all King Rupert the First was openly gay, and acts of homophobia were now dealt with severely.

Jimmy swallowed down his last forkful of haggis and wiping his mouth with a napkin, he switched on the room kettle to make himself some tea. The sheep's *pluck* artfully combined with oatmeal amongst other tasty ingredients had been served with an onion and whiskey sauce, and it had been absolutely delicious.

He had been hoping that the same porter as before might have brought his meal up to him, but instead it was a young man sporting a beard. Jimmy loathed all types of facial hair. He only just tolerated his DSI's moustache. He did pluck up the courage though to enquire about his predecessor. "I think you mean *Veronica*, sir," the hirsute man had stated.

Jimmy climbed onto the bed. It was mid-June now, but still a little chilly so he pulled the eiderdown up over his bare legs and took a sip of his tea. Cutting a slice of

Strathdon Blue cheese from the generously sized wedge and laying it gently on an oatcake, he flicked over the channel of the twenty-eight inch television set and settled himself down for the evening. The film was as good as he had anticipated, but it was a struggle to concentrate fully on the story.

"Veronica," he whispered, " I wonder what you are doing now."

NINE

"Good morning, gentleman. My name is DSI Munro. I shall be chairing today's Detective Forum, so please make yourselves comfortable and we shall begin. You will find a copy of the agenda along with various research papers in front of you. Please take a moment to peruse these."

It was nine o'clock the following morning, and the sun was streaming through the hotel window. Jimmy detected an air of anticipation in the function room. He noted that the documents were copies of the ones MacDuff had given to him, so he stretched back in his chair and took the opportunity to glance around at his fellow delegates.

He vaguely recognised one or two of them. One of the women raised her hand to him in salutation. She had been his DCS before Lennox had taken over the post. He made a mental note to catch up with her on their coffee break which was at eleven o'clock, according to the timetable.

The Chairman gave his Keynote Address after the rest of the introductions had been made. There were ten of them sat around the oval table, and all the CID ranks were represented. They listened intently to what Munro had to say, and the applause as he uttered his final words was both warm and genuine.

The underlying statement of the speech concerned a point which Jimmy had often brought up in conversation down in Edinburgh, namely how Detectives were becoming invisible. Jimmy was shocked to learn that in some parts of England, *the noble role of the Detective was descending into some kind of quasi-investigation-agency run by civilians*, in an attempt to cut costs.

****

It was public knowledge that the country was still in debt, although this had technically become *sovereign* rather than *national* when the monarchy was granted absolute power seven years previously. The deficit had slowly dwindled since the BTP had taken up the reins of office twelve years ago, but their accounts were still hovering *in the red*.

On election the party had ceased all foreign aid, and the British troops out in Afghanistan had been brought home. The previous government had promised to pull out the soldiers years before, but it had never happened. There were still three armed services, but the Secretary of State for Defence only permitted the employment of troops if the borders of the United Kingdom were deemed to be literally threatened. No longer were soldiers used as *peacekeepers,* or for constructional tasks such as building bridges or repairing school buildings. Mine clearing become an operational duty only ever boasted about by the retired soldiers, fortunate enough to have survived their dangerous occupation. Currently there were no overseas bases, but Great Britain was well defended. Since withdrawing from the European Economic Community the country's military ties with mainland Europe had also fallen away.

There was now a caucasian gentleman residing in the White House again, and King Rupert the First had established a mutually beneficial relationship with the incumbent president. Despite this, he would not sanction any of his own troops to support the Americans unless the aggressors were directly endangering his shores.

****

Jimmy felt certain that the King must be unaware of the cost-cutting measures being imposed by the Home Office. Detectives after all played a pivotal role in policing, and diluting their role by civilisation would ultimately lead to lower detection rates.

If he recalled correctly, the monarch's next scheduled regional visit to Edinburgh was in two weeks' time. Jimmy had scribbled the details in his diary. He had yet to meet the first openly gay royal. He wondered if he was as good-looking in person as the newspapers and television broadcasts would have him believe. Perhaps the King should pay more attention to the financial aspects of his kingdom, or maybe the BTP was just becoming too conceited for its own good.

The rest of the morning's agenda held little interest for Jimmy. He was not particularly concerned about the shenanigans of the English which tended to dominate the topics up for discussion. He was looking forward to the item scheduled for after lunch though. Indeed he had prepared a thesis for the debate. It was simply entitled, *Unsolved Crimes*.

****

Operation Seven Hills had been shelved just a year after the third body had been found. Further evidence of the cost cutting measures perhaps, but Jimmy had felt confident at the time that the team had explored every avenue possible to bring the murderer of the three women to justice, but they could not gather sufficient evidence to satisfy a jury.

The owner of the pornography firm where all the victims had worked had been brought to trial, but a *not proven* verdict had resulted in an acquittal with no possibility of a re-trial. The media's response had been intense and full of outrage. The general opinion was that Christopher Jones had indeed strangled all three females.

A witness had seen Melanie Gordon enter the premises of Naughty But Nice on the day that she had disappeared. She stated that she had been working at the cafeteria across the road until late that evening. Mr. Jones's solicitor had argued that it was possible that the deceased could had left without the witness spotting her. *After all*, he had said, *it was a busy café.*

None of the bodies had had any traces of foreign DNA on them. DCI MacDuff had pinned his hopes on the trademark red kisses found at the top of each woman's thigh, but in all three crime scenes the DNA had either been destroyed, or washed away by rainwater.

The weather in the Lowlands of Scotland during November and December of 2024 had been dry, but below freezing for weeks. Ice crystals would have formed in the cells of any secretions or tissue left by the murderer on the bodies. The samples taken back to the forensic laboratory for examination were frozen, too damaged to accurately match with the suspect's. If the corpses had been dumped indoors somewhere DNA profiling could have been actioned using the perpetrator's saliva, or any of his or her skin cells found beneath the deceased's fingernails.

DCI MacDuff had remarked darkly on receiving the results that *they could no more prove that Jones had committed the homicides than suggest that King Rupert had had a hand in the grisly events!*

The marks had been made by a waterproof lipstick

which could be found in any High Street chemist. None of the product had been found on any of the actors or actresses employed by Mr. Jones when they had been searched the day after MacDuff's original visit.

From the post mortems the pathologist had concluded that the pattern of bruises on each of the victim's necks indicated that they had all been manually strangulated by a female, by the prolonged compression of their carotid arteries. MacDuff had observantly noted during his initial questioning that Mr. Jones had remarkably small hands for a man. As a consequence, he had been taken into St. Leonards Street Police Station for questioning. He was their only suspect.

Christopher had essentially provided Kathy with an alibi, and he had threatened his other employees with instant dismissal if they disclosed any information to the police. He was determined to keep his loyal conspirator a secret. She had obviously committed the murders, but only under orders from himself. He felt so guilty, not in the taking of the three women's lives, but in letting Kathy down. He had sworn to her that his plans to make them both rich were foolproof.

His fatal mistake was to use a woman recommended by one of his employees. The other two had been common prostitutes. At their interviews Kathy and him had quizzed them carefully as to whether they had any family ties. Both had been single, and being drug users were unlikely to have anyone who cared for them.

Heroin addicts were after all the new *lepers* of society.

If only they had been more careful and kept to their original plan of using anonymous women off the street who were all too glad to work inside for a change, then Christopher felt sure that the police would never have linked the murders to Naughty But Nice. Maybe it had been an error as well to employ those two rent boys for their third snuff film. Their inclusion had certainly made the pounds come rolling in, but Christopher was unsure whether they could be trusted to maintain their silence. Their pimp was a close friend of his, and he had threatened them in a far more coercive fashion than Christopher had his *girls*, but even so it was something else to worry about.

Mud had been found on the tyres of his Land Rover which was parked in the firm's garage. On analysis this did match up with the soil particles of the first crime scene.

In his spare time Christopher enjoyed taking his four-wheel vehicle off-road, and after much careful research online he had found a local company that could supply him with *Super Swamper Boggers*. The sales chap had informed him that this particular make of deep tread tyre could *claw through even the gooiest slop holes with ease*. They had puncture and tear-resistant sidewalls, and despite costing rather more than his previous ones they are certainly proved their worth as Christopher had explored the Perthshire countryside of a weekend.

Although he had allegedly picked up the mud two months previously the subsequent freezing temperatures had ensured that there was no rainwater to splash through, and the mud of Calton Hill had stayed stuck fast in the treads. Again Christopher had cursed his carelessness. *Why, oh, why had he not hosed down the wheels of his vehicle more carefully?*

The police had made door-to-door enquiries in the vicinity of the hills where the bodies had been discovered. They had drawn a blank at Calton as well as Braid and Blackford hills, but one of the residents of Cairnmuir Road had seen a man climbing out of an olive green Land Rover on the Saturday in question. She had been looking out of her kitchen window, awaiting the return of her son. He had gone along to the Murrayfield Stadium that afternoon to watch Scotland playing Wales in the Six Nations rugby contest. The sighting had stuck in the woman's mind because she thought the man had looked particularly *shifty*.

He appeared anxious, she had said. *He just stood in the car park at the base of Corstorphine Hill, glancing all around him.*

Her son had come in then, and by the time she had looked out of her window again the man had gone. At the trial Mr. Jones's solicitor had asked the resident whether she could be absolutely certain that the accused was without doubt the man she had seen in the car park.

The witness had looked uncomfortable. Seeing as it had been November he had been well wrapped up in winter attire. She reluctantly admitted that she could not be certain that the man in the dock was the Land Rover driver, and the vehicle had been parked in such a way that the registration plates had not been visible.

All of the employees had made statements to the effect that they knew *nothing about anything*. All the dead women had only worked on Saturdays, and although the third victim was a friend of one of them, even she could be of no assistance except to disclose that Melanie had told her that she had played opposite an actress by the name of *Kathy* in the three porn films which she had participated in prior to her death. Kathy was interrogated at length, but swore that she had called in sick on the Saturday in question.

Mr. Jones repeated over and over again that Miss Gordon had indeed reported for work, but on explaining to her that her *co-star* was unwell she had left the premises. Her mother who stayed with her had said that the last time that she had seen her daughter was at nine o'clock that morning when she had left for work. She had assumed that that would have been at the care home as she had no idea that Melanie was a part-time porn actress as well.

DCS Lennox had become increasingly anxious for a

conviction. He submitted a report to the Procurator Fiscal who after interviewing the witnesses and reviewing the forensics had surprisingly considered that there was sufficient evidence to prosecute. The Crown Counsel decided that Mr. Jones would be tried at Edinburgh High Court.

In the public gallery a sixty-five year old man had sat motionless for the entire proceedings. Barely blinking, he had stared at his son with a mixture of pride and disquiet. When Christopher had been arrested Mr. Jones senior had had an uneasy feeling. He had retired from the pornography business himself fifteen years ago. The staff who were working for him were more than happy to have a new younger boss. There was plenty of money in the bank by then, and Christopher had decided that it was about time that Naughty But Nice had some more salubrious premises. No longer did the *girls* have to trail through the Easterhouse estate and spend their shift in a poky little flat, laughingly called *a studio*.

Mr. Jones senior had never revealed his entire business practices to his son. As far as Christopher was concerned his father just made standard pornography films. The snuff movies were a secret which he would take with him to the grave. Truth be told, the police finding the last girl floating in the Clyde had seriously undermined his self-confidence, and he began to wonder if the risk taking was really worth it. He had made six snuff productions in total, but as far as he was aware the other five people were still resting at the bottom of the river.

On questioning his employee after the girl's body had turned up Mr. Jones senior had concluded that his henchman had had a touch of the collywobbles, and in an effort to cure his affliction he had consumed rather too much of the *hard stuff*. Usually he was extremely skilful at weighing down the corpses with rocks before tipping them into their last resting place, but this time his calculations were obviously askew.

As he watched his son being interrogated by the Advocate Depute Mr. Jones senior began to question his offspring's innocence. *Could he have actually ordered the deaths of the three women found on the hills? Was history repeating itself?*

On hearing the jury's decision the accused's father had burst into tears. He had not uttered one word during the whole trial. Now his sobbing was accompanied by hysterical banter. His son had looked up from the dock, and was alarmed to see his father winking at him as if in conspiracy. Christopher had almost collapsed with relief on hearing the verdict. He vowed to only make movies in future in which he could re-use the actresses.

The verdict had not surprised Jimmy. He had suspected

all along that they had been *scraping the barrow* over this case. Like his governor he had always believed that the pornography firm had had nothing to do with any of the murders. He thought it more likely that all the victims had been apprehended by an unknown local man which essentially meant that there was still a killer on the loose. On kissing his wife goodbye the previous day, he had made her promise him that she would not go out alone whilst he was up in Inverness. She had not been in the best of moods, and wiping the saliva off her cheek she had dismissed his comment. The cases had been marked as *unsolved*.

****

Jimmy could not eat much of the complimentary buffet kindly provided by the Police Federation. He had sat with his former DCS. Apparently, she was now working locally, and he grudgingly accepted her offer to show him around Inverness before he left. He had had no problem with her as a work colleague, but intelligent dominant women scared him somewhat. Being married to one had resulted in that.

His mind had flashed back to the sexy porter who had carried his luggage up to his room. She was certainly a bright young lady, but she had come across as pretty submissive, in her working role at least. He still hoped to ask her out for a drink before he made his way home.

Having to engage in small talk with his ex-boss, whilst nervously anticipating presenting his paper that afternoon had diminished Jimmy's appetite.

He made his excuses and disappeared into the foyer's Gents. Thankfully, it was deserted. He supposed most of his associates had returned to their rooms to ready themselves for the next two hours of discussion. He rested his head against the cool metal of the hand drier and sighed. It would be good to receive some feedback from the other detectives on his paper, but just at the moment his stomach felt like a whole flutter of butterflies were swarming about inside it.

He unzipped his fly at the urinal and as his stream hit the back of the stall he felt immediately calmer. His presentation would soon be over. Tonight he would be out *on the town,* and hopefully his hands would be encircling a few more members!

"Whilst investigating the Seven Hill murders I carried out a little research into similar unsolved homicides."

Jimmy paused in his presentation and looked around at his audience. One or two of the nine detectives appeared to be covertly dozing, after too heavy a lunch perhaps but the remainder seemed to be in a state of rapture, listening intently to his every word. Despite the gruesomeness of his subject, Jimmy allowed himself a faint smile. At first he had had serious doubts whether even revealing to the other forces that the Lothian CID had failed to secure a successful prosecution was a good idea. The last thing he wanted was to bring his colleagues' reputations into disrepute, but now as he was beginning the concluding part of his speech he felt confident that he had done the right thing. His was the first of four presentations scheduled for the afternoon, and there was time set aside at the end of each for *a question and answer* session.

"Fifteen years ago a female body was found floating in the Clyde down in Glasgow. The post mortem clearly indicated that the woman who was forty years of age had had her throat slashed. The deep laceration had severed both carotid arteries. The process of adipocere had occurred. This transformation of the fatty layer beneath the skin into a soap-like material requires many weeks or months."

Jimmy paused for breath, gazed quickly around the room and continued, "Other immersion artifacts were evident as well such as *anserina cutis,* which as we all know is roughening or pimpling of the skin. The pathologist therefore thought it was most likely that the woman had been dead when she had entered the water, and that she had been immersed for a considerable period of time. There were marks on her body suggesting that she had been weighed down with rocks of some description before she had floated to the surface."

The detective took a few sips of water from the glass in

105

front of him and concluded, "The identity of the deceased was established from her dental records. Her name was Stacey Connelly. Apparently, she had worked as a prostitute in Glasgow for all of her adult life. Her sister was eventually traced. They had had little contact during the previous ten years. Despite extensive investigations the woman's murderer was never found."

There's daggers in men's smiles, the near in blood, the nearer bloody, Veronica had recited to herself as she had cleared away the detritus from the detectives' buffet lunch at the far end of the room. Although this was not the usual job for a porter she had volunteered to help out the waiting staff as one of their team had been off-sick. It made a change from lugging heavy cases all day.

On hearing the speaker's words she had almost dropped the pile of plates precariously balanced on her arm. Shakespeare's lines had entered her mind automatically. She had achieved an *A* grade in her English Higher, and could now almost recite his *Scottish play* verbatim.

The detective is talking about my Mum, she thought. Suddenly feeling rather nauseous and choked with emotion, she let the plates slide back onto the table, and sobbing ran back out into the foyer.

TEN

The tantalising aroma of freshly prepared hot food, and
the sound of friendly banter emanating from the terraced
beer garden greeted Jimmy warmly as he approached
the Castle Tavern. It was his last night in Inverness, and
he so wanted to make it a memorable one. Whatever
happened it had to be an improvement on the previous
evening.

He had been planning to go out on his own, after
discovering that the young porter had been excused
from her late shift. All day he had been trying
desperately hard to pluck up the courage to ask her out
for a farewell drink. Becoming increasingly anxious that
his nerves would overwhelm him he had discreetly
questioned a fellow member of staff as to her
whereabouts during the afternoon coffee break.
Considering that he had only met her once Veronica had
had quite an effect on him, and so it was with a heavy
heart that he had learnt that she was unavailable. He had
been tempted to make further enquiries, but as a
member of His Majesty's Police Constabulary he did
have his reputation to consider. He would probably
write to her instead on his return home.

As if that was not enough to contend with, his old
governor had literally grabbed him as he had been
gathering up his papers at the end of the forum. He had

tried in vain to wriggle himself out of her insistent invitation. It is with great reluctance that he finally acquiesced, and agreed to have supper with her in the Ash Restaurant which was part of the hotel complex. She was undeniably lonely, and in a way Jimmy felt sorry for her.

He had ordered a chicken and mushroom pie, topped with a puff pastry lid whilst his loquacious companion plumped for one of of the Royal Highland's classic dishes. Monica's meal was indeed a culinary delight. Described on the menu as *Bacon Kilted Haddock*, the Scottish white fish had been baked with French mustard and white wine, wrapped in smoked bacon and served with a creamy chive sauce. Jimmy had thought, *at least the food's impressive.*

Then much to his embarrassment the DCS had tried to seduce him after downing her nightcaps like a lost soul out in the desert. Monica was a very attractive woman, but he was not interested in having torrid sexual relations with a female. He had Mrs Jack at home for that. He made the clichéd excuse of having a headache after a rather intense day, and politely made his escape.

The following morning the Home Secretary was booked to make a speech to the Federation. Jimmy smiled at the slightly grey-looking Monica as their paths crossed in the foyer fifteen minutes before the scheduled start. She reddened and whispered, "I'm sorry," into his ear. Unsurprisingly, she did not repeat her suggestion

that he might like to take a wander around the city with
her later that day.

The bar was heaving with people and Jimmy almost
turned tail. The public house was very popular with
locals and tourists alike. It always had three guest real
ales on tap and the food was inexpensive, but of a good
quality. If his stomach had not already been full with
local game, even the wild ducks up North were friendly,
then Jimmy, glancing at the specials board would have
ordered himself a bowl of Cullen Skink, which was
essentially a smoked haddock chowder. That tasty dish
would have swiftly been followed by a darne of
Shetland salmon served on a bed of spinach and cream.
Jimmy was still ravenous though, but for the attentions
of a gentleman rather than the gastronomic delights of
Inverness.

Despite his better judgement, he waited his turn to be
served, and just when another wave of impatience
threatened to engulf him the young barmaid asked him
what his pleasure was. Jimmy grinned and was tempted
to make a lewd comment. He ordered himself a pint of
ale with a whiskey chaser. Both were apparently
brewed, or distilled in the district known as Badenoch
and Strathspey which was thirty miles or so away from
the city. The beer went by the name of *Wildcat,* and
although it uncomfortably reminded him of his wife its
strong distinctive flavour proved to be most satisfying to

his palate.

Jimmy glanced at his watch as he wandered into the beer garden. It was just nine o'clock and still light. A warm breeze and, for once no rain created too pleasant a condition for him to sit inside. He chose a picnic table at which a middle-aged couple were sitting. He would have preferred to have been on his own so that he could covertly use his well tuned *gaydar,* but the area was almost as busy as inside. He sat down and smiled in greeting.

Taking the first sips from his drink, he let his gaze fall on the castle which was perched on a cliff overlooking the River Ness. He had read in one of the tourist pamphlets at the hotel that the original fortress had been built by Macbeth of Scotland back in the eleventh century, but the current building now housed the Sheriff's Court.

Jimmy had become a recent convert to the works of Shakespeare. Whilst at school he had dismissed his plays as *a load of old nonsense*, being rather more interested in the sciences. Macbeth had become one of his favourites. Once he had slightly misquoted one of the lines to his wife, *I chastise you with the valour of my tongue*, but she had not appreciated its irony. She had simply cuffed him around the head like some errant schoolboy, and told him *not to be so silly*.

He took a long draw from his beer, and looking up again caught the eye of one of the two men who had just settled themselves on the adjacent bench. From their body language Jimmy made the assumption that they were a couple. They were of a similar age, perhaps in their late twenties and both appeared to be intelligent professionals.

Jimmy did not really have a type when it came to men, but he loathed obesity in either gender. Fortunately, nowadays there seemed to be far fewer fat people in Scotland than there had been five years previously. The up-and-coming generation took the matter of their health very seriously, or at least their parents did. The old people's homes were currently full of the overweight folk who had lacked self-discipline in their younger years, and were now paying the cost.

In a classic case of serendipity the man and woman sat at his bench rose and disappeared through the garden gate. Jimmy non-verbally suggested to the two friends that they might like to join him. The blond one shrugged his shoulders at his companion, and in a few seconds they were sat opposite him.

They made the usual introductions. Jimmy had been correct. They were in a gay relationship. He felt emboldened by the alcohol. The Speyside single malt was slipping down nicely, and he felt warmed not only by the spirit, but by the genuine friendliness of the couple. It had been several months since he had indulged his homoerotic tendencies, and it was much safer to play a hundred and fifty miles away from home.

He took a deep breath, and asked them whether they would be up for a threesome.

"Come on in, Jimmy. Welcome to our humble abode," the red-headed man stated as he stood back to let his boyfriend and their guest walk into the small terraced house situated on Ness Walk, overlooking the river. Jimmy felt the nervous excitement building up within him. He had never tried a threesome before. Usually he just meet up with a single chap whom he had contacted via a gay chat line. It seemed that his new friends were very experienced at this kind of thing. In the public house they had informed him that they had been dating for two years, and six months ago they had decided to buy their first house together.

Both of them were registrars at the local hospital. Indeed they had met each other whilst working at Raigmore General, which was situated just off the A9 near the Northern Constabulary Headquarters. Tonight marked a rare occasion as neither of them were on-call.

Mark took Jimmy's jacket and asked him if if was partial to red wine. Nodding, the detective followed Carl into the lounge. A few moments later the three men were relaxing and chatting companionably. Mozart was discreetly playing in the background. It was still light outside for this far north it was only truly dark for three or four hours of the night, but Mark had drawn the lounge curtains as a path ran along the front of the house.

"If a passerby happened to peer in he might see *three* Loch Ness monsters," Carl had remarked, drolly.

Jimmy kicked off his shoes, his nerves dissipating in the convivial atmosphere. He usually took the passive role in a homosexual setting, but this evening he was impatient to proceed with the promised activities. He was also acutely aware that it was almost eleven o'clock, and although he guessed it would only take him approximately twenty minutes to saunter back to his hotel he did have a long drive back to Edinburgh in the morning. Taking the initiative for once, he carefully placed his glass of wine on the coffee table to the right of him, and pushed himself up from his easy chair.

Mark had an attractive face, and he smiled his approval as Jimmy knelt in front of him. As the zipper on the flies of his cotton trousers was lowered, he moaned gently in anticipation of what was to come. Reaching inside, Jimmy felt the hardening penis and gently drew it out. Almost reverently, he took Mark into his mouth and slide his lips down his shaft. Pulling back a little, he concentrated on the head as Mark became fully erect. He licked around the corona, paying particular attention to the frenulum, and then traced a line with his tongue all the way down the underside of the penile shaft to its base.

Jimmy was all too aware of the ever-increasing bulge in his own crotch. It was becoming really uncomfortable, and the urge to release himself was threatening to dominate his mind. As if by telepathy, Carl was at his side, and to Jimmy's enormous relief he felt his manhood being set free.

Mark then took over the proceedings with a cheeky glint in his eye. He playfully kicked Jimmy out of the way, and pushed him back towards the chair. He grabbed hold of his boyfriend's shoulders and pulled him into a standing position. Mark's penis was now protruding from his body at an angle of about hundred and ten degrees, and it was bobbing slightly as the corpora cavernosa, now completely engorged prevented the blood from draining away. A drop of pre-ejaculate dribbled down onto its dorsal side. His foreskin had automatically retracted, exposing the glans.

Carl just stood in front of him as Mark undid the button on his own fly, and pushed his trousers and Calvin Klein underpants to his ankles. He deftly stepped out of the garments and swiftly removed his T-shirt, exposing his defined torso. Carl's eyes grazed his lover's body, and in a similar fashion he stripped off his own clothes so that the two men were stood barely touching, and completely naked.

Jimmy quickly realised that his new friends were intending to put on a show for him. They were obviously exhibitionists and although he yearned to join them, in a strange kind of way being obliged to just watch heightened his own arousal. It was warm in the room as Mark had switched on the central heating, so Jimmy too was at this moment in the nude, lazily caressing his penis, making the most of his never-before-experienced voyeuristic role.

The two men were now in a close embrace, writhing and rubbing their crotches together. Carl ran his hands lovingly all over Mark's chest which was matted with curly red hair, and tweaked his nipples. He sucked the pert nubs for a minute or two, then sank to his knees to resume the service which Jimmy had been precedently employed in. Carl was pulling on his own penis as he massaged the head of Mark's fine member.

Jimmy started to rise from his chair to partake in the oral activities, but Mark scowled at him to remain where he was. Jimmy was used to taking the passive role, but not to this extent. He was unsure whether he really liked being so completely dominated.

Whatever objections his mind had, his body had other ideas. He could feel his orgasm building, almost sense the semen rising from his testicles. The warm tingly sensation in his groin intensified, and as waves of pleasure spread throughout his body he stared at Mark who had his tongue deep between Carl's buttocks. He was pushed up against the chair, and Mark was licking all around his boyfriend's anus.

The compact disc had reached its end, so all that could be heard in the room apart from the sound of the occasional car crossing the Ness was heavy breathing and deep moaning. As the first shot of white sticky fluid was expelled up through Jimmy's shaft and forced out the meatus of his penis, Mark slowly slide the head of his organ into Carl's well-lubricated orifice. He unhurriedly slid it in and out, building up a rhythm and penetrating deeper as Carl's muscles relaxed. Much to Jimmy's surprise, Mark suddenly coughed to attract his attention.

"Carl is versatile," he stated. "He'll take you whilst I'm busy here, if you like!'

Jimmy felt a little scared for some reason. He had resigned himself to just watching the show, and was enjoying the warm afterglow that always followed a decent ejaculation, but it felt rude to refuse his guests. After all, it had been his suggestion in the first place that they had a threesome. Jimmy nodded his agreement and stood up.

Mark reached around Carl's upper body, and pulled him into a vertical position so that his face was up against his blond hair. He indicated to Jimmy that he should lie on his back with his legs in the air. It continued to amaze and puzzle Jimmy for months afterwards quite how Mark managed what he did next.

With his boyfriend still buried deep inside him and clinging onto his back, Carl lifted up Jimmy's buttocks, smothered his penis with lubricant and lunged into his welcoming orifice. Mark resumed his thrusting, and as if by some telepathic clock they both withdrew at the same time. Carl's semen warmed Jimmy's abdomen as Mark's coated his boyfriend's back. On reflection Jimmy would wonder if it had all been a fancy of his imagination, although the next morning he did find himself cuddled up with the two doctors in their double bed.

ELEVEN

"Well, if this is what retirement is all about, bring it on!" Caroline laughed, wrapping her arm even more firmly around her wife's back.

They were snuggled up together a week later on the observation deck of the MV Loch Nevis, one of several ferries run by Caledonian MacBrayne, on their way to Eigg, which was the second largest of the Small Isles. With just over sixty inhabitants, it formed part of the Northern Inner Hebrides, an archipelago situated off the west coast of Scotland.

The two women had decided that it was about time that they re-visited Maggie's cousins on Skye. Whilst discussing their travel plans Caroline had suggested that, seeing as she was now *a lady of leisure,* and Maggie had some annual leave as-yet-unspoken for, they ought to make a real holiday out of it and take a tour around the group of islands which lay between it and the Ardnamurchan peninsula. In advance they had booked accommodation for two nights on each of the four islets.

By the time they made an appearance at Dunvegan they would be able to tick off Rum, Canna, Muck, as well as Eigg from the list of places which Caroline was determined to pay homage to. She was so looking forward to Maggie finishing work in three years' time.

"We will be able to join the local Old Age Pensioners' club then," she would tease her beloved. "Two little old ladies shaking their walking sticks at the world!"

As they drew ever closer to the distinctively shaped island, the general chatter aboard increased with excited anticipation. "Look, there's An Sgurr," Caroline pointed breathlessly at the near vertically-sided crag which was looming above the southern end of Eigg. "Perhaps we could climb it tomorrow. I read in the guidebook that one can see Ben Nevis from its summit. It's only 1,289 feet in height, so hardly a Munro but-"

"Only *1,289 feet*? Well, that's OK then. I'm sure we could conquer that before supper," Maggie laughed, poking Caroline in the ribs. "Just remember you're a damn sight fitter than me, even though you're five years my senior."

Her wife's expression changed from one of childish excitement to crest-fallen disappointment.

"Oh, all right then. As long as this fine weather holds, we'll have an early breakfast and tackle it tomorrow morning. Will that stop your daft sulking?"

Caroline grinned and leant over to place a firm kiss on Maggie's lips. "I so love you, darling," she stated emphatically.

"Only because I let you have your own way. Come on, we need to go down to the car deck."

Maggie carefully steered their silver Vauxhall Vectra off the ferry ramp into the village of Galmisdale. She asked Caroline whether she wanted to stop off at the An Laimhrig building which housed the island shop, tearooms and craft centre, but they decided to drive straight to Cleadale instead on the north-west side of the island where their guesthouse was situated.

"This place is *so* beautiful," Caroline remarked, staring out of the window at the rocky landscape. There did not seem to be anyone else around now that they had left the relative hustle and bustle of the port. She placed her hand on Maggie's thigh and absent-mindedly caressed it.

"It reminds me of Skye. Sometimes I think we ought to to move permanently to one of the islands."

Caroline's attention was distracted from the wild scenery for a moment. "Are you serious, darling? Leave your home town of Stirling? I thought it was me who was the *country bumpkin*, having spent half of my life in the far-flung corner of Cornwall."

"I do love Stirling, and of course until I retire we shall have to stay living there, but what is there to stop us relocating to somewhere more peaceful after that? As long as you are by my side, I don't really care where I spend the rest of my days but-," she pointed at the island of Rum on the horizon which had just come into view, "wouldn't it be *fantastic* to wake up of a morning and not hear any traffic? No children screeching on their way to school. To be able to do our weekly shopping in a community where the locals greet us by name-"

"OK, I receive the message loud and clear!" Caroline interrupted. "What *has* got into you, Maggie?"

"I'm sorry for going on. I guess I'm missing Veronica, and oh, I don't know. We've stayed in that house for almost eighteen years now. For all our married life in fact. Now that our daughter has grown up and fled the nest I'd like to move before we're too old to do so. It would be so good to settle down somewhere new where the ghost of my late husband is not haunting us."

Caroline looked aghast. "I had no idea that you even thought about Andrew anymore. He died twenty years ago. Do you feel guilty, or something?"

Maggie's visage crumpled. She mumbled something indecipherable and pulled off the road. She switched off the engine and glared out at the shimmering sea, but her thoughts were far away.

****

She did still think about her late husband. Even after all these years her feelings for him were very confused. She did not love him anymore, or at any rate she was not *in love* with him, but her memories of, and for him were ones of affection.

Sometimes she would catch glimpses of him when she was alone in the house. She was more likely to see him if Veronica was with her. His appearances had never frightened her. In fact the very opposite was true. He would always be smiling benevolently at the two of them. He never spoke but would just stand there, watching them both, almost in a protective, or an approving kind of way.

Now that Veronica had left home she had only seen him once or twice in the last eighteen months. Maggie had always been very open-minded when it came to matters of the supernatural. She knew for certain that his appearance was not some symptom of an overactive imagination.

She loved Caroline to bits, and there had never been a single second in all the time that they had been together that Maggie had regretted falling in love with her, or indeed sacrificing her marriage so that the two of them could become lovers. She did not feel one ounce of guilt over what had happened. What did bother her was that Andrew still seemed to be part of their lives. It almost felt like she was being unfaithful to Caroline, even if she had no control over the manifestation of Andrew's ghost.

Shortly after Veronica had started at primary school, and Caroline had become the main breadwinner for the family Maggie would sometimes sit down at about two o'clock of an afternoon to take a break from the household chores before she set out on her two mile walk to collect their daughter. Anticipating seeing Veronica's smiling face again at the school gate, Maggie would repeatedly formulate the words to describe her supernatural experiences to her wife. Unfortunately though, every time the opportunity arose to explain to Caroline about her ghostly apparitions Maggie would become timorous, and her secret was never disclosed. Her wife was very pragmatic and would no doubt have dismissed such things as *a load of old nonsense* anyway.

Once she had retired Maggie wanted the two of them to stay in a house that she had not shared with her late husband. He had been a part of her life now for over thirty-five years, either corporeally or as an eidolon, and she was so looking forward to spending the rest of her days with just Caroline by her side.

Veronica now had her own life, and although she telephoned her parents every week she was by nature fiercely independent. Compared to Caroline, it was Maggie who had always had the strongest bond with their adopted daughter. She put that down to the fact that in reality it was her who had brought Veronica up, whilst Caroline had provided for them financially. *It would be so lovely to wile away the remainder of our days on some deserted island*, Maggie would often think.

****

"Oh, just ignore me. I'm having one of my silly days," Maggie reassured her concerned spouse. "But it would be wonderful to buy somewhere together. It would almost be like our first home."

Caroline still looked bemused. Maggie used to have mood changes like this when she was going through the menopause. One minute she would be *right as rain*, and then the tears would come. At the time Caroline had wondered if her beloved was suffering from the beginnings of depression, or from some sort of anxiety problem.

****

In moments of quiet contemplation, Caroline put herself through the proverbial wringer as to whether they should have adopted little Veronica at all. Dealing with the tantrums of a ten year old would be trying for any mother, but when neither of them were exactly *in the first flushes of youth*, or genetically related to the child it made the situation even more difficult.

Maggie had insisted on returning to work on a part-time basis once Veronica had started at her first school, even though as a household they could have managed on just one salary. She stated that she would have *gone mad* if she had remained at home every day. She cut her hours so that she was employed at Eaglesham Properties for just three mornings a week. By the time Saturday came around, Maggie was exhausted, but she insisted to Caroline that all was well, and that she was coping. When Veronica left home Maggie increased her hours again.

For just over a year the two of them had worked full-time again, as they had done after Caroline had recovered from her renal transplant, before little Veronica had become part of their lives. Now that the older woman had retired, it was Maggie who left their marital home of a morning, shouting, *Goodbye*, up the staircase to her sleepy wife.

Caroline just hoped that their two week holiday would rejuvenate the woman she loved so much. They did need to spend more quality time together, to simply relax in each other's company without worrying about *anything*.

****

Caroline unbuckled her seat belt and climbed out of the car. She walked around to the driver's side and opened the door. Maggie smiled up at her weakly. As the two of them were leaning against the vehicle, admiring the coastal view, Caroline with her arm flung around Maggie's shoulder said decisively, "I'm worried about you, love. I have an idea. Why don't you take early retirement? We could put our house on the market then, straightaway. I would love to move out here, just you and me."

"Do you really mean that?" Maggie asked, her features brightening. "I just want to spend every day with you, not go off to work, leaving you at home. I think I liked it better when you were the breadwinner. It feels wrong somehow, you being in the house on your own all day."

Caroline felt uneasy again, and possibly a little indignant. "Well, I am sixty-two. I reckon that I have earnt my rest after all those years of selling mortgages."

"Of course, you have, darling," Maggie laughed, poking her playfully in the ribs, in an attempt to lighten the atmosphere. "All I meant was that I want to be with you, rather than with my work colleagues. I *will* have a chat to my line manager when I get back. *Early retirement* does sounds great!"

Caroline sighed with relief. It seemed her assumptions were correct, Maggie was just stressed out and tired. All of a sudden she had an overwhelming desire to show the woman next to her how much she really did love her. They were on vacation, after all. "Just hold that thought. What time are we expected at the guesthouse?"

"I told the lady that we'll be there *sometime* this afternoon in case we wanted to do a wee bit of exploring first. Why do you ask?"

Caroline just raised her eyebrows and sauntered to the boot of the car. "Oh, good, we did remember to bring this with us."

She took out the Montgomery tartan blanket and shook

it out. Laying it on the grass on the far side of the car, so that they could not be seen by any passing motorists, she sat down and stretched out her legs.

Maggie giggled, "What are you up to now?"

"Let's mark the start of our holiday in style. I've always wanted to make love to you *al fresco*." She reached up and pulled Maggie down beside her. "Nobody can see us from the road."

"What if there are people out walking? It wouldn't be a good start if we ended up in the local papers. I don't fancy being had up by the police for acts of indecency. You know how strongly the King feels about public displays of affection."

"*Bugger* his Majesty! I hear he's rather partial to that!"

"Caroline, you can be so crude at times. You could be accused of treason for saying something like that."

"Well, I won't tell, if you don't. Now shut up and let me kiss you."

She rolled on top of Maggie and stroked the side of her face. "I love you so very much," she whispered, placing a tentative kiss on her lips.

"I love you too. Now let's act out that fantasy of yours!"

Caroline kissed her wife again, but this time it was full of passion and tenderness. A light breeze was blowing in from the sea, and the late afternoon sun warmed Caroline's back.

Her tongue explored the depths of Maggie's mouth as

she slowly slide her hand up under her skirt. She caressed the area between her wife's legs. The soft cotton was already slightly damp. Maggie gasped and spread her lower limbs further apart.

All thoughts of work and, ghosts were firmly pushed from her mind. Here she was being made love to by the most gorgeous person in the world on the beautiful island of Eigg. They had nothing to do for two whole weeks, except to be together.

Her clitoris ached and she could feel her nipples hardening. She felt special and adored, and just at this moment she would not have swapped places with anyone else. She gazed into Caroline's eyes. "I shall remember this vacation for years to come."

"Me too," Caroline confirmed as her fingers slipped into her wife's vagina. Maggie was more aroused than Caroline realised. Perhaps they ought to have sex in the great outdoors more often!

She massaged the nub of her clitoris and taking a precautionary glance around them, she pushed up Maggie's skirt and deftly removed her pants. As she flicked her tongue inside her, tasting the moisture there, Maggie had gorged herself on strawberries the evening before so her secretions were deliciously sweet, Caroline could sense that her orgasm was building. Over the years they had perfected their lovemaking techniques, and each knew meticulously how to bring the other to an exquisite climax.

Caroline, still fully dressed in her navy summer trousers and white blouse manoeuvred herself, so that once more she was laying on top of Maggie. She could see the desire in her eyes, and it took but a few digital penetrations for her orgasm to break.

Caroline smiled as she felt Maggie's vaginal muscles contracting against her two fingers, as her body bucked beneath her. Then it was all over. Maggie closed her eyes for a second or two.

"Wow, that must be the best one yet," she stated delightfully, holding onto Caroline who was now lying by her side, seductively licking her fingers. "Did you come too? I was so carried away that I didn't even touch your bits!"

"No, I didn't, but it was pleasure enough to see you in the throes of passion. You can make it up to me later. Mind you, I shall feel rather damp on the way to the guesthouse!"

Maggie laughed. She felt wonderful, but all that stimulation down below had made her want to urinate.

"Don't worry, I promise I'll have you convulsing later. Sorry to break the mood, but we really ought to get going. I am dying to see what our room for the night looks like."

Caroline clambered up and assisted Maggie to her feet. "Me too. That was quite a start to our Hebridean get-away." She folded up the rug and tidied it away in the boot.

"Before we set off though, I must have a pee," Maggie said. "You know what my bladder is like. I thought I would be OK, but I reckon you must have massaged it as well as everything else, not that I'm complaining, I hasten to add."

She checked for any passersby and satisfied, lifted her skirt and squatted down by the side of the car. She giggled like a teenager, "I forgot I don't have any knickers on!"

Caroline pulled the ball of material out of her trouser pocket and waved them in the air, laughing as well. She watched as the stream of urine ran across the grass. Maggie gathered her skirt so that her vulva was just visible.

Caroline blushed and thrust a hand between her own legs. "Bloody hell, I've just come," she stated, her voice full of incredulity.

"And I've just marked my territory," Maggie said, standing and straightening her clothing. Before she opened the door of the car and resumed her place back behind the wheel, she took Caroline in her arms and whispered, "I always forget how much of a turn-on my peeing is for you."

TWELVE

"Look, Maggie that must be Muck, the final stop on our whirlwind tour of the Hebrides," Caroline exclaimed the following morning, pointing to the low-lying, almost treeless landmass on the horizon. The cloudless blue sky offered it the perfect backdrop. "You can just make out the ruins of its round buildings."

Maggie clambered onto the back of the ridge and joined her wife. She held desperately onto her arm, breathless and exhausted. "To hell with the buildings, you have a lady in *ruins* here!"

It had taken them four hours to reach the summit, the final section involved a steep climb and a short rocky scrabble, and the younger woman had been pushed to her physical limits. Thankfully, the June weather had stayed fine, and the view from the top was certainly impressive.

An Sgurr was originally a lava flow from a now extinct volcano on Rum. The magma had followed an old river bed, filling the glen. Millions of years of erosion had worn away the surrounding basalt rock, leaving the harder pitch stone lava standing proud as a mile-long ridge.

It was on on this promontory that the two women were now sitting, Maggie's legs having finally given out on her. It was very windy on the top, and Caroline's lips felt chilled on her cheek as she kissed her in appreciation of her efforts.

"Are you all right?" Caroline asked, slipping a hand beneath her beloved's anorak.

Maggie had tugged the zip down as her exertions had generated an uncomfortable amount of body heat during the ascent. Caroline lay her palm just under Maggie's left breast, and felt her heart racing.

"Any opportunity to have a grope, and you take it," Maggie laughed. "I'll be fine in a minute. I did warn you that I'm not as fit as you are."

She covered Caroline's hand with her own, outside of her jacket. "Just promise me one thing. *Please* don't ask me to accompany you on any more mountaineering exhibitions on this holiday, or I'll never make it back to Stirling in two weeks, let alone be in a fit state to relocate with you. Unless you want to be a grieving widow I suggest we stick to low-level walking in future."

The gusts and Maggie's breathlessness made it difficult for Caroline to hear all her words clearly, but she understood her meaning perfectly well. Despite giving up her extreme sport activities shortly after she had met Maggie, Caroline still went to the local gymnasium every week, as she did when she was working.

As a couple she had always been the stronger partner, both physically and mentally, and the most dominant. She knew that more often than not her spouse just went along with her plans to placate her. That was one of the reasons why Caroline was so glad that it had been Maggie who had suggested that they adopt a more peaceful rural lifestyle in the future.

****

Their accommodation in Cleadale last night had been delightful. A converted croft house, *Lageorna* was the proud holder of a Gold award from the Green Tourism Business Scheme. It was a recognition of the guest house's extraordinary efforts to do things as sustainably as possible.

Despite it now being the twenty-first century, Eigg had never been supplied with mains electricity. Over the years the islanders' reliance on their micro-generators had slowly decreased, as entrepreneurs had installed the technology necessary to harness the power of the waves, sun and wind. Now ninety per cent of the energy used was renewable, and Lageorna was a supreme example of this.

Their king-sized bed had been locally made, and it faced the bay window through which the granite islet of nearby Rum could be seen in all its glory. They had been warmly welcomed by the owner, a Mrs Fraser, and after unpacking they had taken a power shower together before dining in the four-star restaurant.

Maggie had kept her promise. Caroline had taken her

place at their table wrapped in a metaphorical blanket of euphoria. They had made love as the piping hot water had pounded their bodies, Maggie plunging her fingers deeply inside Caroline this time, so deep that she could feel her cervix.

Much later with their stomachs full of roasted local pollock and homemade rhubarb crumble, Caroline achieved her third orgasm of the day as the two of them had engaged in the *scissoring* aspect of tribadism.

Maggie had laid on her back whilst Caroline faced away from her, locking their crotches together. She gripped Maggie's left thigh between her own, and moved backwards and forwards so that their two vulvas rubbed together. They had climaxed simultaneously without the requirement of any manual stimulation.

Caroline had thrown away her strap-on years before, as wearing it usually elicited squeals of laughter from her lover rather than groans of arousal. Most of their lovemaking consisted of tribadism in some form or another, but usually with Caroline gazing into Maggie's beautiful green eyes rather than her looking out of the window.

The older woman prayed that in years to come osteoarthritis did not set into the joints of her fingers. She still took enormous pleasure in penetrating her gorgeous wife, as Maggie did in being taken, but they both much preferred to do this digitally rather than using any kind of sex toys.

****

"So, that's the *bloody* volcano that almost put me in my grave," Maggie remarked, glowering at the Rum Cuillins the next day.

Caroline nodded in confirmation and took her hand. They had made it back down from An Sgurr on Eigg, and were now exploring the mountainous landscape of the largest of the Small Isles.

Yesterday morning they had arrived by boat into Loch Scresort on the island's east coast. Eider ducks were waiting patiently on the shore for the low tide, so that they could wander out to the extensive mussel beds to feed. Maggie had gasped at a white-tailed sea eagle as it had swooped down to the water's surface, grabbing a wriggling fish in its mighty talons. She had squeezed Caroline's hand in excitement.

As they waited at Kinloch to disembark they had marveled at the red sandstone battlements of the castle which was standing proud at the head of the bay. Their home for the next two nights was originally built as a private residence for Sir George Bullough, a textile tycoon from the industrial town of Lancashire in the north of England.

At the ferry pier they had been advised to park up next to the slipway, and take advantage of the complimentary minibus provided. Along with their fellow passengers they approached the castle from the south, through a tunnel of trees. Caroline had remarked, as they were bouncing along the three quarter of a mile unmade road that, *their Vauxhall's suspension would have had a bloody good workout along here*. Maggie shushed her, not wishing to break the sense of enchantment that she had felt since stepping onto this most romantic of the Small Isles.

They had taken up the offer of a formal guided tour from one of the Scottish Natural Heritage volunteers who now acted as caretakers for the place, shortly after their arrival. It was evident from the numerous mounted heads adorning the walls of the Grand Hall that it had primarily been used as a hunting lodge. Maggie had been more impressed by the monkey-eating bronze eagle perched beneath the sad mementos of the once magnificent beasts.

****

Caroline had really splashed out on the accommodation. She had booked them into one of the *Oak Rooms*, rather than at the adjoining hostel. Last night they had slumbered upon a gothic style four poster bed surrounded by romantic paintings of cherubs, and the like.

Duncan, Maggie's gay best friend had a sister-in-law who had spent her honeymoon at The Witchery Hotel in

Edinburgh. From his description of their suite it seemed likely that Kinloch Castle was of a similar standard. Maggie could not be certain which of the establishments had the most ornate rooms, but there was one thing which she could be sure about. Both had been witness to so *very* hot lesbian lovemaking as Clare had also married a stunning blonde. Her bride's name was Lyn.

****

"Well, love it will be island number three tomorrow. Are you enjoying our whistle-stop tour of the Northern Inner Hebrides?" Caroline asked Maggie as they made their way back to the castle. Suddenly she caught the glimpse of a red deer stag silhouetted against the azure sky. He was standing on a granite boulder, proudly surveying his kingdom. Caroline squeezed Maggie's hand to focus her attention. Then he was gone.

Rum currently had a population of just thirty people, and as a guest one was either obliged to stay with relatives, or at the old hunting lodge. There was a basic camping area by the shore of Loch Scresort, but one was likely to be attacked by the hungry Highland midges there, a particularly ferocious sub-species of the tiny swarming insect.

Maggie stopped in her tracks and took Caroline into her arms. "It's been wonderful, darling. I am so glad that you suggested that we divided our time between the

Small Isles and Skye. I shall never forget these islands, and it's been so lovely to just spend time with you."

Caroline kissed her tenderly on the lips. "Well, I suppose considering that I even accompany you to the lavatory we have not been out of each other's sight for a single minute!"

"That's true. That lady did look at us a little strangely yesterday when you followed me into the public convenience at the Bistro."

The following morning they were once again on the MV Lochnevis. Their destination this time was Canna, the most westerly settlement of the archipelago. It appeared small and whale-shaped from afar.

As they approached the island's buttressed cliffs aboard the ferry, Caroline abruptly grabbed Maggie's thigh in elation, and shot her arm out towards the solitary stack rising from the sea.

Maggie whooped in excitement as she watched the eagle fly towards the coast through the pair of binoculars which they had bought at the general store on Rum. Suddenly, it swooped down low and caught a young rabbit. Maggie felt very sorry for the small furry creature.

"I thought they only ate fish," she blurted.

Whilst idly looking around the village shop as Maggie was choosing her field glasses Caroline had recalled her

conversation with the owner of the accommodation on
Canna. He had informed her that there was no electricity
on the island between the hours of midnight and six
o'clock in the morning. He had explained that this was
because the power was produced by three generators
which were very expensive to run. Canna had no mains
electricity. She had purchased a torch just in case either
of them needed to answer the call of Nature in the
middle of the night.

Caroline also felt sad at the lagomorph's demise, but
she was rather more practical than her spouse. She
explained the harsh reality to her, "That is their food of
choice, but there are so many rabbits on Canna that they
like to supplement their diet with a little fresh meat on
occasions. They are quite partial to mutton as well
which was *the nail in their coffin,* really. They
eventually became extinct earlier this century, but back
in the 1970s the RSPB and SNH set up a re-introduction
programme. A total of eighty-two eaglets, nearly
fledged were imported, under special licence from their
nests in northern Norway to Rum, and the rest, as they
say is history."

Maggie stared at her wife in astonishment. "Well,
who's the walking encyclopaedia then! How come you
know so much about them?"

Caroline grinned. "You know what I'm like. There is
only so much housework *a lady of leisure* can do in a

day whilst her beloved is slaving away at the office. I took your advice and borrowed a few books from the local library."

"I never saw any tomes hanging around the house. You struggle to get through Clare's novels. I'm sure you only read them out of politeness to Grant. We always seem to end up discussing his sister's latest masterpiece when they invite us around for supper."

"You're probably right, but I think it's Duncan who is obsessed with all things literary. Grant confessed to me once that sometimes when they are entertaining Clare and her wife of an evening, he has the strongest of desires to just get down to some good old surgery. *I would rather repair a hernia than read some damn novel*, he said to me once."

Caroline had stowed away the reference books in her bedside drawer. She just wanted to act as Maggie's personal tour guide whilst they were on their holiday. She had a feeling though that perhaps she was being over-enthusiastic, showing off her new-found wealth of knowledge.

As the boat landed at the small quay, another couple of facts came into her mind. She was just about to tell Maggie that Canna was currently in the care of the National Trust for Scotland, as was the island of Sanday which could be reached by simply walking across a wooden bridge, but she thought better of it. Instead she just took hold of her hand and assisted her to disembark.

They had left their car on Rum as they would have required special permission from the National Trust to bring it onto the island. Canna was only five miles long and a mile or so across, so even without their beloved Vectra traveling around would not prove to be too much of a problem.

As the boat landed Maggie was almost jumping up and down with excitement and anticipation. She too had done some research on the Small Isles, but online rather than poring over any *coffee table* books. Of all the islands, it was Canna that she was secretly looking forward to exploring the most. On the Internet it had seemed the most isolated. Just the thought of relaxing in such a wild landscape filled her with great joy.

They had arranged to meet Mr. Donaldson, the owner of *Tighard*, the guesthouse where they were to spend the next two nights, straight off the boat.

Caroline spotted a stout-looking man holding a placard on which had been written, *Mr. and Mrs Montgomery*. She whispered to Maggie, "Will you look at that! Which one of us is the *Mister*, I wonder!"

The man sauntered over towards them and enquired of Caroline whether she was indeed Mrs Montgomery. She reassured him that she was, and said, "And this is my *wife,* Maggie."

Mr. Donaldson looked startled. "I assumed that you

were a married couple when you made the booking on the telephone," he stuttered, his cheeks taking on a ruddy glow.

Maggie shuffled her feet in embarrassment. She had a sense of foreboding about the outcome of this debacle. An overwhelming feeling of disappointment had started to creep through the very bones of her. "We are a *married couple*, sir," she retorted. "We've been wed for eighteen years."

"I'm sorry, ladies. There has been some misunderstanding," he explained, leaning casually against his Land Rover. "We don't allow same-sex couples to stay at Tighard, married or not."

Caroline could not believe what she was hearing. She bristled with indignation. Like a bull about to paw the ground before a charge, she could practically feel her blood boiling. Just as she was about to let out a tirade of abuse, she become aware of Maggie's hand on her arm.

"Leave it, love. He's not worth it. If we hurry we can get back on the boat before it departs," she said wearily, her voice threatening to break with emotion.

Caroline hesitated. Part of her accepted Maggie's resignation, and she was loathe to create a scene, if only because she knew that her wife disliked confrontations. If the guesthouse owner was so homophobic on an island which only had a resident population of twenty what chance did they have? This was the first time that either of them had ever experienced even an inkling of prejudice.

The boat was sounding its horn, signaling that it was about to leave. She picked up both her own and Maggie's holdalls.

"That's a disgusting policy to have," she almost spat at the arrogant man who now had his arms folded defiantly.

On his face was a look of revulsion. *Bloody lesbians*, he thought. He had heard about women sleeping with other women, but he had never actually met one, let alone a *pair* of them before!

Mr. Donaldson had stayed on Canna for all of his fifty years, and apart from his monthly trips to Mallaig to stock up on provisions he never went off the island. He was for once literally lost for words, so he just shrugged his shoulders and turned to open the door of his vehicle.

"King Rupert will hear about this. Acts of homophobia are now punishable, you know. You could serve five years in prison for your insults."

Mr. Donaldson could not hear Caroline's words over the roar of his V8 engine kicking back into life. His tyres screeched, churning up the gravel.

The two women threw themselves onto one of the ferry's benches, panting. They had made it with but a few seconds to spare.

"Let's forget Muck. I've had enough of the Small Isles to last me a lifetime," Caroline stated.

Maggie burst into tears. "That was awful. I've never

been treated so appallingly before," she sobbed, wiping her eyes with a proffered handkerchief. Blowing her nose loudly, she exclaimed, "That man made me feel unclean, as if us being together was something shameful. And there was me, thinking that homophobia was a thing of the past."

Caroline took back the now sodden handkerchief and gave Maggie a fresh one. "It is, love but obviously the news has yet to reach Canna. Let's just go straight to Skye. I know your relatives will welcome us with open arms. I am proud to be a lesbian and even prouder that you're my wife. *Mr. Montgomery*, indeed. Mr. *Donaldson* will be hearing from our solicitor *very* soon!

Maggie gulped lungfuls of the tangy sea air. She took the older woman's face in her hands and kissed her. "I love you so much, Caroline. Ours is a marriage made in heaven. May all those bigots on Canna rot in hell," she whispered, tears once more welling in her emerald green eyes.

THIRTEEN

Up in the Highlands several days later it was a hive of activity. Gritting her teeth and mustering up all her strength, Kathy wrapped her arms around the oil drum which was three quarters full of a sticky coffee-coloured liquid, and tried to tip its contents down the drain which was by the back wall, but it would not budge.

Resigned, she glanced quickly around her garden, and then ran back into the house. Panting from exertion, she laboriously bailed out the drum with a pint Pyrex jug, beads of perspiration forming on her top lip upon which a fine line of hair could be detected.

She wrinkled her nose at the aroma. The liquor had the consistency of motor oil and it smelt awful, like a cat litter tray that had not been emptied for weeks.
Eventually the drum was light enough to lift, and Kathy tipped the rest of it directly down the drain. Her dog barked excitedly.

There was a soggy residue at the bottom. According to her research if she placed the drum back over the fire and let it all dry out a wee bit, then by the morning the remains would look rather similar to the ashes that the crematorium had given to her in an urn after her grandfather's funeral. The plan was to then scoop them out and bag them up. She would hide it amongst her usual kitchen rubbish, all ready for the municipal bin men to collect on Wednesday. Peering into the bottom of the container Kathy noticed something metallic. Reaching now, it looked like some kind of screw. She had not realised that Angie had been into DIY, or carpentry for that matter. She shoved it into the pocket of her jeans for safekeeping.

****

Kathy had found out online that the best way to dispose of a body was to dissolve it in a solution of potassium hydroxide, a strong alkali used in soap-making amongst other things. It had been easier enough to purchase the chemical over the Internet, but keeping the fire going underneath the drum for the required five hours had been rather more taxing.

Ideally, she needed to heat the solution to a temperature of three hundred degrees in a pressurised environment, sixty pounds per square inch was recommended, but that would have required specialized equipment. Angie might have been very petite, but even if she had dismembered her there was no way that she could have fitted her into a domestic pressure cooker.

Alkaline hydrolysis was apparently used to dispose of cadavers donated for research to medical centres. Kathy had considered using sulphuric acid instead which would have liquefied the bones and teeth as well, but she had been concerned about the toxicity of the fumes, and acquiring some nasty third degree burns. The *lye*, as strong bases such as sodium or potassium hydroxide were known as, was a much safer option.

Thankfully, she had discovered an old barbeque stand at the bottom of her garden on Sunday morning. Angie's body now lay under her bed, rather than on it. Whilst out foraging around the grounds of the now dilapidated farmhouse later that day she had came across the disused oil drum.

Wow, that's a classic example of pure serendipity for you, Kathy had thought to herself. She had been rather concerned that her carefully researched plans would not prove practical.

Somehow she had kept the chemical solution at boiling point long enough to do the required job. She used a discarded piece of corrugated iron as a makeshift lid. Every once in awhile, standing on a chair which she had found in one of the outbuildings she gingerly lifted it up with a pair of old kitchen gloves, and peered inside. She had wondered if it would be necessary to stir her grisly stew, but the lye seemed to be working perfectly well without the need for agitation.

At one occasion she had nearly toppled backwards, glimpsing the partially decomposed face of her late lover. She was certainly not looking her best. It was all a lot of hard work, but much safer than dumping the body into a loch somewhere. This way she did not mess up her car, and the likelihood of anyone linking her to Angie's disappearance was very slight indeed. It felt like she was simply clearing up after her weekend of fun and frolics.

****

The disused farm which Kathy now stayed on was well off the main road. Her nearest neighbour was a mile away.

After the court case in which her employer and co-conspirator Christopher had been accused of murdering the three women, she had began to suffer from panic attacks, ever fearful that the police would come looking for her after they had failed to secure a conviction. She become paranoid about her neighbours, and even the other parents who took their children to the same riding school as her daughter. She suspected that they were gossiping about her, although no public connection had ever been made between her and Naughty But Nice.

One evening whilst trying to relax in her house in Liberton Kathy's thoughts had become so scrambled that she began to fear for her very sanity. After yet another sleepless night she decided to relocate to the Highlands.

The housing market was buoyant, and within two months of a *For Sale* board being erected in the front garden a buyer was found, and with a bulging bank account she moved almost two hundred miles north to a rambling cottage on the outskirts of Laggan, a sleepy village nestling at the foothills of the Monadhliath and Grampian Mountains. A tributary of the River Spey ran along the bottom of her garden.

Her parents who stayed in Edinburgh had been most concerned about Kathy's mental health and the effect her capricious behaviour was having on their granddaughter, so they kindly offered to look after her for a while, until her mother was well again. Kathy had raised no objections, in fact she was secretly relieved. In her present state of mind she could hardly care for herself, let alone a nine year old girl.

Once she had settled in Laggan and found herself a job Kathy had started looking for someone to share her life with. She now worked in a large supermarket in Inverness and although being sat behind a till all day was not exactly mind-blowing, at least she could keep her clothes on.

With nobody at home to worry about she was free to spend her time off as she wished. Most evenings she simply drove for the required forty-five minutes, and wearily collapsed in front of the television after supper, but once a week she treated herself to a night out.

For ever since she could remember Kathy had considered herself to be bisexual. In a way it had been a blessing as it meant that she could participate in both straight and lesbian films, without feeling the least bit uncomfortable.

Since the original murders she had kept a very low profile, but now the delights of Inverness were hers for the taking. She had carried out some extensive research online and discovered that despite there still being a certain degree of homophobia in the Highlands, which meant that gay people kept to their own pubs and clubs, unlike down south where it really did not matter what sexuality you were, there was still a vibrant queer culture in the city.

Each week she went to a different establishment. Once she had caught a woman's eye in the Castle Tavern and had woken up in her flat overlooking the supermarket where she worked of all places, but usually she returned home alone with just her daft golden labrador to keep her feet warm in bed at night.

One Friday after her shift had finished, she drove over to Aberdeen which was a hundred miles in the easterly direction, booked herself into a bed and breakfast, and then spent the whole night in a gay club. On Saturday she repeated the experience. Kathy wanted to explore the whole of the Highlands, not just the environs of Inverness and Laggan. She had loved the granite architecture of Aberdeen, but even more so the thirty year old lady that she had picked up there. They had gone back to her place, a flat in the heart of the city, and made passionate love well into Sunday afternoon.

Angie was exactly the kind of woman that Kathy went for. She was slim, intelligent and her breasts were the perfect size for her to cup with one hand.

Kathy would have described herself as buxom and she was proud of her assets, but in a lover she preferred a more boyish physique. Brunette herself, it did not matter one iota to her whether the lady was dark or blonde, but she liked somebody who could hold a decent conversation.

Angie worked as a legal clerk in Aberdeen, and having just split up with her long-term girlfriend she had been feeling particularly lonely. As a couple the two of them had steered away from *the scene*, preferring their own company so it had been Angie's first time in the Caberfae Nightclub.

When Kathy had suggested to her as they were lying in bed together on that first Sunday afternoon whether she would like to visit her in Laggan she had responded with positive enthusiasm.

Two weeks later she found herself parked up in front of an isolated farm cottage. Kathy ran out to greet her, and as they entered the low-ceilinged entrance hall the two women had literally fallen on each other.

The next morning whilst she was making a pot of tea for them both Kathy reflected on the night before. Angie had been as sexually exciting as in Aberdeen, but there had been a very worrying development. As far as she was aware Angie had had no idea that anything was amiss, but Kathy had felt scared. As she was thrusting into her lover, her trusty strap-on securely attached to her groin a strange sensation had crossed her mind. Flashbacks to the last film she had made increased her arousal, and without realising what she was doing her hands had reached up to Angie's neck.

Her lover moaned loudly, and Kathy stopped what she was doing. Angie had climaxed at just the right moment. A split second later and what she assumed to be a loving caress would have been, in reality her last breath.

****

Kathy had never felt any guilt about taking the three lives, but she had been very concerned that her employer might be hanged in proxy. Not only did she feel no remorse but ever since had subconsciously yearned to do it again.

Every time she had placed her hands over the women's carotid arteries and applied enough prolonged pressure to ensure that their brains were starved of oxygen, she had experienced the most intense of orgasms. Since then she had tried in vain to achieve a similar climax, but despite being somewhat of an expert when it came to the art of masturbation none of her nightly fondles ever came close.

Like a addict desperate for her next fix Kathy gradually became almost obsessed by the need to feel that high again. She knew for certain that she would have tried to kill the woman whom she picked up in the Castle Tavern in Inverness if she had not been quite so intoxicated. *Every Christmas the government launched an advertising campaign with the slogan, Alcohol kills! Well, she had definitely disproved that one.*

****

"Kathy, darling, where are you?" Angie called from the bedroom. She had just woken up, and scrabbling out of the unfamiliar bed she had drawn back the heavy curtains to gaze in wonder at the magnificent view. The rolling heathland seemed to stretch from the cottage walls right over to the hills themselves, the purple heather interspersed by the yellow of the gorse.

Angie threw open the window and savoured the very quietness of it all. She could not hear anything aside from the occasional call of an unknown bird, and perhaps the faint trickle of the stream. What a difference to waking up in the vibrant city, with its noise and fumes, she had mused.

There were less cars now than there used to be. Rather like in the 1930s the vehicles had character and were manufactured to the highest of specifications. One no longer saw clones of *a box on four wheels*. These automobiles had style, but they were expensive. Rolls Royces and Rover V8 SD1s were particular favourites, and behind the steering wheel there was as likely to be a chauffeur than the owner himself.

Only the middle and upper classes could afford a brand new car. They soon become bored with them though, and for ever striving to keep up with the latest fashion they would discard them, rather like people did clothes years before. Charity shops sold second-hand cars now, not garments. It was acceptable to wear one's older brother's jacket for example, but even the working classes turned their noses up at donning the rags of a stranger.

Kathy entered the bedroom carrying a tray loaded with cups of steaming tea, and two plates of deliciously smelling toast and marmalade. She had gathered herself together in the kitchen, but had decided that however much she might like Angie to stay for another night she had to persuade her to return to Aberdeen. She just could not trust herself.

"My, my, breakfast in bed. You are spoiling me!"

Kathy placed the tray on one of the bedside cabinets and handed a cup to Angie. "You looked so peaceful there. I didn't want to wake you, so I made myself useful," she said, smiling.

Angie beamed, her eyes full of lust. The sex last night had simply been *out-of-this-world*. She had never been penetrated with a strap-on before, but now she could not imagine being made love to without one. To feel Kathy's hips moving on top of hers so that she could match every thrust had been marvelous. She had orgasmed so many times that she had lost count. She could not recall her lover climaxing but that had not seemed to bother Kathy at all, so selfless had she been. She put down the tea, took a huge bite from her slice of toast and grabbed the object of her desire.

Twenty minutes later she was dead.

FOURTEEN

"Are you sure that's all right, Marcus?" Maggie spoke into her mobile telephone.

The two women had climbed down the steep staircase to Deck Two of the MV Lochnevis, and were now sat at one of the tables near the *Coffee Cabin*. Caroline cradled her cup of tea in both hands, she had started to shiver despite the sun's warmth shortly after they had boarded the ferry, and smiled at her wife. Despite her bravado, their treatment on Canna had really shaken her up. In the end it was Maggie who had had to comfort her.

At least it seemed Anne and Marcus were happy enough to offer their hospitality two days earlier than originally planned. Caroline had met Maggie's cousin, his plump jolly wife and their children three times before. On the second occasion the five of them had made the journey from their then home in Portree, Skye's main town, to Stirling.

****

Before he retired Marcus had owned a thriving garage business just up from the bustling port. He used to run it with his brother Gerry, but sadly he had succumbed to a massive myocardial infarction and died.

Terry, his nephew had just turned sixteen by then, and he decided to accept his father's offer of an apprenticeship. He loved his new job, being able to use his hands and having the time to have a blather with the customers. The turnover had been good whilst Gerry was alive, but once Terry was qualified and able to turn his hand to any mechanical problem word had spread around the island and their profits had soared.

Terry's reputation became such that within two months he was known as *the best mechanic in the whole of the Hebrides*. Many believed that, given the opportunity to prove it, that would probably be the *best mechanic in the whole of Scotland*, but Terry had no plans to leave his beloved Skye.

To mark his twenty-fifth birthday Marcus had made him a partner in the business. Two years later his father officially retired, and Terry became the sole proprietor of the garage. Now fifty-five years of age, Marcus had had enough of spending every bath time scrubbing his hands clean of oil and the like.

Six months before his early retirement Terry had presented him with his first grandchild. Rupert, named after the monarch was a happy baby, and the apple of his grandfather's eye. Terry decided to employ a local mechanic, so that he could take time off to visit his parents who both now stayed in Dunvegan, which was about six miles from Portree.

Terry was very fond of his second cousin, and he was to coincide his fortnightly trip to the north-west of the island with her holiday so that he could spent a few days with her and Caroline. He had been just a child when Maggie had re-married after the sudden death of her husband. Despite being of an above average intelligence, he had not really understand her new circumstances.

One December whilst helping his mother to write her Christmas cards, he enthusiastically slapped a stamp onto each of the envelopes, Terry had pointed to the words, *To Maggie and Caroline*, on the card to Stirling, and asked innocently, *Whose's that?*

It had taken him a while to come to terms with the idea that one of his family was now a lesbian, and his first meeting with his cousin and her new wife when he was a precocious eight year old had not gone well. After reluctantly accompanying his parents and his younger sisters to the mainland two years later his opinion had dramatically changed. He could see how happy Caroline made his cousin. His father told him that he could not remember Maggie laughing so much, when she had been married to Andrew.

When he was twenty-two Terry had fallen hopelessly in love with a local lass, and of course Maggie and Caroline were invited to his wedding just eight months later. It was really this family celebration which cemented the bond of friendship between them, despite Terry being less than half of Caroline's age.

He was so looking forward to showing off his son who was now a bubbly toddler to his extended family. It was just a pity that their adopted daughter Veronica would not be able to join them. Terry had met her just once five years ago when she had accompanied her parents to witness his nuptials, but they had kept in touch by e-mail ever since.

Terry's wife was not the easiest of women to live with, although as far as his Mum and Dad were concerned everything was *just fine* in their marriage. Secretly, he had fallen in love with the stunning Veronica on his wedding day. Consequently, their correspondence did tend to border on the flirtatious, although Terry had never been quite sure how serious she was about him until fairly recently.

Perhaps one day he might take a well earned vacation of his own and drive up to Inverness to see her. The main reason why he had been putting off the trip was because he feared that when they did meet again something physical would happen between them. Despite the difficulties in his marriage, he still loved his wife, and even now his conscience struggled with the fact that he had romantic feelings for two women simultaneously.

Last year Veronica had sent him a gift for Valentine's Day. He had experienced palpitations on opening the box. An animal's face was gazing up at him. Apparently, according to the wee note inside it was a *dipped sheep*. This was essentially a soft toy which had been immersed in scented candle wax, so that it could be used as a rather cute room freshener. Amazingly, if the perfume ever needed reviving one just warmed the wax with a hairdryer.

Terry had covertly loved it, but he had panicked something rotten. *What the hell was he supposed to do with it?* He could hardly put it on a shelf in the marital bedroom, or even in their lounge for that matter. It had a red heart resting on its lap, saying *I Love You*!

He thought about hiding it away in his chest of drawers like a dark secret. In the end he had simply left it in its original packaging, and shoved it to the back of his wardrobe.

Feeling confused and guilty, for two months he had ceased all communication with Veronica despite her profuse apologies and her reassuring him that she was not, and never would be a threat to his marriage. She explained to him by e-mail that the red heart was in fact removable. He could then openly display it in the house. After all, his wife knew that they were friends. *What was the harm in one pal sending a present to another?*

Eventually, he could stand it no longer and they

tentatively started exchanging e-mails and texts again. He knew that he had treated her badly. After all, she could not help how she felt about him. In a way he admired her loyalty and persistence. Despite his protestations, she did make him feel special and appreciated.

According to her recent e-mails she had about eighteen months left of her course at the Royal Highland at which point she intended to secure her first job, managing a hotel. Veronica was very ambitious, and Terry had no doubt that she would fulfill her dreams. He made a promise to himself to take that trip north, before the Highlands were once again covered in a thick blanket of snow.

****

"Welcome to Dunvegan!" Marcus threw his arms around his cousin, almost knocking her off her feet. "It's been a long five years, but you haven't changed one bit!"

Maggie playfully punched the big built man on his shoulder. "I don't know about that, but I must admit marriage has been good for me. You've changed, though. You seem to have lost that magnificent beard of yours, and dare I say, gained a few extra pounds."

Marcus laughed, which seemed to begin as a deep

rumble somewhere in his bulging waistline. "You can blame Anne for both of those. She got fed up with her face being scratched every time I felt frisky, and you know me, little cousin, that feeling overwhelms me at *least* once a day. After some persuasion she allowed me to keep my *little slug*." He fingered his trimmed auburn moustache. "As for the other thing, well, I never could resist decent home cooking!"

Maggie chortled as well, and sighed with relief. Canna was just a fading memory, now that she was once more in the bosom of her family. Any idea of relocating to the Small Isles had been firmly erased from both her and Caroline's minds, but on the boat they had discussed the possibility of moving to Skye. Aside from the undeniable advantage of having her cousin near by, the island was the only one of the Hebrides to be linked to the mainland by a bridge. They could simply drive over, rather than being reliant on the ferry. It was still wild and remote enough to offer them a peaceful retirement.

Marcus turned to Caroline who was smiling with pleasure at the joyful reunion. "And how are you, my love?" he asked her, embracing her warmly.

"I'm fine, now that we are here. It's great to see you again, Marcus. How's that strapping boy of yours?"

"Terry? Not so much a *boy*, anymore. He's twenty-seven now, and a proud father. He'll be over next week. He's really looking forward to seeing you both again."

The three of them walked into the house. The detached property was situated at Claigan, a small coastal settlement on the north-east shore of Loch Dunvegan.

Anne greeted them in the airy kitchen. The smell of freshly baked bread made Maggie's nostrils twitch, and her mouth water. She was wrapped in arms even bigger than her cousin's. *Evidently, the government's healthy eating drive has yet to reach the Hebrides*, she thought, but she returned the plump woman's embrace fervently.

"Hello, Anne. It's so wonderful to see you again. You are looking well!" She spied a rackful of apple scones on the table. "And I see you have been busy."

"As soon as you phoned I said to Marcus, *No doubt the pair will be ravenous after their adventures.* I've a date and walnut loaf in the oven too, and there'll be a ham and haddie pie ready for our supper."

She turned to Caroline. "It looks like you could do with fatting up, love."

Caroline laughed. "It's all the running around after this one," she paused, poking Maggie in the ribs, "that keeps me so trim."

Anne laughed as she wiped her floury hands in her apron. "Why don't I show you to your room, and then we can all have a nice cup of tea and a bit of a catch-up before we eat. I expect you could both do with freshening up after your journey."

Caroline winked at her wife. Despite not seeing Maggie's cousin and her family for five years, and never having visited their current residence, she felt very much *at home*. They both followed Anne's swaying derriere up the narrow staircase.

To Maggie's delight their room overlooked the coral beaches. Anne had explained before she left them to unpack that, in reality the sand consisted of pieces of dried calcified seaweed known as maerl, as well as thousands of tiny delicate snail shells. She promised that tomorrow, if the weather held they would take a walk up there.

Caroline's eyes had lit up when she mentioned that there was a fine example of a *souterrain* close by as well. Anne did not seem to know much about the structure, aside from the fact that it was a pre-historic chamber which disappeared horizontally into the earth for about thirty-two feet. A flashback to her caving trip in Sutherland came back to Caroline, and it filled her with a strange kind of excitement.

As soon as they were alone Maggie took her wife into her arms. It had been an emotional day for both of them. They were stood in the middle of the room, and as Maggie placed her lips on Caroline's she felt herself being gently lowered onto the double bed.

"I know we don't have time to get up to anything *too* naughty," Caroline whispered in her ear as the aroma of freshly washed bedding assailed her senses, "we have all night for that, but I just wanted to hold you."

"Oh, darling. Hold me, and never let me go! I love you so much," Maggie stated, her voice choked with emotion.

They kissed each other with a terrible urgency as if by confirming their love for each other, they could obliterate from their memories what had happened on Canna. Caroline knew just how much Maggie had been looking forward to exploring the island, and it was a shame that they had missed out on Muck too, the smallest and most fertile of the Small Isles.

I must remember to ring the hotel there in the morning to cancel our booking, she thought as she deftly removed Maggie's lower garments.

They were awoken a hour later by the sound of Marcus's voice from below informing them that their supper was ready. Both their holdalls sat untouched by the window.

Maggie stretched languidly. "Now let's go and have our main course," she said, pulling Caroline up from the bed. She discovered her slightly crumpled trousers laying in a heap by the en-suite bathroom door.

FIFTEEN

"Talking of seaweed," Marcus interrupted his wife, waving a forkful of smoked haddock in the air, "two hundred years or so ago the kelp on the beaches here became a *very* valuable commodity."

"Marcus, you're as bad as Caroline. She thinks she's *Scotland's answer to the Encyclopedia Britannica*!" Maggie gazed around the groaning dining table and smiled contently.

Her cousin was sat at its head, and as a gesture of honour she had been offered Anne's usual setting directly opposite him. The matriarch was now seated next to Caroline, whilst the two daughters whose ages were either side of twenty faced their doting mother.

Huge portions of Anne's famous Bacon and Haddie Pie adorned each plate, and all six of them had just helped themselves to the numerous steaming dishes of fresh local vegetables. These made a fitting centrepiece placed as they were around the base of a five branched silver candelabrum. Anne had drawn the curtains even though it was barely dusk outside to create a cosy atmosphere.

Marcus cleared his throat, took a mouthful of his wine which he had explained earlier had been produced in the Orkney Islands from hops of all things, and continued, "When kelp is burnt it releases soda ash, a chemical crucial to the glass making industry. Up until the late 1700s Britain's source of soda ash was Spain, but the war with Napoleon put pay to that. Cutting the weed was filthy work, but at least it put food in the bairns' bellies."

"Very interesting, Marcus," his wife informed him with perhaps just a touch of sarcasm in her voice. "Now stop your blathering and eat your supper before it gets cold!"

Marcus reddened and feigned obsequiousness. Most of the time Anne let him have his own way, but just once in a while she gave him a gentle reminder as to which one of them was really the boss.

Whilst the two young women were helping their mother to clear the table in preparation for the next course Marcus asked his cousin about her daughter. He did not exactly approve of gay adoption, but that was probably due to his own traditional upbringing.

He had only met Veronica once at his own son's wedding five years previously. Like Terry, she was very bright and had a fiery temper if provoked, but it was plain that she adored her two mothers. He did cross his mind at the time whether having two lesbians for parents would affect her sexuality. He knew his son kept in touch with her. He had never mentioned her having any girl, or boyfriends. Marcus was just curious, that was all.

"Well, we haven't seen her for six months. She's on a

two year hotel management course up in Inverness. Caroline suggested to her before we went to Eigg that we could pop up there before we return to Stirling, but she fobbed us off. Sometimes I think our daughter is *too* independent! I really miss her, well we both do."

Later that evening Marcus was snuggled up in bed with his wife. Whilst cleaning his teeth he had begun to wonder about his cousin and Caroline. Nobody could accuse him of being homophobic, in fact he had been shocked at their treatment on Canna which Maggie had related to him as they were relaxing over their postprandial coffees, but despite them being together for almost two decades he really could not understand how his cousin could have fallen in love with a woman in the first place.

****

As children, and indeed rebellious teenagers Marcus and Maggie had spent most of their school holidays together, playing on the Skye beaches and paddling in the sea. Marcus's grandparents had owned a small farm at Carbost, and they were all too pleased to welcome their grandson's pretty playmate. Usually the children spent four weeks of their summer break there, and the rest of their vacations in Portree.

Marcus and Maggie used to run around amongst the

cows. At first the motley collection of beef cattle would start and become agitated, but they soon learnt that the youngsters meant them no harm. Once exhausted the two cousins would flop themselves down onto the grass, taking care to avoid the cow pats, and gaze down at the fishing boats moored up on the shores of Loch Harport.

On her first visit to the farm Marcus's grandmother had introduced Maggie to their Black Rock chickens. There were just six hens who were all out in the garden, industriously pecking at the grain scattered amongst the grass. Maggie had been concerned about how they would cope with the winter, but their proud owner reassured her that much of their bulky bodies consisted of feathers which served as excellent insulation against both the wet and the cold.

Later when she was back home in Edinburgh, Maggie had pestered her mother to buy her a book about the breed. Many an hour she would sit crossed-legged on her bed, reading all about the fascinating birds. She learnt that they were *hybrids*, her father had had to explain what that meant, originating from a single hatchery in the east of Scotland Maggie had gazed in wonder at the photographs. She thought it was truly amazing that *her* hens had come from two such different looking breeds, the Rhode Island Red and the Barred Plymouth Rock.

Even to this day she would never forget the old lady proudly handing her a box of brown eggs on the morning of their departure. It became a tradition which she kept up every year until Maggie started studying for her Highers, and school holidays were filled with homework instead of carefree days on her beloved Skye.

For some reason Maggie's parents never invited Marcus back to their family home on the mainland, but that never seemed to bother the boy. Even now Marcus felt uncomfortable when he traveled over the bridge.

As Maggie had blossomed into a beautiful young woman she had attracted the interest of several of the local lads. She regarded Marcus as her best friend, seeing as she was an only child.

She had confided in him one afternoon as they were sat out on their verandah, watching the fishing boats landing their catch at Portree. "I let that boy have his wicked way with me, Marcus." Her green eyes were transfixed on an imaginary speck of dirt on her thigh, at just the point where the beige of her cotton shorts met her pink skin.

Harry who at fifteen was about the same age as the pair of them had been pestering Maggie for most of the summer vacation. She could not look at Marcus, so ashamed and embarrassed did she feel as she confessed the loss of her virginity. Apparently, so Marcus learnt, feeling both jealous and proud of his cousin, he had yet to even kiss a girl, she had just wanted to find out what it was like.

"Did you enjoy it then?" he had asked her, curiously.

"It was all right. The worst part was afterwards. He came inside me, and his sperm dribbled down my leg!"

Marcus stared at her in horror. He might have lacked experience, but he knew all about the *facts of life*. His mother had given him a book about it when he was twelve, and the boys at school had filled in the rest.

He was aware that Maggie had started her periods as one day she had told him that she was not well enough to go out for a walk with him. He had looked so worried that she had sat him down and explained that she had her *monthlies*. He had asked her all sorts of questions, keen to learn more about the fascinating world of women. She told him that she had a sore stomach, and that her legs ached something chronic.

Using his initiative, he had boiled up a kettle and filled a bottle for her. With some of the water he had made her a cup of tea too. She sniffed the steam rising from the china mug. "This is certainly not my usual *Typhoo*. It smells kind of herby. What is it, Marcus?"

He had explained that it was *raspberry leaf* tea. His grandfather swore by it, and he would always add a cup to the cows' molasses when their calves were due to make their appearance in the world. Logically, Marcus thought it might help his favourite cousin with her *women's problems*.

Maggie had laughed and kissed him on his cheek. "I'm

not quite sure what to say to that, but anything's worth a try." She had gingerly sipped the brew, and fifteen minutes later had joined him in the garden where he was quietly sitting reading a book.

He had looked up as she came towards him and smiled. "You certainly seem better!"

She kissed him again."Well, that's one *old wife's tale* that certainly works! What would I do without you, Marcus?"

Sitting on the verandah, hearing about his cousin's first sexual experience had caused him great anxiety. "You do know that you could be *pregnant*, don't you? Why didn't Harry use a rubber?"

Maggie had burst into tears. She was pretty naive for a fifteen year old, and it had just not crossed her mind that she could now have *a bun in the oven*.

"What am I going to do, Marcus?" she pleaded to him.

He took his curvaceous cousin in his arms and tried to think rationally. "When is your next period due?" he asked her, anxiously.

Maggie pondered for a moment, counting the days on her fingers. "Next week if I remember correctly."

Marcus signed with relief. "Well, that's all right then. Your father's not coming over to collect you for another two weeks, is he? Let's just wait to see if you *come on,* " he laughed, "if that is the correct expression."

Ten days later Maggie ran into Marcus's room early

one morning and shook him awake. "It's okay, I've *come on!*"

****

Marcus whispered to his wife, "Are you still awake, love?"

She groaned and opened her eyes. *Thank God, I'm ten years younger than the randy old goat*, she thought. She could feel his erection stabbing into her back. *At least I don't have to contend with that awful beard anymore.*

Marcus might not quite have understood the appeal of lesbianism, but all that speculating about what his cousin might be up to right this minute with her lover, as he was taking his shower had aroused him. That was something that he could never ask Maggie about.

He reached around his wife's ample body and massaged her breasts. She had given birth to their son when she was just twenty, and had never regained the slim figure of her youth. Of course all that home baking did not help. Marcus could hardly comment as he was not exactly tiny, and anyway he liked something to cuddle of a night.

Maggie's better half was very fit and trim for a lady in her early sixties, but Marcus would not exchange his buxom Anne for anyone. He stroked her stomach lovingly, the way she liked it, and he could have sworn that he heard her purr.

"That damn cat's come up again!" Anne exclaimed, kicking the animal off the bed. Leo meowed in protest and slinked out of the room. Marcus was of the opinion that their fluffy feline was a wee bit of a sex maniac.

Once his wife had settled again on her side, he slide his hand further down her voluptuous body and idly played with her pubic hair, which was still as red as his moustache. With his other hand he fondled his penis. Mental images of Maggie and Caroline enjoying themselves on the other side of the house made his member tingle even more. If he was not careful Anne would be accusing him of premature ejaculation, yet again!

He gently slipped a finger into her vagina and used the moisture there to lubricate and stimulate her clitoris. Anne moaned. Her sex drive was a fraction of her husband's and lovemaking to her was more of a marital duty than a pleasure, but give Marcus his due he still knew how *to press the right buttons*.

Sometimes she would tease him that the only reason he had wanted to move to Claigan was because there were far fewer people around to disturb their *al fresco* activities. Marcus adored having sex outside. When they had first explored the area and discovered the souterrain he had grabbed her from behind, underground in the pitch dark. Accommodating as Anne was, even she had *put her foot down over that*. She had wriggled out of his embrace and ran back towards the car. Ten minutes later he was plunging into her behind a rock on the coral beach.

Marcus gripped his throbbing penis and placed it between Anne's buttocks. She wriggled and he pulled her bottom towards his groin, so that its head rested at the entrance of her vagina. She had never experienced anal sex, and Marcus never suggested it. For their age, they were an open-minded couple, but that would have been going *too* far.

Anne gasped involuntarily as she felt her husband's large member push inside her. *Spooning* was her favourite position, and for two amply proportioned lovers probably the most comfortable. Marcus lifted her top leg so that it rested on his hip. Her thighs were now spread apart. She arched her back and moved with him, matching his every thrust. His fingers were still massaging her clitoris and they orgasmed together, Marcus's chest hair tickling Anne's back, and his arms wrapped tightly around her.

SIXTEEN

"Dunvegen is the the oldest continuously inhabited castle in Scotland, and has been the stronghold of the Chiefs of MacLeod for eight hundred years," the guide informed the group of tourists.

It was pouring with rain outside, and as usual the inclement weather was a blessing to the estate. The family owned the magnificent Cuillin hills as well as the Castle.

"Over the years, we have given a warm Highland welcome to thousands of visitors including Sir Walter Scott, Dr. Johnston, Queen Elizabeth the Second *and* the Japanese Emperor Akihito. We now look forward to welcoming you."

Maggie shivered. The sudden downpour had been most unexpected and she had come out without a jacket. Caroline shrugged her rucksack off of her shoulder, and stepping back from the huddle of sodden people she pulled out a sweatshirt and handed it to her wife.

"Thank you, darling! I bet you were a Girl Guide in your youth. You're always prepared for any circumstances."

Caroline grinned and kissed her wife's lips as her head emerged from the garment. Nobody took a blind bit of notice which was an enormous relief to Maggie. The last thing she needed was a repeat performance of the

homophobia that they had experienced on Canna.
Caroline had always been overtly affectionate with her
in public, although according to Anne she was *a cold
fish* compared to Marcus. At the souterrain earlier that
afternoon she had related what he had tried to do to her
on their first visit to the strange antiquity. The plan
today had been to then take a walk along the coral
beach, but instead they had run for cover inside the
castle.

Anne had served them all such an enormous breakfast
when the four of them had gathered in the kitchen that
morning, the two girls had left early to join their
mountaineering club for a spot of rock scrabbling, that
no lunch was required. Caroline was to treat them all to
dinner at one of the local hotels that evening.

Maggie marveled at the family portraits and antique
furniture as she wandered from room to room. Various
showcases held an eclectic selection of relics. A lock of
Bonnie Prince Charlie's hair held her attention, but
Caroline was more interested in the Fairy Flag. She
learnt from the information handwritten on a piece of
card pined next to the scrap of material, that the sacred
banner was believed to have dated back to the seventh
century.

According to legend, the flag would bring success to
the chief, or his clan if unfurled in an emergency.
However, the charm would only work on three
occasions. It had already been used twice to secure

MacLeod victories in battle.

Marcus smiled to himself as he watched his cousin exploring the historic house. Any doubts he had about her relationship with Caroline were now fatally squashed. Deep in his subconscious, he knew that they had been instigated by jealousy. If life had turned out differently then perhaps it would have been him gripping her hand excitedly, as Caroline was doing now, as the two of them stood transfixed in the Pink Drawing Room.

He turned to Anne and suggested that they took a walk in the grounds. He could see through the window that the rain had stopped, and once more the sun was making an appearance.

This surprisingly was his first visit to the seat of Clan MacLeod even though he only stayed a mile from the fortress. He had heard that one could *walk through a shady woodland glade, and end up at a shimmering pool fed by a cascading waterfall.* It all sounded rather too poetic for him, after all he was just a retired car mechanic, but if they made a quick exit before the tourists he was sure that they could find a quiet spot. He whispered something lewd to his wife and discreetly grabbed her curvaceous bottom.

"Sleinte!" Marcus toasted his family in the traditional Scottish fashion later that day. The six of them were sat in the Tables Hotel which was situated in the centre of

Dunvegan village, just two and a half miles away from home. Maggie was staring out of the restaurant's window, but she was not really seeing the flat tops of the mountains on the horizon. Her thoughts were many miles away north, in Inverness with her daughter.

Veronica had called her as they were changing for dinner. At the sound of her distraught voice, Maggie had felt her heart begin to race. She was quite accustomed to her offspring's fiery temper, she had shouted at them both in anger several times in the past, but this verbal display of vulnerability was a rarity.

The last time that she had showed such emotion was eighteen months ago when she had found out that her late mother's body had been discovered thirteen years previously, floating in the Clyde. As far as Maggie was aware, Veronica had put her grisly findings to one side to concentrate on her studies. She had never mentioned Stacey again to either her or Caroline, and both of them had agreed that it was best to let the proverbial sleeping dog lie. After all, there was nothing the three of them could do about it all these years later, was there? The case had been closed, according to the police records.

"Oh, Mum, I feel awful!" Veronica had burst into tears on hearing her mother's gentle accent. She had been so preoccupied with her work at the hotel that she had quite forgotten how much she missed her parents. She had just started her stint as a receptionist, and although she was enjoying it rather more than being a hotel porter she was finding it increasingly difficult to give it her full attention.

Veronica had deliberately pushed all thoughts of her late birth mother to the back of her subconsciousness as she found it too painful to contemplate. After uncovering the tragic truth about her she had grieved privately for the the woman who had brought her into the world, even though they had never met. She did not even have a photograph to remember her by.

Even now she felt uncomfortable burdening her adoptive mother with her worries. It just did not seem fair after all the love she had cherished upon her. Whatever the circumstances which had led her real Mum to her watery grave the fact still remained that she had given her away. Maybe it was a mere childish fantasy to imagine that one day she might have held her in her arms and said, *I'm sorry for giving you up.* That was never going to happen now unless she came back as a ghost!

Overhearing that detective at the police conference had made it all come back in a rush. It had been such a shock to hear her real mother's name being mentioned. Perhaps it was mere wishful thinking, but the speaker seemed to hint at the possibility that Stacey's death was somehow linked to the more recent murders of the three prostitutes.

Veronica remembered reading in The Times about the trial of Christopher Jones. He had been acquitted due to insufficient evidence. For weeks afterwards he needed police protection, so whipped up and furious was public opinion. During all the debates and discussions both on the television and in the newspapers there had literally been only one or two people brave enough to suggest that *maybe* Mr. Jones had been innocent.

Veronica secretly believed that he was too. She had a strong inkling that he had been involved in some way, but she could not see him actually committing the murders himself. Perhaps he had had a hatred of sex workers, and he had hired someone to cull them like the gamekeeper did the sickly deer on the hunting estate close to where she grew up. But what did she know?

That detective had seemed rather taken with her when she had carried his luggage up to the room. Veronica had been hoping to *accidentally* bump into him again before he left, if only to discreetly *milk* him for more information, but she had been so overwhelmed by his words at the Forum that she had felt physically sick.

The following morning on reporting for duty one of her colleagues had informed her that a certain DS Jack had been asking after her the previous evening. Veronica had blushed. She had been rushed off her feet all day, and unfortunately they never had a chance to meet again.

After all the delegates had left the following morning Veronica discovered a business card poking out of her staff pigeon hole. She had smiled to herself and popped it safely into her uniform pocket.

That was when Veronica's problems really began, and she began to feel that her usually ordered life was spiraling out of control. She had up to now been a very sound sleeper, but now every night she was plagued by bad dreams. More often than not, these would result in her waking in the middle of the night, perspiring profusely with her heart thumping in her chest. She tried desperately to recall her nightmare, but all she could see in her mind's eye was the body of her mother, bloated and disfigured with her eyes staring heaven-ward. Once she woke up screaming and remembered with vivid clarity the corpse's mouth trying to mouth some words. The image kept invading her consciousness whilst she had been stood behind the reception desk. One minute she was telling a guest about Inverness Castle, then she suddenly felt faint and was forced to sit down.

"Are you all right, love?" the concerned gentlemen asked her. "It looks like you've seen a ghost!" In a way she had.

"What on earth is the matter, sweetheart?" Maggie had grabbed the arm of the easy chair by the window. The two of them were lazily preparing themselves for their evening out when the mobile had rung. Caroline was buttoning up her cream coloured blouse, and she quickly joined her wife at hearing her tone of voice.

Maggie whispered, "It's Veronica. It sounds like she's in some kind of trouble." She switched on the speaker function of her phone so that both of them could hear her troubled words.

Between sobs and gasping for air, their daughter explained to them about the police conference, and the effect that it had had on her. By the end of their conversation, Veronica began to feel a little silly and immature, but when Caroline suggested to her that perhaps she ought to come back home for a while Veronica had jumped at the chance.

"Are you all right, love?" Marcus asked his cousin. She had eaten very little of her meal and, was obviously preoccupied by something important.

Maggie jumped and looked apologetically at her family. "I'm sorry, I was miles away. It's just that we received a call from Veronica earlier."

Anne looked concerned. She had really enjoyed her and Caroline's company over the last two days, and had already made plans as to how to entertain them over the following week. Amongst them was a drive over to Carbost.

Marcus's father still stayed on the family farm over

there, even though he was now in his nineties. Now a widower, and reliant on carers to wash and dress him, he was nevertheless fiercely independent in his mind. He was so looking forward to seeing Maggie again.

Maggie took a deep breath. "I hate to say this, but we really ought to go home tomorrow. Our daughter's in a bad way at the moment. She's traveling back to Stirling in the morning, and we want to be there to greet her."

Anne swallowed hard and was about to explain about her father-in-law, and Terry's visit. Her son had rung last night and told her about his trip to Mallaig to buy his wee boy a new set of clothes for the occasion, but instead she bit her lip and assured Maggie that she quite understood. A solitary tear rolled down her plump cheek.

SEVENTEEN

Five hundred miles away, King Rupert, looking resplendent as usual in his purple robes trimmed with white fake fur entered the ballroom of Buckingham Palace attended by two Gurkha orderly officers, a tradition began in 1876 by his great-great grandmother.

The British Traditionalist Party had enforced their manifesto pledge to disband the brigade which was composed of soldiers from India and Nepal, but on his accession to the throne and the imposition of his absolute monarchy the King had decided that for ceremonial purposes tradition took precedence over racial purity. The right of Gurkha veterans to settle in the United Kingdom had been refuted, and the serving officers and men became an independent fighting force with no allegiance to the British Army. They gained their independence as India had done in 1947.

Out of respect to their former allies, two men were chosen every six months to travel over to England to take part in the Investiture ceremony. The representatives initially regarded it as a great honour, but with the passing years it was becoming increasingly difficult to persuade the chosen officers to participate.

There were now no foreigners living in the United Kingdom, and even though Rupert made sure that the

Gurkhas were well looked after during their stay they felt like museum exhibits. People would gawp at the visitors, thinking them strange and exotic-looking, with their brown skin and non-native tongues.

Last month a classical concert had been held in the one hundred and twenty feet long stateroom, but now it held a dozen nervous men and women all waiting to receive their honours from the monarch. Two decades previously there had been twenty or so investitures held each year in which over two thousand people would be awarded some form of decoration or medal. Nowadays just two services took place annually, and one was simply awarded an order of chivalry for which the motto was, *For God and the Empire.*

This scaling back and simplification made it much easier to manage administratively, and since only about thirty citizens were selected every twelve months the privilege held greater significance. Before the BTP came to power the whole thing had descended into a farcical affair. Almost everyone seemed to have some sort of lettering after their surname.

There were five classes in both the civil and military divisions, ranging from a *Knight Grand Cross of the Order of the British Empire* to a mere *MBE*. The first rank automatically resulted in an individual becoming a knight or a dame, an honour allowing the recipient to use the title *Sir* or *Dame* before their first name. It was this award that Grant was having bestowed upon him today for *Services to Medicine*.

He was sat in the front row which allowed him room to stretch out his long legs. Now fifty-two, he was considering taking early retirement in three years' time.

He still had no idea who had nominated him for the honour. All it had said in the letter from the Palace was that *he had been recognised by his peer group as inspirational and significant, and that he had demonstrated sustained commitment in his field.*

On reading the invitation, Grant's pulse rate had increased dramatically. Feeling faint, he had sat down heavily and called out in excitement to Duncan who had just popped into the downstairs lavatory.

Still drying his hands on a towel, his husband had grabbed the letter, and then given Grant the biggest of bear hugs. He tried to lift him off the ground, but even fired up with adrenaline he failed to do so. Instead he planted a wet kiss on his lips.

"Services to medicine, eh?" he had exclaimed. "I'll shall have to call you, *Sir Grant* then. Wow!"

Unfortunately, Duncan had been struck down by some new strain of the influenza virus two days before they were due to go down to London. Grant had generously suggested that he postponed the presentation until the next Investiture ceremony, but Duncan would not entertain that.

So, here he was at one of the milestones of his life, all alone. His sister, Clare had offered to accompany him to Buckingham Palace on hearing about his knighthood, but he had turned her down in favour of his spouse. Grant had contacted her the day before he was due to travel, but she had already made plans of her own to attend some book signing, or some such like. What made it all the more sad was the fact that everyone else seemed to have their *significant other* with them, or at least a family member or friend. Grant mentally chastised himself for being so pathetic, and concentrated on the proceedings.

On the dais were five more men attending the monarch, but these were all caucasians. Their dress was startlingly different too. They wore red and gold tunics in the Tudor style, with red knee-breeches and stockings.

Grant remembered reading somewhere that these gentlemen were all retired service personnel, and that they were drawn from a corps known as the *King's Body Guard of the Yeomen of the Guard.* To his eye they looked rather camp, as if they were going to some gay fancy dress party, but what did he know about the eccentricities of Scotland's neighbour? This was the first time that he had ventured south over the border for ten years.

To complete the ensemble were four Gentlemen Ushers decked out in three-piece suits, rather similar to

Grant's own. Music was provided by the Band of the Household Division.

The national anthem had already been played, and now with the King standing on his left-hand side the Lord Chamberlain announced the name of each recipient, and the achievement for which he or she was being decorated.

Ten minutes elapsed and then he called, "Mr. Grant MacLeod, for Services to Medicine."

Grant took the ten or so paces required to take his position in front of King Rupert. He knelt on the dark blue velvet cushion as indicated by the Lord Chamberlain, and solemnly received the Accolade.

The King laid the flat side of his late father's sword on Grant's right shoulder, and then gently raising it just above his head he placed its blade on his left in a similar fashion. The surgeon thereupon rose up as *Sir Grant MacLeod*. Smiling benevolently, the monarch presented him with his Grand Cross award. The Badge of the Order was affixed to a gilded silver star which was secured to a sash of the same hue as the cushion.

With the ribbon diagonally crossing his chest, Grant once more took his seat. For a million Scottish pounds he could not have recalled what the King had said to him. His thoughts were whirling around inside his head. He felt so incredibly proud. It was just such a shame that Duncan could not have been by his side at such a glorious moment. One of the attendants had informed him earlier that the entire ceremony would be filmed. The footage would be quite something to flaunt to his family, friends and work colleagues when he returned home to Scotland.

After the ceremony all the recipients and their guests made their way slowly along the West Gallery with its four ornate Gobelin tapestries to assemble in the State Dining Room. The red silk damask on the walls made a fitting background to the numerous state portraits. The huge table was meticulously laid with the finest of silver plated cutlery and lead crystal glasses. The centrepiece was a delightful seemingly haphazard display of pink roses, winter greenery and cream coloured candles.

It looked like it had just been thrown together, but Grant suspected that it was an example of *organised chaos*. He found his place card, and his exulted mood reached a new height when he realised that his dining companion on his right would be no other than the royal consort himself, Prince Stephen.

"Good evening, Your Royal Highness! It appears that I have the good fortune to be seated next to yourself," Grant addressed the elegantly attired prince. As protocol dictated, he waited for the young man to settle himself at the table before taking his own seat.

"It's Sir Grant, I believe. Please do sit down. It is a great honour for me to be in the presence of such an imminent surgeon as yourself." He smiled graciously, but there was a twinkle of mischief in his eye.

Stephen used to take part in the actual Investiture ceremonies, but he had become bored with all the pomp of such occasions. Being quite the gastronome, he never missed the subsequent celebratory banquet though.

The prince had spotted the mature handsome medical practitioner as the party was admiring the textile art in the gallery, and being rather fed up with having to entertain *ladies of a certain age* at dinner he had covertly swopped Grant's place card with a *Dame So-and-So's*.

****

The last two years as a member of the royal family had not been easy for Prince Stephen. His relationship with the King had become almost business-like, rather than personal. He still fulfilled his royal duties. The two of them were always together for the regional council audiences, and although he now found the overseas trips to be more of a bore than a pleasure he was without exception at Rupert's side.

Away from the public glare though it was a totally different story. His husband had even less time for him than before, or so he made out. The frequency of their lovemaking had become like that of an old married couple. They were more like good friends and companions than passionate lovers. Rupert was so exhausted of a night that he practically fell asleep as

soon as his dark locks touched the pillow, and in the
morning his valet awoke him at seven o'clock.
Breakfast was served punctually an hour later which
allowed little time for anything of an intimate nature.

He did not doubt that his spouse's protestations of love
were genuine and heartfelt, but Stephen was still only
twenty-five and not quite ready for *his pipe and slippers*
yet! He did enjoy the trappings of wealth and power
though that such a lifestyle afforded him. The prince
had toyed with the idea of taking up the thrilling sport
of powerboat racing as his late father-in-law had done,
but a heated argument with Rupert had put pay to that.
The King had lost one of his parents prematurely, he
could not have beared the sudden demise of his darling
husband too. Stephen had no intention of rocking any
other boats, he just wanted to have some fun.

****

The two men leaned back in their regency chairs as the
footman ladled steaming vegetable soup into their bowls
which were made of white bone china trimmed with
gold. Grant regarded his fellow diners. He counted
twenty-six in total, including the monarch who was sat
at the head of the table. He observantly noticed Rupert
acknowledge his consort who was at the foot.

It pleased Grant greatly that in these modern times a
same-sex couple now ruled the country. To think that

just over sixty years previously it had been illegal to be gay, let alone marry on the same terms as a heterosexual. The thought brought a satisfied smile to his craggy features.

"You seem very content, sir," Stephen remarked, interrupting his thoughts. "Is the good lady on your left, your wife?" he discreetly enquired.

Grant took a surreptitious sideways glance. A forty something plump woman with mousy brown hair was slurping her soup noisily.

"Good God, no! I'm afraid I bat for the same side as you, dear boy. Mind you, if I *was* of the straight persuasion I reckon I would have given that one a miss. She looks *terribly* common!"

Stephen grinned and discreetly sighed with relief and anticipation. *So, this one is on his own,* he mused. *I reckon he's in his fifties, obviously very successful in his field,* and looking at the timepiece on his neighbour's wrist, concluded that he was *very* wealthy too. He had always been attracted to powerful dominant men. Bedding the King of England used to give him such a thrill, but the novelty was wearing a little thin now.

"That's a *Dent* watch, isn't it, sir?" he asked.

Grant shook his left arm to display its adornment to the best effect. "That's quite correct, sir. Not many people would recognise it as such though."

Then he remembered that the company had proudly held a Royal Warrant since Queen Victoria's day. Grant had always been very patriotic, long before the current government had come to power. He had tried in vain to find a Scottish watch manufacturer, but in the end he had been forced to choose a bespoke company down south. He had had every intention of buying the timepiece for himself, but to his greatest surprise and absolute delight Duncan had presented it to him during his birthday celebration.

Edward John Dent had established the firm in 1814. He had embraced the Victorian fervour for technological innovation, creating precision chronometers for the Royal Navy. Mr. Dent also made the famous clock, known as Big Ben. Grant had smiled to himself yesterday on seeing the Houses of Parliament, and feeling silly and excited had flashed his wrist at the Great Clock. *Say hello to your big cousin!* he had quipped.

Stephen admired the hand-stitched alligator skin strap with its eighteen carat rose gold buckle, and its casing made of the same precious metal. The dial with its Roman numerals was obviously made of the finest ivory.

"That must have set you back a few thousand pounds, sir. It's gorgeous."

Grant whispered, "I'm not quite sure how much it cost, it was a fiftieth birthday present from my husband, but between you and me I think it's worth about *seventeen* thousand pounds. By the way, do please stop calling me

Sir, it makes me feel like some kind of headmaster."

Damn, he's married, thought Stephen. *All the best ones usually are. I wonder where his beloved spouse is right now. Fancy him missing all of this!*

"Okay, so long as you call me *Stephen*. So, where is your ever-so generous husband? Surely he should have been by your side on the day you receive a knighthood from the King, or is he one of the retiring sort?"

They paused in their conversation as the crockery was cleared away. Grant explained about Duncan's illness. By the time they had finished their main course, the Beef Wellington was to both their cultivated tastes, he had felt Stephen's hand on his knee so many times that when it was not there he missed its warmth.

The next morning Grant woke up in his hotel bed. For a moment he thought it was Duncan gently snoring by his side. With a start he suddenly realised that the tousled dirty blond mop of hair did not belong to his husband, but rather the spouse of the King of England. *Bloody hell*, he thought, alarm bells ringing loudly in his mind as a wave of intense panic threatened to engulf him. *I could hang for this. If sleeping with the royal consort doesn't count as treason, then pandas really do hate bamboo!* The materialization of Grant's quirky sense of humour more often indicated that he was stressed, rather than being a sign of his contentment.

Prince Stephen moaned and mumbled in his sleep. Lying on his back, he was dreaming about the night before. He had a full erection, and just before he sleepily opened his eyes a damp patch could be seen forming on the bed sheet.

EIGHTEEN

God, I hate lying, Veronica thought to herself as she
boarded the bus outside of the Barcelo Stirling Highland
Hotel two weeks later. The establishment was situated
just five hundred yards from the castle. She glanced
over her shoulder at the fortification perched atop its
intrusive crag, and sighed deeply. *Well, at least the
manager agreed to my transfer, I suppose. I can now
continue with my course, and still find out what really
happened to Mum.*

After discussing her concerns with her adopted parents
back home in Stirling Veronica had decided to forget
about Inverness and look for a local placement. She had
indubitably loved her work, but researching her
mother's background had become an overwhelming
obsession. She wanted to find out all about her life, not
just how she had ended up in the Clyde.

Veronica calculated that she could only have been four
years old when the woman who had given birth to her
had had her existence so cruelly snuffed out. It was
incredibly important to Veronica to discover every little
detail about her life before she had been adopted.
Maybe she could track down some family members,
become reunited with an as-yet-unknown sister or aunt,
or and sometimes she would dream about this, make
contact with her father.

She had watched films where some girl or other would be knocking at an imposing front door, and a handsome kindly gentleman would appear at the threshold.

I'm your long-lost daughter, the girl would say, and the man's face would crease up into a huge smile, and he would throw his arms around his often dreamed about, but until now undiscovered child. If it could happen in the movies, then why not to her? Maggie and Caroline were fantastic, but to have a man in her life who loved and cherished her, someone whom she could call *Dad*, now would that not be simply wonderful?

It had taken a few days to re-adjust to living back home again, but she had only been away six months so it had not proved too difficult. She much preferred to have a big house to roam about in rather than just a single room to call her own, and Maggie's cooking was certainly superior to her own culinary efforts. At first Veronica had felt uncomfortable talking about her natural parents, guilty even. When she had learnt that her *two Mums* had cut their long-awaited for holiday short, just so that they could be at home to welcome her back from Inverness she had felt most contrite.

All her worries had been unfounded though. Both her parents seemed to support her in her quest, and to understand her need to discover who she really was. Caroline had even offered to drive her to the hotel interview that day, but Veronica had politely refused.

Even though it was great at home sometimes she felt suffocated, and just needed some time to herself.

Her old boss at the Royal Highland had been most sympathetic too, but she could not bring herself to tell him the full truth, as to why she wanted a transfer. She had concocted a story about Caroline being unwell and needing her at home. A tale which she had repeated at the interview as if she was reading from a script. It almost felt like she was tempting fate, making up something like that, but Veronica imagined that her new manager would feel more sympathetic to her case if she was acting the dutiful daughter rather than being some neurotic twenty year old.

The three of them had celebrated her metamorphosis from gawky teenager to young adult two days ago by dining out at the establishment where she hoped to be working for the next eighteen months. It had been Caroline's idea. *Call it research*, she had said, grinning.

The hotel used to be a High School until twenty years ago. It was now one of the most renowned establishments in Stirling. The elegantly dressed waiting staff served the diners both traditional and international classical dishes beneath the vaulted beams of the Scholars Restaurant, which was thankfully open to non-residents as well as the hotel guests. Veronica had delighted in her chicken breast stuffed with tarragon mousse, and Maggie had remarked that her vegetarian choice of main course was *divine*.

Her interesting looking meal was served in a earthenware dish, and its cheese topping was still bubbling as the waitress had placed it in front of her. According to the menu, it was called *Rumbledethumps*. Its main ingredients were potatoes and cabbage boiled together until tender, and then baked with onion until golden brown.

Caroline had whispered something lewd about flatulence, and the three of them had burst out laughing, causing their fellow diners to pause, their forks halfway to their mouths. Maggie had reddened with embarrassment and kicked her wife hard under the table. She had almost choked on her Crispy Duck pancake, the soya sauce drips narrowly missing her new velvet trousers. It was at that point that Veronica had vowed to herself to not take advantage of her adopted parents' love and generosity, or for herself to be lead into a false sense of security. The last thing she wanted was to hurt either of them.

****

Two weeks later Veronica was stood behind the reception desk of the Highland Hotel, chatting to one of the guests. She had settled in quickly and despite her initial doubts was glad that she had made the decision to transfer down from Inverness.

Her new employer owned and managed almost two hundred hotels scattered around the world. Seventeen countries proudly boasted one of the Spanish four star-rated establishments. The Barcelo Group had been established a century ago in Palma de Majorca, and was now one of Spain's leading tourist companies. Over the years it had been run by three generations of the Barcelo family.

The UK division was acutely aware that the company would never have been granted permission to take over the old school if they had tried to set up a business in the last twelve years. Foreign companies were now prohibited by the government to invest in the country. If the present monarchy had been merely constitutional rather than absolute all foreign owned firms, however profitable would have been forced to close down and their employees made redundant, but the King had stepped in and ruled that all existing businesses would be given leave to remain in the UK, so long as they only employed British nationals. Gone were the days when hotels, whatever their origin were staffed by mainland Europeans or people from further afield.

Most of the ethnic restaurant owners had packed up and gone home in protest. They refused to employ English people to cook their spicy food. It was now more difficult to find an Indian or Chinese to eat out in than to buy a *chocolate teapot*. The Far East still traded with Great Britain as did many other countries, so the citizens of the archipelago bought their suppers online and ate their curries and chop sueys in the comfort of their own homes, if they wanted a break from cooking. The Highland Hotel in Stirling was very fortunate to have a head chef who had worked extensively abroad. He had taught his staff how to prepare a diverse menu.

Out of the corner of her eye, Veronica spotted a man in his late sixties entering the hotel lobby. He seemed vaguely familiar, but she could not figure out why. Although outwardly he looked respectable enough, quite dapper in fact, Veronica shivered involuntarily. A quote from the play she had studied for her Highers unexpectedly entered her mind. *By the pricking of my thumbs, something wicked comes this way.*

The guest approached the reception. "I'm Mr. Jones. I have a reservation for the next week," he stated firmly.

Veronica smiled professionally and completed the necessary paperwork. She handed him his key card, and wished him a pleasant stay in Stirling.

"Are you here on business, sir?" she asked him courteously.

"No, for personal reasons. I am here to see my grandson for the very first time."

"How lovely. What a pity that your son or daughter couldn't put you up though," Veronica retorted, regretting her words almost as soon as she had uttered them. *Bloody hell*, she thought, *me and my big mouth again.* She blushed at her tactlessness.

Mr. Jones seemed unperturbed. "Christopher, my son did offer to put me up, but his wife and I don't rub along too well. It's better this way, to have my own space, and when I'm not playing the doting grandfather I can take advantage of all this," he said, waving his arm expansively. "I see from your brochure that you have a jacuzzi, a swimming pool *and* a gym, so I shan't be bored!"

Watching the man slowly ascend the staircase behind the porter, Veronica was surprised to find herself gripping the edge of the reception desk. She felt a little nauseous too, but for the life of her she could not figure out why. *Perhaps that was a premonition,* she mused. That's just plain daft, she scolded herself, but nevertheless she surreptitiously scribbled down the guest's address on a piece of hotel writing paper, and tucked it into the pocket of her uniform.

****

Truth be told, there was no grandchild to visit. Mr. Jones's son was not even married. For him to find a wife, let alone to make her pregnant would have required Christopher to leave the security of his flat, and go out and meet people. After the trial, even though he had been acquitted his son's mental health had gradually deteriorated. His condition became such that he had been obliged to hand over the day-to-day management of his pornography firm to a trusted friend of his.

Christopher still owned the company which continued to be highly profitable, but now his days were spent pacing around his luxurious apartment in Cooperage Quay overlooking the River Forth, rather than making erotic films. He experienced frequent flashbacks to the three murders which he had both ordered and witnessed, and had become paranoid and delusional. He heard *voices*, and regularly saw the ghosts of the dead women, or so he thought.

Christopher clung on desperately to the remnant of insight which he still possessed. It was enough for him to realise that he was probably psychotic, and most definitely suffering from a post traumatic stress disorder. In any other circumstances he would have sought professional help before his illness became such that he regarded his symptoms as completely normal, but how could he now?

That would mean confessing his involvement in the demise of his employees, and ruining the life of his co-conspirator. Kathy had sent him a greeting card a few weeks after the trial. *Thank you. I owe you one*, was all it had said. She had obviously placed her made up mouth under the words for a red lip kiss completed her message. He had stared at the crude image, for what seemed like hours. It seemed to be mocking him. Their owner had got away with murder, whilst he was slowly going mad.

****

Christopher had lost contact with his mother five years ago after she and his father had divorced. He had always meant to track her down and try to repair the damage to the filial relationship, but now it was too late. He just about managed to feed himself and keep on top of his hygiene needs, there was no way that he was in a fit state to deal with his overdemanding mother. They had had one too many arguments over him running Naughty But Nice.

When his mother accepted his father's proposal of marriage Mr. Jones senior had just started working in the pornography business through a contact he had made whilst out drinking one night in his home city of Glasgow. He showed a flair for production and within a year had graduated from a mere runner, a dogsbody in reality, to the firm's producer and director.

Mike had a broad Glaswegian accent, and his manner at times was as equally difficult to decipher. He was a deep man who kept himself to himself, but he loved the ladies. Patricia Lally, the daughter of a former Lord Provost of Glasgow somehow managed to infiltrate his barrier, and within six months they were wed. Pat's parents always considered that their daughter had rather married beneath her, and regarded her new husband as a bit of a rogue, and not particularly likeable at that.

Oh, Mum, he's my rough cut diamond. He may not have our airs and graces, but I know he'll look after me, she would repeatedly tell them.

The Lally's could not dispute the fact that their son-in-law certainly had the means to support their darling girl. It was where he sourced his money from that was their biggest concern. They never realised how lucrative being a supporting artiste, or *extra* could be. They suspected Mike was a drug dealer, or something. In reality the twenty-five year old was not supplying illegal substances, in fact he was vehemently anti-drugs, but churning out good quality, but extremely explicit blue DVDs.

Despite the difficulties, Mike proved to be a good husband. He kept his business dealings very close to his chest. He was always impeccably dressed, and made sure that his family enjoyed the trappings of his success. When all was said and done, he did earn his income legitimately, for now at least.

One night when their only child Christopher was ten years of age, Pat found out the truth. She never believed that their family income only came from her husband's acting work for film, television and advertising companies. She suspected that he was heavily involved in the protection racket. Not for one minute did she think that the razor gangs of the 1930s, the notorious *Beehive Boys* for example, had returned to the city, but in the media there were frequent reports of doorstep lenders taking advantage of vulnerable people, and widespread extortion by gang members.

One day young Christopher had been badly beaten up by some boys at his school, and Pat needed to take him to the local casualty department. She had tried in vain to reach her husband, but his mobile phone was turned off. He had been sat waiting for them on their return from the hospital, and most out of character Pat had *lost it*.

Frustrated and worried, she had vented her feelings by throwing several dinner plates at the kitchen wall, and one or two of their expensive drinking glasses were smashed too. Something inside her prevented Pat from directly lashing out at her husband. She reflected afterwards that it was probably self-protection. Mike had never been violent with her, in fact he rarely lost his temper at home, but she dared not imagine what might happen if he was provoked.

Her husband's laid-back attitude only served to fuel her agitated state. *Her precious son had been attacked!* Mike stated that he had been drinking all afternoon in one of the city public houses. She did not believe him. There was hardly a whiff of alcohol emanating from his person.

After settling her son upstairs in bed, he had some

nasty abrasions to his face and one of his ribs was cracked, a full-blown argument had blown up between the two of them. Fed up with being accused of things which he would never entertain, Mike had come clean about his operations.

He confessed that his business partner was indeed a so-called *loan shark*, and perhaps his methods of extracting money from his clients were at times a little heavy handed, but neither of them had ever extorted funds from local traders, or used violence or intimation to deter witnesses from testifying to crimes in court, as his wife was insinuating.

I make porn movies, that is all, he had shouted at his wife.

Pat had surprisingly been more disgusted by that revelation than the thought that her husband might have been some kind of modern day *Kray twin*, the infamous gangster pair who had ruled the East End of London in the 1950s and 60s. Sex, as far as she was concerned was only for procreation and to express one's love for another person, preferably of the opposite sex. To think that her husband directed and watched nude men and women fornicating, and recorded it for other people to masturbate over appalled her.

Their marriage become one of pure convenience. Pat had little money of her own and her religion forbid her to divorce, she was too proud to ask her parents for financial support or to admit to them that her marriage was failing, so she had no choice but to stay put. Now that she knew how Mike made his living she could not bear him touching her.

Their day-to-day life went on much as before. To the outside world they were a perfect couple, but as the years passed Pat's unhappiness turned her into a bitter frustrated wife, and an overbearing mother. Eventually she could it stand no more. The last proverbial straw smashed her world completely.

Her son had always sided with his father, and one night he audaciously stated that he would be taking over the grubby firm, re-naming it of all things, *Naughty But Nice*. He proudly told her over the kitchen table that he wanted to find them new premises and expand the business.

Pat for once was speechless. She simply went upstairs and calmly packed her clothes and personal possessions. Fifteen minutes later father and son heard the front door open, and close. They never heard from, or saw Pat again. Mike received a divorce petition from her solicitor a month later.

****

"I think I understand what you're going through, son," Mike informed his offspring.

They were sat across from each other, two Denby

mugs of tea cooling between them. Christopher dragged his eyes from the mallard that he had been watching through his window. Its head had just re-emerged from the surface of the river which ran parallel to his flat. It always tickled him to see their little tails sticking up as they sieved the water with their broad bills, to extract the small crustaceans and vegetable particles which made up the staple part of their diet.

He tried to focus on what his father was saying. After all it had been six months since he had last seen him. It had taken that long for them both to recover from his previous visit. Things had not gone well.

There had not been any arguments as such, but the tension in the apartment had become unbearable after a few days, and Mike had cut his trip short to return home to Glasgow. At least this time they only had to tolerate each other's company for an hour or two. It seemed his father was keen to try out the swimming pool at the hotel.

Mike could feel his heart thumping against his chest wall. He had decided that he would tell his son all about the six snuff movies which he had made when he was the owner of Naughty But Nice. It was a huge decision to make, but he strongly suspected that the murders for which his son had been tried were rather similar to his own. Mike had vowed to keep the illegal side of his past business dealings to himself, to take his secrets to the grave in fact, but he loved Christopher and was desperate to relieve him of his mental torture before it was too late.

At night Mike kept experiencing a recurrent dream in which he was visiting Christopher in a psychiatric hospital. As he approached the door of the ward he could hear his son screaming. He hoped that by confiding his past demeanours in him Christopher would not feel alone anymore. He told him during his last visit that he saw the ghosts of the women whose bodies had been found at the base of the Edinburgh hills. If Christopher was indeed completely innocent, and it had been pure coincidence that all of three of the victims had worked for him, then so be it.

Truth be told, Mike was desperate to clear his own conscience before he *shed his mortal coil,* as his mother had been fond of saying. Unlike his ex-wife, he was not a religious man, so he could hardly go to his local priest for the absolution of his *sins*. Neither did he fancy dangling from the hangman's noose which, now that the death penalty had been restored would be his inevitable fate if he confessed to the police.

Of course he had not actually killed the six women himself, but as he suspected of his son he had certainly ordered their deaths and the disposal of their bodies, so that would make him liable to a *conspiracy to murder* charge.

As far as he knew five of the six would have provided gourmet meals to the loch fishes. The final one was buried in a cemetery on the outskirts of Stirling. The Clyde had eventually given up her water-sodden body four months after she had sacrificed her mortal coil for the sake of art. Another month had elapsed before her sister, her only surviving relative apparently, had laid her to rest.

****

"I don't know what really happened to those women you were accused of murdering, son but, I have something to tell *you*."

Christopher took a gulp of his now cold tea, and listened intently as his father explained to him his part in the demise of six of his employees. After he had finished, his features pale and visibly shaking Christopher pushed himself up from his chair, and sunk to the floor at Mike's feet.

He wrapped his arms around his waist and said, "Oh, Dad, I never knew how much of a chip off the old block, I really was. Your suspicions were spot-on. I was making snuff movies too."

The older man's tears ran down his face. It felt so good to have unburdened himself after a very long sixteen years, but what now? If any of it ever reached the public's ears then both of them would be facing execution.

Could he trust his son to keep both of their secrets?

Was it such a good idea to burden him further, a mentally ill man? He seemed to be going slowly crazy, dealing with his own crimes. How the hell could he cope with the fact that, for all intents and purposes his father was a killer too?

NINETEEN

In the leafy suburbs of Aberdeen a month previously
Mrs James had been absent-mindedly washing up. The
day before she had reported her daughter missing to the
police. Angie rang her mother most days, but last Friday
she had texted her instead.

The message had read, *I'm off to see a friend
tomorrow, won't be back until late Sunday, so I'll ring
you Monday evening if that's OK. Have a good
weekend. Love you xx.*

Mavis had been pleased to know that her daughter was
starting to get out and about again. Breaking up with her
long-term girlfriend had hit Angie hard, it had almost
broken her heart finding the love of her life in the arms
of another woman, and for months she had simply
buried herself in her work, trying desperately to blot out
the pain and despair. She spent hours talking on the
telephone to her mother, they had become very close
since Angie's father had been killed in a horse riding
accident two years previously, and eventually life
started to feel better again.

Her work colleagues had been supportive, but not
overly intrusive. Angie had been the Middle Clerk at
Oracle Chambers, a small law firm practising in
Aberdeen. She had joined the company as a legal

secretary twelve years previously.

In the sixth form whilst studying for her Highers she had crammed in a Distance Learning course. It had taken her a year to complete, but the sense of satisfaction she had felt on acquiring her diploma had been amazing. After seven years of typing up endless legal documents and correspondence her post had evolved into that of a legal clerk.

Her new role stimulated her mind, and of a morning she looked forward to traveling across the city to tackle another day's work in Chambers. She loved researching case law, and retrieving information from the clients' files to assist the advocates with their briefs. She looked after two members of the Faculty of Advocates, both of whom were Queen's Counsel. One preferred to prosecute, the other to defend.

Angie had had an inkling that if she had been born heterosexual the Senior Clerk, a good-looking man five years older than herself might well have made her an ideal husband. A year previously Tony, much to everyone's surprise had stated one morning that he had just asked his *boy*friend to marry him, and he had said, *Yes!* Everyone had been stunned into silence. They had all assumed that their colleague was strictly heterosexual. It seemed like he was indeed destined to become an *ideal husband*, after all.

In comparison, Angie had always been completely overt about her sexuality. She had proudly told the interview panel on applying for her original post that she had a girlfriend. Charlotte would accompany her to work events, and her colleagues had always made her feel most welcome. They would tease her, asking if or indeed when, Angie would *pop the question*.

Charlotte kept her affair discreet for as long as she could. How was she to know that Angie would appear unexpectedly at their bedroom doorway one afternoon, having returned home early from work? She was never sick. In reality, the onset of a migraine had heralded the end of their six year relationship.

There was a rap on the door. Mrs James started, her reverie rudely interrupted. She dried her hands on her apron, and hurried to see who her visitor was. She knew who she did *not* want it to be, but her worst fears were realised.

"Mrs James?" the young policeman asked.

Mavis nodded, as he pulled his identification card out of his pocket. *They have found my darling Angie, dead in a ditch somewhere*, she thought, her knees threatening to give out on her. She gripped the pine newel of her staircase for support.

The officer looked uncomfortable. "May I come in, Mrs James? I believe you reported your daughter missing yesterday. We have received a packet at the station which might be pertaining to the situation," he said, feeling his palms grow moist.

The delivery had arrived by Royal Mail, but it was certainly not the usual type of correspondence that the desk sergeant took possession of. As he followed the distressed woman into the house, he enquired hesitantly, "This may be a strange question to ask, but did your daughter ever break one of her legs?"

Mavis was taken aback. "I don't understand, sir," she said. "She did smash up her right femur a few years back when she was knocked off her bicycle by a drunk motorist, but what has that got to do with anything?"

The constable took a deep breath. "This morning a padded envelope arrived at the station. Inside was a stainless steel screw. We made a few enquiries. Apparently, it came from an orthopaedic implant supplier, rather than a carpentry firm. It was wrapped in a piece of plain paper, on which was typed, *This used to belong to Angela James.*"

The blood drained from the woman's face, and gripping the side of her armchair she gasped, "Christ, what sort of sick joke is that? Have you heard from my daughter? Are you suggesting that *bolt thing* used to be inside my Angie?"

Mavis's words came tumbling out of her mouth. She knew that her speech was probably incoherent, but it reflected the thoughts whirling around in her mind. If it had really belonged to her daughter, then how come it was at the police station. *Why, in the Devil's name would anyone send in something like that?*

****

A hundred and twenty miles away Jimmy Jack rubbed his eyes in disbelief. Feeling rather peculiar he addressed the young woman with her back to him, discreetly admiring the simplistic beauty of the female form, "It's Veronica, isn't it?"

The detective had been wandering around Edinburgh Castle on one of his rare days off, both from his police work, and his wife. The One O'clock Gun had just been fired, a tradition which was instigated in the late nineteenth century as a time signal to ships in the Firth of Forth, and the port of Leith.

Funnily enough, he had been thinking back to the conference in Inverness just that morning, or more specifically to the stunning porter who had carried his bags up to his room. Although he had dismissed the foolish notion that he might have fallen instantly in love, the detective's thoughts were often filled with images of the young, and mysteriously sexy hotel worker.

Things were still no better between him and Mrs Jack, her latest trick was to slam the internal doors of the house so violently that the wood of their jambs split, and daydreaming about Veronica provided him with some relief from his domestic troubles. He pinched the flesh on his bare arm, just to make sure that the vision before him was not some fantasy conjured up by his overactive imagination.

Veronica had been staring out at the panoramic view across the city which the Argyle Battery afforded, reflecting on her experiences that morning. From her elevated position the pedestrians on Princes Street looked like ants, busily going about their business.

Two minutes ago she had been reciting a speech from Shakespeare's Hamlet. The wind had carried away her words.

Fillet of a fenny snake,
In the cauldron boil and bake;
Eye of newt, and toe of frog,
Wool of bat, and tongue of dog,
Adder's fork, and blind-worm's sting,
Lizard's leg, and howlet's wing-
For a charm of pow'rful trouble,
Like a hell-broth boil and bubble.

She was in such a peculiar mood that for a split second she had been tempted to stand in the centre of the Middle Ward of the Castle, and entertain the tourists with her rendition, but her plan was to return home to Stirling later that day, not to be arrested by the local police for a breach of the peace!

Half an hour previously she had wandered through the spectacular gatehouse, and bought her ticket at the kiosk. Having meandered around the gift shop like some tourist, she had finally decided on a decorative plate to commemorate her day out. Her parents would appreciate her thoughtfulness.

She listened patiently to the sales assistant as he explained that the room that they were standing in had originally been the old guardroom. Veronica smiled at him. His words had seemed rather muffled, as if her ears were stuffed with cotton wool. Truth be told, she had only walked over to the castle to kill some time before catching her train back to Stirling.

That morning she had spent an hour or so at the Records Office, or *New Register House*, as it was formally known. The impressive building was at the east end of Princes Street, just a few minutes walk away from Waverley railway station. She had calmly searched through the archives for any trace of a *Stacey Connelly*. The entry stated that her maternal grandfather's name had been *Edward Connelly*, and before marriage her grandmother had been, of all things a *Montgomery*. A wave of sadness had engulfed her as she realised that they were now both dead, but another realisation pushed the grief to the back of her mind.

Oh, my God, thought Veronica, pulling out a chair and sinking herself onto it, *I have the same surname as my grandma*. A shiver coursed through her body as if she had walked across a grave. *Bloody hell, I wonder if she is related to Mum.*

All of a sudden she felt really hot, but the dribble of perspiration rolling down her back was cold. Don't be so silly, she chastised herself, there are probably millions of Montgomery's in the world, but whatever the truth was Veronica's face glowed with pride. By sheer coincidence she carried her family name. She genuinely belonged to the Montgomery clan, it was her birthright, not just a name given to her on adoption.

Taking a deep breath, she peered once more at the document. Under the *Cause of Death* entry it said, *Violence*. Veronica leant back heavily in her chair. That detective had been right then. She remembered him telling his fellow delegates at the conference that the woman they had dragged out of the Clyde had had her throat cut. She could not recall much more than that. Just hearing her late mother's name had been enough.

Anger surged through her. *Somebody murdered my Mum!* Again she reprimanded herself, fighting to gain control of her emotions. She dug her nails into the palm of her hand.

Veronica rested her head in her arms, and sighed deeply. She had spent long enough poring over the dusty records. A female voice made her start. She had not even realised that there was anyone sat next to her. They must have been as quiet as the proverbial church mouse.

"I used to know her, *Stacey Connolly*."

The elderly lady pointed at the entry with a digit which more closely resembled an emaciated sausage, than a human finger. "Going back a bit it was, but-," she remarked before Veronica interrupted her by asking in astonishment, "You knew my mother?"

"Well, not exactly. My younger sister and *your aunt* went to the same school. In the same class, in fact. I remember seeing in the papers about poor Stacey being fished out of the Clyde. Terrible business, it was."

Veronica stared at the wizened face of the woman peering at her. She wanted to ask her so many things, but the golden opportunity was cruelly snatched away almost as soon as it had presented itself.

"Love to sit here chatting, dear but I only popped in to register the birth of my latest grandson. His mother's too busy, and his Dad's in prison, so the task was left to *muggins* here. I was present at the birth, see, so I have a right," she concluded, reaching under the chair for her handbag.

Veronica gripped her bony shoulder. "Congratulations on your new arrival, but before you go, what was the name of my mother's sister?" she asked, with just a hint of desperation in her voice.

"Wouldn't you like to know, dear."

Veronica could have sworn that she heard her cackle. "Please, it's very important!"

The woman who was bent over with age turned back to face Veronica, one gnarled hand gripping her walking stick. "Stacey's sister was called *Lisa*, not that it did her a lot of good!" With that, she gave her a toothy smile, and hobbled towards the exit.

Veronica felt rather disorientated. She had not anticipated meeting anyone that morning, let alone an eccentric old crone. "Double, double toil and trouble, fire burn, and cauldron bubble," she muttered under her breath. Some of Caroline's black humour must have rubbed off on me, she thought, laughing to herself.

A lump had formed in Veronica's throat when she had realised that, by pure chance her birth mother had a surviving sister. *That is my aunt*, she thought. "Auntie Lisa," she muttered to herself over and over again, rolling the phrase around her tongue.

If the police had deemed her mother's case as unsolvable, what hope did she have in finding her murderer, but just to meet and chat to one of her relatives would be fantastic. She had never known anyone before who actually shared her genes.

She found Lisa Connelly's birth, marriage and divorce certificate, but that was little use really, except that she now knew that her aunt's surname was Davidson, unless she had reverted to her maiden name after splitting up from her husband. She had guessed that the two sisters had been born in Glasgow. She traced her finger over the name, and tried to imagine what her aunt might look like.

What I need to do now is find her address, she thought, but she did not have the faintest idea of how to go about it. What had struck her most about her strange encounter with the old lady was her accent. It certainly had not been Scottish. Veronica was sure that she had watched a film once where most of the characters had sounded similar to her. I reckon she came from London, Veronica concluded. That piece of information was insignificant. Her priority was to track down Lisa. The woman had said that her *younger* sister was in the same class as her, so at least perhaps her aunt would not be as ancient as her creepy visitor.

The newly revamped Data Protection Act would no doubt prove to be quite an obstacle to her search. Suddenly the face of the detective whom she had met in Inverness formed in her mind's eye. *Perhaps he could help me.* She grinned to herself. There had definitcly been a frisson between them, although Veronica's heart already belonged to her adopted cousin Terry, even though she had only met him once.

Caroline had informed her after they had returned from Skye that he had rescheduled his regular visit to his parents to coincide with her and Maggie's holiday, but of course they had cut their time short on the island to welcome her back home from Inverness. He had e-mailed her two days later to say that he had not been particularly bothered about missing them anyhow, seeing as she would not have been with them. He had promised that he would come over to the mainland as soon as possible to see the three of them, but *especially you, my dear one,* he had written.

Terry had never actually said, or typed that he loved her, Veronica had always worn *her heart on her sleeve*, but she knew that he did. If only she could persuade him to leave that wife of his.

He knew that she liked women, as well as men. On occasions he would e-mail her photographs of attractive ladies, and they would compare their scores. *She's definitely a ten*, he would write. *Ach, no, I've seen better legs on a giraffe*, she would reply.

Of course, the detective need know none of this. Veronica would track him down. She was sure that he stayed in Edinburgh. She would flirt with him, and persuade him to tell her the whereabouts of her aunt. *The art of female persuasion*, as Maggie whispered to her once, after Caroline had eventually given in to some plea of hers.

" Hello! It's Detective Sergeant Jack, isn't it?" Veronica retorted, swiveling around to face the beaming man. She could not quite believe that the very man she had been thinking about was now standing directly in front of her, a gentle breeze ruffling his hair. "Wow, that's spooky. I was just daydreaming about you!"

Jimmy beamed at her. "Me too," he stated. "Well, what I mean is that I was *thinking* about you. To be honest, you have been on my mind ever since

Inverness."

He blushed, aware that he had probably just made a complete fool of himself, *but God, what man wouldn't, with such a vision of beauty before him, silhouetted against the city skyline.*

"You look great," he mumbled, feeling like some lovestruck teenager, instead of a man just turned forty.

Veronica laughed, the sound reminding him of water trickling over rocks. She playfully grabbed his hand.

"Tell you what, I'll let you treat me to a cuppa and a piece of sultana cake. I saw a lovely wee teashop in Princes Street. Their window was full of all manner of tasty afternoon delights."

She glanced at her watch. "I've had enough of this old castle, anyway. My train's not for another hour. That'll be plenty of time to catch up, but-," she paused for effect, "this time you can carry *my* bag"

She handed over the carrier containing the plate you had just bought. "After the morning I have had I could do with a sit down, and a blather!"

Jimmy laughed too, more out of relief than anything else. He just hoped that they would not bump into anybody he knew. *God knows, how he would explain to his wife that sharing refreshments with a beautiful young lady on his day out was purely innocent!*

TWENTY

"I could hang for this!" Grant muttered as he thrust himself ever deeper into Prince Stephen's bottom. He looked around him. The place was gloomy and smelt of horses. It was hardly a fitting place for either a member of the royal family, or a Knight of the Realm.

Both men knew that they were playing with fire by meeting up again, but after their dinner together in London Grant felt that he had no choice but to see the young prince for a second time. He was so fired up with lust and longing for him that it was driving him slowly crazy.

The full schedule of the monarch's regional council visits were always listed in the broadsheet newspapers. For the sake of discretion Grant had been obliged to wait until a Court was held in Edinburgh, even though this meant delaying their tryst for a whole agonising month. He had no intention of destroying his marriage for the sake of a little fun. This way he could incorporate an afternoon of extracurricular activities into his day without arousing suspicion. He had made sure that no appointments were booked at the Clinic for that afternoon, he informed his secretary that he had a matter that he wished to discuss with the King, and so at two o'clock Sir Grant was sat behind the wheel of his Silver Ghost, heading into the city.

The Palace of Holyroodhouse was situated at the end of the Royal Mile. Although King Rupert used less prestigious settings when he held an audience in his English constituencies outside of London, he always chose the former monastery when he traveled by Royal Train to Scotland.

He loved having his own private locomotive. As he had stepped into one of its distinctive maroon and grey carriages at King's Cross railway station early that morning, and turned to wave back at the hordes of people gathered on the platform a bubble of excitement had coursed through his veins. His loving husband and consort, as well as several members of the royal household were already on board.

It would take eight hours to reach Edinburgh, but he had plenty of business to attend to which would help to pass the time as they rolled through the countryside, the late summer sun burnishing the fields. Ideally, he would have liked some time to unwind after his long journey, but his timetable was too tight to afford such luxuries. Their party was to stay overnight in Scotland, but it would then be another *crack of dawn* start the next day.

Sometimes he yearned for the days when his father was on the throne. Although as the heir apparent and the Prince of Wales he had had his assignment of royal duties, there had also been plenty of time to enjoy the company of his family and friends.

Nowadays he hardly ever saw Stephen except on official business, and when they were able to grab a few private moments together Rupert was too exhausted to pay his husband the attention he deserved.

Once they reached Oxenholme on the edge of the Lake District he knew that Stephen would grip his hand excitedly like a child, and they would stare out of the window at the rocky boulders together. That night they would make love in their opulent bedroom, the sensation and sound of the wheels on the tracks below them only heightening their now rare enjoyment of each other. Later as they lay in bed completely sated the same sound would soothe them into a restful sleep.

Mary, Queen of Scots had used the Palace as her main residence in the sixteenth century, and Rupert always felt that link with his past as he entered the Presence Chamber. As was his custom he gazed up at the ornate ceiling which was adorned by a hundred carved oak heads

Unfortunately they were not the same ones as the Queen had admired, as in 1777 the ceiling had been taken down. Some of the carvings had been destroyed, others had been scattered throughout England and Scotland. Shortly after his first visit to the Palace following his accession Rupert had instructed a team of local craftsmen to make a full set of copies from the thirty-four that had turned up around the country. Once again images of such historical figures as Julius Caesar and Henry the Eighth smiled down on the royal visitors.

His mother had told him once that Mary had witnessed the brutal murder of her secretary by her jealous second husband in the private apartments. As the current sovereign he had no such fears that a similar fate would befall his Personal Assistant. The person's gender ensured that!

Usually Stephen would be by his side as the twenty or so local representatives gathered in the Chamber, but this time his throne would be empty. He had declared that he was suffering from one of his *heads*, and had retired to the State Apartments to recuperate.

The high-backed gothic style armchairs had been made for him by a carpenter who stayed in the Highlands. They were copies of the *King Edward's Chair* upon which Rupert had been crowned at Westminster Abbey.

The original had now been decommissioned after over seven hundred years of service. The aged oak upon which many pilgrims and choir boys had carved their initials had finally split.

Eight gilded lions acted as as the current chairs' legs. To the casual observer the two were identical, but Rupert knew differently. Under both there was a cavity and a platform. Only his contained the Stone of Scone like the original chair had.

Thirty years ago it had been returned to Scotland by the then Conservative Government. Rupert could not see the point of the famous artifact languishing in the museum at Edinburgh Castle in anticipation of the next royal coronation. He had ruled that it would remain at Holyroodhouse, until his brother succeeded to the throne.

"But am I not worth it, O faithful knight of mine?" Stephen asked in between groans.

He had so been hoping to bump into the dashing surgeon again on his trip north. That morning he had almost roused Rupert's suspicions by glancing out of one or other of the Palace windows so many times, but all to no avail.

For once the two of them had had breakfast together, Rupert choosing his usual kedgeree and fresh orange juice. Usually the King was already in conference with his Private Secretary before Stephen had rolled out of the marital bed.

With slices of black pudding and clootie dumpling, two sausages, three tattie scones and half a dozen grilled halves of tomato inside him, Stephen had showered quickly, paying special attention to his genitals and the area between his buttocks. Dousing himself liberally in a talcum powder made especially for him, he proceeded to rub himself vigorously with his monogrammed bath towel.

He loved the local food, and was grateful that he had successfully persuaded Rupert to leave his personal chef back in England for once. Delicious though his habitual mushroom omelette topped with two lambs' kidney was, he had been so looking forward to his full Scottish breakfast, and he had not been disappointed.

He cast a discerning eye over his torso. Despite his healthy appetite and his reluctance to use the Palace gymnasium at home, his stomach was pleasingly flat. Last year he had began to worry that perhaps he was gaining a little too much weight. Rupert's physique was defined and toned. Even after a full day of royal business he could be found working his muscles on the weight machines located in the basement.

After some discussion one of the outbuildings at Buckingham Palace had been converted into a fully equipped squash court. Stephen could be found there several times a week with his personal bodyguard, smashing a small hollow rubber ball against the front wall, the perspiration dripping from them both.

Just as he was about to give up seeing Grant again serendipity had stepped in, and the two of them had made eye contact as Grant had sauntered audaciously into the courtyard. He felt rather like a criminal entering a police station. Maybe he had not yet physically committed treason, but in his mind he certainly had. At any minute he expected armed guards to snap handcuffs around his wrists, or worse.

Stephen had just had lunch with several local

dignitaries, to him all the formalities were an enormous bore, and making his excuses he had slipped outside for a smoke. On catching Grant's eye he had blushed deeply, and became restless. He was all too aware of a stirring in his groin. Glancing around him, he quickly stroked his hardening member, and discreetly indicated to Grant that he should approach.

"Good afternoon, Your Royal Highness. I hope my countrymen are treating you kindly."

"It's Sir Grant, I believe, that dashing surgeon who provided me with such gracious company at the Investiture Banquet last month."

"Indeed it is, sir." Grant dropped his voice to a whisper now that the expected formalities were complete. "Ever since then you have been on my mind, and simply remembering your hand on my thigh stiffens my manhood!"

Stephen pulled him into one of the empty stables which occupied an entire side of the courtyard. This was another alteration made by the King.

Where as the Royal Mews at Buckingham Palace were home to thirty or so carriage horses, the Scottish paddocks contained just four fine beasts, but these were rather more suited to galloping across the heather moorlands than providing road transport for the royal family. They were all American Quarter Horses, a gift from the President of the United States. The breed had originated in the seventeenth century when colonists on the eastern seaboard had begun to cross imported English thoroughbreds with native equines.

Rupert had expressed an interest in equestrian matters over dinner one night whilst staying at the White House three years ago. To the King's absolute delight and astonishment, a pair of Quarters were delivered to Holyroodhouse a few weeks later. They had been flown across the Atlantic by an international shipping agent.

Stephen had been concerned that traveling such a long distance would have traumatised the beasts, but after their short road journey from Edinburgh Airport they had been released from their box, looking like they had just taken a stroll up the road. Rupert had immediately placed a call to the President, his voice full of excitement and appreciation. His ally and friend had reassured him that he had used the same company that transported the horses around the world for the Olympic Games every four years. *It is the equine equivalent of sipping champagne on a private jet*, he had proudly informed the monarch.

Both mares had subsequently been artificially inseminated by semen collected from a Quarter stallion in the Highlands. Rupert would have preferred his *girls* to have gone to the stud and be covered naturally, but for the sake of security the royal veterinarian surgeon had both collected the semen, and impregnated them within the safety of their stable.

Eleven months later two male foals were born. In

reality the colts were half brothers. Next year the Head Groom would be breaking them both in, so that they would soon be cantering over the moors with their royal riders, as their mothers now did.

"Come here, you gorgeous man," Stephen growled, kissing Grant full on the lips.

The older man pulled away slightly. "Well, that was certainly worth waiting all those weeks for! To be honest, I wasn't sure whether I had got the wrong end of the proverbial stick at the banquet."

Stephen leant against the wall of the stable, breathing in the sweet smell emanating from the hay rack. All four horses were out in one of the estate fields, so the prince knew that they would not be disturbed for hours yet. He gazed lustfully at Grant. "I don't usually caress the thigh of my dinner companion!"

"Well, maybe not, but I thought perhaps you were just fooling around. After all we are both married men, and I am half your age."

"Were you hoping that I was, just messing about, I mean?" Stephen asked coquettishly, raising his right eyebrow.

In answer Grant pulled him into his arms, all his initial hesitation miraculously dissipated. The sane logical part of him knew that this was a *really* bad idea, but he so wanted this young man with his mop of dirty blond hair, and his boyish good looks.

He kissed him deeply and placed his palm over the bulge in his crotch, a hand more used to wielding scalpels than feeling up some chap's wedding tackle. He and Duncan so rarely made love nowadays.

His husband was just setting up two branches of his publishing company, one in Manchester and the other in London, so he was away from home on business every second week. Duncan had reassured him that once things had settled down, and he felt confident that his staff in England could manage without his physical presence he would have more time for them as a couple, but Grant doubted that very much. His once laid-back spouse with his *devil may care* attitude had turned into an ambitious workaholic, without either of them realising it.

Grant's sister was due to relocate down to London in a few months, once she had found somewhere to stay. Her wife had been offered a promotion at the firm. She was to play a pivotal role in their new Charing Cross Road branch. Duncan and him had had a flaming argument over it. Grant had accused him of driving his only sibling away to satisfy not only his, but Lyn's desire for success.

Pushing all such thoughts from his mind and just trying to concentrate on the here-and-now, Grant unzipped the flies of the prince's trousers, and carefully released his semi-erect penis. He knelt down, grateful that the King had spared no expense with his animals' bedding, and took Stephen's member in his mouth. He could feel the sponginess of the rubber mat, and smelt the woody scent of the pine shavings. Sliding his lips down the shaft, he undid the waistband, and pushed the garment down to his lover's ankles.

Stephen felt guilty too, but his lust equated to Grant's. He knew that this would probably be the last time that they ever met. It was too risky for both of them. If Rupert ever found out about his infidelity his lover would surely be hanged, and he would be banished, his reputation destroyed. Perhaps once he may have yearned to return to the simple life that he had lived before falling for the then Prince of Wales, but not now. He had grown accustomed to the trappings of wealth and power, and there was no way that he would give it all up for his carnal urges. He groaned deeply as he felt Grant push a finger into his anus.

Still fully dressed except for the penile tumescence poking out of his fly, Grant stuck his tongue between the prince's buttocks, and proceeded to tenderly flick it around the puckered hole. It tasted slightly earthy, perhaps like a flower just pulled out of the ground, or maybe that was just his vivid imagination.

He stroked his own penis a few times, gripping it firmly in his fist. If he was not careful he would climax before he had even penetrated his lover. After all it had been a while since he last had had sex with anyone except himself, and now in his early fifties his prowess was not what it was.

Stephen was massaging himself too, and eagerly anticipating the wonderful sense of fullness that would at any moment engulf him. *Rupert had never taken him in a stables!*

Grant replaced his tongue with the head of his quivering penis, and entered Stephen. *This is a damn sight more thrilling than repairing somebody's hernia*, he thought to himself.

TWENTY-ONE

"I dare do all that may become a man, who dares do more is none," Jimmy stated firmly, lying on his back, Veronica's head resting on his chest.

Veronica pushed herself up onto her elbow, and looked down on the handsome detective with a wry smile on her face. She weaved her fingers through his dark chest hair and pulled the tangled filaments gently.

"So, you're a fan of Macbeth too, eh? Not the type of reading material I would have expected you to be interested in, but I should have guessed that you would be full of surprises!"

"Not *all* of us detectives are complete philistines, you know. Some of us appreciate the *finer* things in life instead, like Shakespeare and Leonardo Da Vinci, rather than being into fast cars and wild women."

"Hark at you, and anyway, you're *into* me, so you must find pleasure in *wild women*!"

Ever since that first afternoon that they had spent together in Edinburgh Jimmy knew that he had been fooling himself thinking that his initial feelings for the beautiful young woman were simply a figment of his starved imagination. He had never believed in *love at first sight*, it had taken him three months to fall for his wife-to-be four years ago, but it seemed his strongly held beliefs were up for discussion. The feelings which had built up inside him for Veronica had been so strong that his heart had allowed him only one course of action.

In the tearoom, just as his new friend was scrapping back her chair, preparing to run for the train he had desperately grabbed her arm. "Can I see you again?" he had blurted out, his face reddening with embarrassment.

Veronica had looked startled. For once she had felt flustered, and out of her depth. Spending a hour or two with an old guest had been pleasant enough, and to be honest she had felt very relaxed in the detective's company, but she genuinely had no idea that they would potentially be repeating the experience.

"I don't know, I'm really not sure. It has been nice bumping into you again, but-," she had stuttered, her own usually pale features taking on a brighter hue.

Jimmy was made to feel foolish once again, as he had done at the castle. *Why would a gorgeous girl like Veronica want to waste her time with an old codger like me, and a married one at that?*

"Look, I'm so sorry. Do please forgive me. I really don't know why I thought such a notion."

Suddenly a realisation flashed into Veronica's mind. *This guy's in love with me! How the hell didn't I pick that one up? He's okay, but I certainly don't fancy him.*

Then she thought back to her morning in the Records Office, and her reflections as she had stood staring out

over the city from the castle. It seemed like her mild
flirting with him had done the trick. She had never
imagined that her plan would actually work, but here he
was practically begging to see her again.

"Look, I'll think about it, okay."

She fished a pen out of her handbag, plucked an
unused serviette from an empty table, and scribbled her
mobile number on it. She thrust it at Jimmy who was
fidgeting nervously as if he had an urgent need to use
the lavatory.

"Ring me sometime. I must dash. My train leaves in
twenty minutes."

The detective smiled in relief. Just as he was about to
suggest that he accompanied her to the station, Veronica
had exited into the street. He stood staring at the door,
and his smile turned into a full beaming grin.

Two days later Veronica was stood behind the
reception at the Highland Hotel when her mobile rang.
She jumped guiltily, not even realising that it was still
turned on. It was clearly stated in the Barcelo policy
manual that mobiles were to only be used during official
breaks. Thankfully, the manager who was on duty
fancied her something rotten.

"Go on, answer the call, it's all right."

Veronica smiled her appreciation, and winked at her
boss. "Later," she whispered, turning towards the staff
door which led out into the hotel garden.

The lady blew a discreet kiss at her employee. She and Veronica had stolen a few moments together several times during the last five weeks. Miss Riley knew that her new receptionist was only flirting with her, but maybe one day soon instead of catching the bus back home after they had finished their respective shifts, the sexy young thing might accept her offer of a lift instead.

Veronica would slide into the passenger seat of her Jaguar, and after a little surreptitious seduction Miss Riley was certain that she could persuade her to warm the chilled sheets of *her* bed. The manager giggled to herself. *If Veronica's kisses were anything to go by, her cotton sheets would be set on fire!*

Miss Riley who was three times Veronica's age had just lost her long-term girlfriend to cancer. She had employed a full-time nurse to care for her whilst she was at work, but right up until the end the two lovers had shared a bed together.

Now living on her own in their spacious cottage in Kippen, a wee village ten miles west of Stirling she often felt lonely. Beknownst only to herself, she always engineered the duty roster so that most of her shifts coincided with Veronica's. A friendly but usually professional rapport had built up between the two of them, enhanced by a frisson of erotic tension. At times Miss Riley could have sworn that the very air crackled with a sexual charge.

She suspected that she was just a little in love with the

trainee manageress, but over the years patience had become Miss Riley's trademark. She was more than happy to wait for her gorgeous plum to ripen. Give it a few months and the sweet fruit would fall off the tree into her welcoming mouth. Veronica was a delight well worth waiting for!

More often than not Miss Riley would lie in her bed on a Saturday morning after she had had her breakfast, and her hand would drift down between her legs. In her mind, and her fantasies she had consummated her friendship with Veronica so many times, bringing herself to an ever more intense orgasm. Hamish the cat would slink off the bed in disgust as his mistress's cries of ecstasy pierced the eerie silence of their bedroom once more.

"Hello, who is this please?" Veronica asked the caller, although she had a pretty good idea of the person's identity. She had been expecting the smitten detective to ring.

"This is Jimmy Jack." He hesitated, his palm sticking to the handset.

The detective was sat in his car in his private parking space outside of the police station. He wiped the condensation from the windscreen, and casually watched a tram making its way towards Edinburgh airport.

He had been trying to build up the courage for forty-eight hours to ring the number on the paper napkin, but each occasion that he had found a spare minute he lost his nerve. "Sorry to disturb you in the middle of the day, but I was just wondering-"

Veronica had it all worked out. She felt uncomfortable using the detective in such a way, taking advantage of his feelings, but needs must. She sat herself down on the bench.

"Whether you can see me?" she finished his question for him.

"Aye, but if you don't want to, I would quite understand."

"I'd love to meet up with you again, but in return I have a favour to ask."

That plucked the wind from Jimmy's proverbial sails. He took a long drag from his roll-up. He had just started smoking again, after giving up ten years previously.

"What can I do for you?" he asked hesitantly.

They had met three days later in a bar on the outskirts of Stirling. It was a place that Veronica had frequented twice before. She still felt pretty certain that one day Terry, her adopted second cousin would finally keep his promise, and come over to the mainland to see her, but until then being a woman with a well developed sex drive she occasionally picked up a lady to satisfy her desires.

Once or twice she had considered asking her

manageress out. It would make a pleasant change to taste the flesh of a more mature woman. She could imagine that a sixty year old lesbian would be able to teach *her* a trick or two!

There was a small hotel just around the corner which she would take her lovers to for a night of unbridled passion. It was here that she now lay, but this time it was a man who had heard her orgasmic cries.

Jimmy was already sat on the far side of the pub as she had stepped into its gloom, and as her eyes were adjusting the detective had appeared at her side.

"Good evening, love. I have bought golden opinions from all sorts of people."

Veronica started. She had not heard Jimmy approach her. She looked at him with a curious expression on her face, then laughed out loud, reminding her suitor of water trickling over rocks again.

"You and your bloody Shakespeare! I've never met anyone before who could quote him quite so proficiently as yourself."

A wave of pleasure had washed over the detective. *God, I have fallen really badly for this woman.*

"What would you like to drink?" he asked her, reminding himself that as this particular moment in time it would be *totally* inappropriate to fall to his knees, and worship the ground that she had just walked in on, although the temptation to do so was threatening to overwhelm him.

After half an hour of idle chit-chat Veronica had suggested that they retire to the cosy establishment *up the road*, so that they could continue their conversation in private. She knew that Jimmy had some information for her about her aunt, and that in return he expected a little intimacy.

She had only slept with two men before, more to see what it was like than anything else. She had enjoyed both experiences, especially the sense of satisfaction as her vaginal walls had gripped each pulsating penis, as the men had ejaculated deep inside her. Back then she had been pretty naive, and the thought of contraception had never even entered her mind.

The sensation of semen running down her thigh had been rather strange. After each occasion she had taken the *morning after* pill. The first time her family doctor had prescribed it for her, but she had been too ashamed to go back to him a year later after she had had unprotected sex yet again. Give him his due her second one night stand had done the decent thing, and paid the pharmacist at Boots for the two little white pills.

For some time afterwards Veronica had toyed with the idea of booking an appointment at the local family planning clinic, but on researching the various methods available online she had concluded that there was really nothing currently on the market which would do the trick.

In her late teens her menstrual cycle had started to go awry, and eventually she had been diagnosed with having polycystic ovaries. Essentially, it seemed her organs were being stimulated to produce excessive amounts of the male hormones, particularly testosterone. The gynecologist had remarked following her ultrasound that she was not exactly a typical sufferer of the condition.

You're not fat and hairy, for one thing, he had remarked. Thank God for that then, Veronica had thought sarcastically. He had pointed out to her that although her condition was mild, her fertility might still be affected.

Veronica had not been particularly bothered by that piece of news. She had no plans to have children, anyhow. Even at the tender age of sixteen she had know that for certain. Her career was her priority, and she imagined that having a screaming brat balanced on each hip might make managing an international chain of hotels rather problematic.

Jimmy stood aside to let Veronica enter the room. "This reminds me of when we first met," he said, "except that this time I am looking after you rather than the other way around!"

"*Looking after me*? I'm not sure that that is quite right, but I appreciate your sentiments."

Veronica slipped off her fleece jacket, and sat herself down on the small sofa by the window. Her heart was racing, not due to the inevitable lovemaking, but with the thought that in a moment or two she would hopefully find out where her mother's sister stayed.

She pulled Jimmy down to her and whispered in his ear, "I believe you have some information for me."

"Indeed I have, my love." He lifted his bottom slightly and retrieved his wallet from his back pocket. Unclasping it, he whipped out a piece of white paper, and with a flourish presented it to Veronica.

With her heart threatening to beat its way out her chest, she read out loud the words scribbled on it, "Mrs Lisa Davidson, Victoria Terrace Apartment, Royal Mile, Edinburgh."

She looked at Jimmy, her face etched with excitement and relief. "Is that really my *aunt*?" she whispered.

The detective grinned, delighted by the pleasure that he had invoked in his young friend, even though he knew that his career would be on the line if his superiors ever found out about his disclosure. Finding out the contact details had not been difficult. He had carried out extensive research in preparation for the Federation Conference, so he knew where to find the relevant records. The lady was after all the next of kin of one of their unsolved murder statistics.

Veronica kissed him fully on the lips. "Thank you. This means so much to me. It looks like I shall be making another trip to Edinburgh, rather sooner than I imagined."

Despite her elation she suddenly felt very indecisive. *Should she just make her excuses and go right now, after all she now had the potential means to discover how her mother had actually ended up in the Clyde, or stay and flatter her informant? What if her aunt had no idea as to how Stacey had met her grisly fate? If she did know what had befallen her sister surely she would have confided in the police all those years ago.* Her mind in a whirl, Veronica knew that the decision that she was about to make could prove to be a turning point in her life.

She gazed into her companion's eyes and saw a look of expectancy, and indeed love there. She felt bad about what she was about to do. This man was not some one night stand, somebody to just relieve her sexual tension, he loved her. Suddenly, her mind was made up.

Damn, damn it all, having my own tame police officer is just too good an opportunity to pass up.

She would have much preferred that a woman had been sat next to her, stroking her thigh tenderly, Miss Riley's face flashed before her eyes, but giving herself to this man was a small price to pay to ultimately find out who had killed her mother.

She tucked the precious scrap of paper into her shoulder bag and placed her hand over Jimmy's crotch, squeezing its contents gently.

"Veronica," the man whispered, "I love you."

Jimmy felt his zip being lowered, and the air on his hardening member. He groaned loudly as the young woman slipped to her knees, and took him in her mouth. All thoughts of professional suicide were obliterated from his thoughts, as he felt his penis swelling within the warm wet cavity.

TWENTY-TWO

Veronica checked the details on the piece of paper again. *Yes, this was definitely the right place*, she confirmed to herself. Jimmy's directions had been spot-on.

In her excitement she had stumbled on the steps which lead down from Johnston Terrace, cursing her own stupidity at her choice of footwear. Thankfully, she had not broken one of her heels. A fine sight she would have looked, appearing at her aunt's front door with her tights ripped, and holding a broken shoe in her hand.

She shivered, detecting the first signs of autumn in the air. The detective had informed her that the apartment was a split-level converted stable. As a young *copper on the beat* he had regularly patrolled the area around the castle.

"Hello, can I help you?" the woman asked, peering out of the crack in the door. "If you're here to sell me something, then I'm not interested. The last thing I bought from one of you lot fell apart the second time I used it, so bugger off!"

Veronica blinked at the smartly dressed woman. Her manner of speech sat uneasily with her appearance. She was wearing a bright red suit, and Veronica guessed that she was in her early sixties. She reminded her of

Maggie.

Lisa stared at the pretty young thing cluttering up her doorstep, waiting for her to speak.

"I am so sorry to disturb you. If you are just about to go out, then I can come back."

The woman's face softened. There was something familiar about the girl. She was certainly quite a looker, reminded her of her late sister, somehow.

Lisa Davidson took herself mentally in hand. Stacey had died sixteen years ago, but she still missed her. There had only ever been the two of them, both their parents had died from alcoholic liver poisoning many years before, and now Lisa was all alone in the world.

To her eternal shame she had walked away from the alcohol sodden home when she was in her late teens, leaving her fourteen year old sister to care for their Mum and Dad. Lisa could not deal with all the drunken arguments which often resulted in her father physically abusing one, or other of them. He would shout and swear, the frustrations of his worthless life evident in his bloodshot eyes.

One night after he had punched his older daughter so hard that her lip had split Lisa had stormed out, and braving the elements and the gangs of youths patrolling the Glaswegian streets at the time, she had reached her boyfriend's flat. The two sisters were eventually reunited at their father's funeral.

Two months later Mrs Connolly joined her husband in hopefully a sober afterlife. Her oesophageal varices had haemorrhaged in hospital, and despite the diligent attention of the medical staff she went into shock, and subsequently passed away.

For the next ten years the siblings saw each other about once every six months. Stacey tried so hard to forgive her sister for deserting her, but the relationship between them never became close.

One Christmas Lisa's boyfriend had an enormous row with Stacey, and this time the younger sister stormed out. Now in her thirties and fully immersed in the world of the sex worker, another thing that rankled her sister, Stacey had practically disowned Lisa, just keeping in touch with her with the occasional text. At the time of her death she had not set eyes on her for ten years.

"Do I know you?" Lisa enquired of the anxious looking girl.

Similarly to her second meeting with Jimmy, Veronica felt completely out of her depth. If she did not calm her nerves and say something the woman would disappear back into her apartment, and her trip to Edinburgh would prove to be a total waste of time.

"My name is Veronica. I have reason to believe that I am your *niece*."

Lisa gawped at her visitor, then it dawned on her that she must look remarkably like a gold, or perhaps that should be a *red* fish gasping for air. *Was this the baby that Stacey had put up for adoption all those years ago?* She never knew about the wee mite until after her sister's death.

Even whilst she had been staring down at the body in the police morgue Lisa had not been completely certain that the bloated corpse was her own *flesh and blood*. A week later the Family Liaison Officer had paid her a visit. She presented her with several large bags which represented Stacey's entire life. After reading her diaries, they meticulously recorded all her sibling's daily activities and emotions, Lisa knew for certain that her identification of the body had been correct.

She peered more closely at the young woman who understandably looked embarrassed and uncomfortable. Lisa guessed that she must be about twenty, so that would fit.

"Look, why don't you come in? I've just got back from work, hence the get-up." She indicated her attire. "I had to come home early. Daft really, I tripped over a cable, and fell down."

Veronica looked concerned. "Are you all right? Did you hurt yourself?" she asked as Lisa opened the door fully, allowing her to walk into the apartment.

There was no entrance hall, instead she found herself in a small kitchen-diner. Lisa indicated that she should sit herself down at the four-seater pine table. The whole of the ground floor appeared to be open-plan. There was a sink unit and a washing machine directly ahead of her, with several pine cupboards fitted around them. To the left of them was a small electric oven with a gas hob. A brand new looking fridge freezer and a dishwasher completed the look.

"I've got everything I could want here. The place might be a tad on the small size, but it's plenty big enough for me," Lisa commented as if she had read Veronica's thoughts.

She sat herself down opposite the girl. "Nice comfy sofa too," she added, taking off her court shoes and rubbing her sore toes.

"It's all really lovely. How long have you stayed here then?"

"I moved in just over a year ago, but enough of the idle chitchat, eh? What makes you think you're my sister's wee girl then?"

Veronica stopped her admiration of the decor, took a deep breath and recounted her visit to the Record Office.

" Aye, I remember Mavis. She looked pretty witch-like even back then. Skinny little thing she was. Her sister and I were pretty close once, but I've not seen either of them since Stacey's funeral. Mavis threw her arms around me after we had laid my poor sister to rest. Hugging her was like embracing a bundle of twigs!"

Lisa remarked after Veronica had described the old lady who had taken such an interest in her research.

Laughing, Veronica reached down to her bag and placed it on her lap. She carefully took out the folded document, and slid it across the table to Lisa. The woman's initial brusqueness had worried her, but now she was feeling more at ease.

Lisa smoothed the creases out of the certificate. She experienced a certain degree of lightheadedness as she saw her sibling's name staring up at her.

Birth mother-Stacey Connolly, it said. *Father Unknown. Adopted Parents-Maggie and Caroline Montgomery.*

"Bloody hell, you really are my niece. Come here!"

Lisa pushed herself up from the table, her bruised knee forgotten. She re-adjusted her spare pair of spectacles on her nose.

Truth be told, the only reason why she had been obliged to return home after her stumble at work was because her glasses had fallen off, smashing one of the lenses. Her boss at the contact centre where she was employed as their Human Resources Co-ordinator had suggested that she took the rest of the day off. It was hardly worth her driving back to Glasgow to continue her shift.

Now she thanked her lucky stars that she did. Ironically, she had watched a film called *Serendipity* last night on her state-of-the-art plasma television. It looked like that for once her clumsiness had brought her some marvelous good fortune, rather than just making her look like a blundering elephant. She threw her arms around her newly discovered relative.

"Steady on, you're squeeze the life out of me! You really are my aunt, aren't you?" Veronica said, disentangling herself from the embrace.

"It sure as hell looks like it, girl. Unless there is another Stacey Connolly around."

"Well, I suppose we could get a DNA test done or something, just to be sure," Veronica ventured, her optimism slightly dented. Maybe Jimmy had got it all wrong. She dared not reveal her sources.

"Ach, don't be daft. You're my Stacey's, all right. Just give me a second, and I'll show you a photograph of her. You'll see then."

Lisa strode over to the living area and picked up a photo frame. "See, even a blind man could tell that you were mother and daughter. You even have her green eyes."

Veronica gripped the object, and for the first time she found herself looking into her mother's face. She was laughing at the camera. It must have been windy on the day that it was taken for her long blonde hair was blowing around her face. Despite her obvious cheerfulness, the photographer had captured her tiredness. Veronica could see the lines etched into her mother's features.

"How old was she when this was taken?"

The older woman sat herself down again heavily and started to sob. This time it was Veronica's turn to stand up. She went to her aunt and gripped her shoulders. Lisa swiveled around in her chair, and buried her face in the soft material of her niece's coat.

Veronica was really not sure how to react to this sudden outburst of emotion. "Shall I make us a nice cup of tea, love?" she asked. "I'm sure I can find the necessary things for myself."

Lisa straightened herself, wiping her tear-stained features." I'm sorry about that. It's just that I never expected any of this. If somebody had suggested to me at seven o'clock this morning that today I would not only smash my best pair of specs, but also become acquainted with my long lost niece, well, I would have strapped them into a strait jacket! Sod the tea, we need something harder than that."

Once again, Veronica laughed at her aunt's humour, it was so like her own. She accepted the tumbler of whiskey proffered to her gratefully, and cupped her hands around the glass. "Sleinte, to us!"

"Ach, where are my manners? In all the excitement, I never even offered to take your coat."

Veronica smiled and slipped off her yellow jacket. "Don't hold it too close to you. It clashes something awful with your suit."

Lisa slipped the garment over the back of one of the

chairs. Facing Veronica once more, and lighting up a cigarette from a packet which she had retrieved from the coffee table earlier she asked, "How much do you know about your mother?"

"Not much really. I discovered that she worked as a prostitute, and that the police found her body floating in the Clyde, when I was about four years old. Of course by then I had been adopted. That's about it really, but," she gripped her aunt's hands earnestly, " I so want to know *everything* about her."

Lisa smiled at the girl, a feeling of warmth pervading her body. Perhaps it was just the effect of the whiskey, but seeing her Stacey's bairn sat there in front of her was such a comfort. Of course she was a stranger to her in reality. She did not know anything about her, but finding out was going to be such fun.

"Look, why don't you go over there," she pointed to the settee at the far side of the room, "make yourself comfortable, and I'll just pop upstairs and change out of my work clothes. We can have a proper blather then."

Veronica nodded her agreement, and watched her aunt disappear up the stone steps leading to her bedroom.

"I still feel guilty after all these years, leaving the poor mite to mop up after two drunks," Lisa confessed. She refilled her glass and offered another wee dram to her niece.

They were sat side by side on Lisa's squashy sofa. Two

pairs of feet, one sporting fluorescent green socks, the other encased in tan coloured tights were resting on the mother of pearl inlaid coffee table. The two of them had been talking for almost three hours, and Lisa was more than a little tipsy.

"That's enough of the hard stuff for me, thanks," Veronica said. "I've a train to catch in an hour. Mum worries about me if I am back too late."

She now knew all the intricate details of her birth mother's life, practically from the hour that she was born in the family home in central Glasgow, to her funeral. It was a very sad tragic story, and many tears had been shed by them both.

Veronica had learnt how her mother had had little option but to *go on the game* after the premature death of her parents, how she had never realised her dream of becoming a hairdresser, and about her addictions which proved to be as devastating to her life as alcohol had been to her Mum and Dad. It seemed fruit machines, and the buying of expensive designer clothes had been Stacey's two main weaknesses.

Veronica surreptitiously glanced at her watch. It had been quite a day, meeting her aunt for the first time and feeling that at long last she now really knew who her natural mother was, but there was something more pressing on her mind.

"Lisa, look, I'm really sorry to bring this up, but before I go I have to ask you something."

Her aunt took her feet off the table and straightened
herself. She felt rather whoozy, and the harshness of the
spirit was playing havoc with her gastric ulcer. She had
just popped an antacid into her mouth.

"What is it, love? Feel free to ask me anything."

Veronica drained the last drops of whiskey from her
tumbler, and placed her stockinged feet firmly on the
floor, digging her toes into the deep pile of the carpet.

"What do you think happened to Mum on the day she
disappeared?"

The issue had been carefully skirted around until now.
Veronica knew that the two sisters had exchanged texts
a few months before Stacey's body was found by a local
fisherman, and that it had taken the police weeks to
trace her next of kin.

"As you know we were never very close, and I really
could not tell the police anything of significance when
they appeared at my door. It wasn't all my fault, it was
Stacey who washed her hands of me. The image of her
bloated body lying on that slab in the morgue still
haunts me of a night, you know."

She belched discreetly and grimaced as a stabbing pain
shot through her stomach. She waved away Veronica's
hand.

"Don't be kind to me, I shall only start crying again.
The last thing Stacey told me was that she had found a
way to clear all her debts, but considering that our only
means of communication was by text, she refused to

speak to me on the phone, I don't really know any more than that."

Veronica felt a fluttering in her stomach. Somehow she knew that this piece of information, albeit limited, was vital in the search for her mother's killer.

"Could you give me her last address please? Maybe one of her neighbours remembers something."

Lisa shook her head doubtfully. "I am happy to tell you where she was staying, but Veronica, I know you mean well, but all this happened sixteen years ago. What's to say that anybody staying there now was a resident back then? She had a flat near Central Station. The area was quite nice up until five years ago. Some of the undesirables who were staying in Easterhouse shacked up there under the radar of the local council. It's a pretty dangerous place now. I wouldn't want to lose you, not just after we had found each other."

Veronica stood up and slid her feet back into her shoes. She picked up the piece of paper on which Lisa had scribbled her mother's last known address, along with half a dozen old photographs taken during their childhood. Her aunt had carefully extracted them from her album for Veronica to keep. The younger woman threw her arms around her only surviving relative and hugged her tightly.

"Don't worry, I'll be careful. I'll do a bit of poking around, see what I can find out. It's about time Stacey's ghost was laid to rest. The only way that will happen is by us discovering who murdered her."

Lisa smiled weakly. "Good luck, Veronica. Keep me posted, won't you? I am so glad that you knocked on my door today. Come and visit me again soon."

She kissed her niece on her cheek and let her out onto the street. As she waved, a tear dribbled down over the place where Veronica had just placed her lips. *Take care, dear one*, she thought.

TWENTY-THREE

Veronica stopped for a moment to catch her breath
outside of the Theatre Royal. So, this is Hope Street, the
place where my mother spent the last years of her life,
she thought.

Journey's End was currently showing at the playhouse,
according to the billboard. Quite fitting really, she
mused as she read the preview notice. Essentially, it was
a wartime drama following one Captain Stanhope and
his young band of men as they awaited an enemy attack
in the trenches. It was written by a chap called R. C.
Sheriff, apparently.

Veronica recalled a episode of *Blackadder* which had
had a similar theme. She had studied all four of the
series as part of her coursework for her English Higher
examination. The scripts of the popular television
programmes had provided a hilarious relief from
Shakespeare and Wilkie Collins. She had roared with
laughter at the historical situation comedy starring
Rowan Atkinson which had been broadcast throughout
the 1980s. Veronica had quoted one of her favourite
lines to her tutor when she suggested to her that such
was her love of literature that perhaps she might like to
become a classical actress.

*I'd rather have my tongue beaten wafer-thin with a
steak-tenderizer, and then stapled to the floor with a*

croquet hoop.

Miss Brodie had nearly wet herself with hysterics.

Veronica strode purposefully along the pavement. She passed a couple of restaurants, and thought about her lunch nestling in the bottom of her rucksack. She had bought it at the Bagel Factory before leaving Central Station earlier that morning. Now she imagined biting into the doughy ring, and tasting the free-range egg, and its salad complement beneath. Her stomach grumbled.

Maggie had cornered her in the kitchen just as she was about to sink her teeth into a piece of marmalade coated toast hours before. Veronica's original plan was to leave the house unnoticed, but Caroline had had a bad night and her spouse had popped downstairs to make them both an early morning cup of tea.

Although she had received her new kidney almost twenty years previously, Caroline was yet to find a combination of anti-rejection drugs that she could swallow, which did not blight her with side effects. Taking the *Cyclosporin A* had resulted in her growing a moustache. Maggie had wittingly commented that it was a shame that she no longer used her strap-on as sporting facial hair might have made her role playing more realistic. After the family doctor had changed her prescription the new medication had made her brown locks fall out instead. Eventually that problem had been overcome by careful monitoring and adjustment of the dose, but on occasions the other pills that she was obliged to take on a daily basis gave her abdominal pain. Last night was one such occasion.

After careful consideration Maggie had taken early retirement, but seeing as Veronica was now living back home again she had persuaded Caroline that staying in Stirling was not so bad after all. Their dreams of relocating to Skye were put on the proverbial back burner for now.

The two of them, although understanding of their adopted daughter's need to find out what had happened to her birth mother were both very wary. The family had had several rather heated discussions over the matter. That was why Veronica had so wanted to slip out of the house that morning unseen.

Her appetite lost, she had had no option but to explain to her mother that she was off to Glasgow to try to find somebody who might remember Stacey. Maggie had not been happy when Veronica had tracked down her Auntie Lisa, jealousy and a fear of losing her beloved child had been the main instigator of those feelings, but the thought of her trailing around Hope Street filled her with great worry and fear. Veronica's fiery temper had flared up, causing her to storm out of the front door, its glass quivering in her wake.

"Excuse me, I'm sorry to disturb you but are you familiar with the name, Stacey Connolly?" Veronica asked yet another resident of the block of flats.

"Bugger off!" she was told by the scruffy looking man, still clad in his dressing gown, even though it was now eleven o' clock.

As the door was slammed rudely in her face, Veronica sighed deeply. Her aunt had informed her that the whole place had deteriorated somewhat over the years. For her dear mother's sake she sincerely hoped that that was the case.

She recalled reading in the newspaper that Caroline bought each day that this part of Glasgow was next in line for refurbishment. Considering the king's antipathy to users of illegal drugs, alcoholics and single mothers Veronica dared not even think what would happen to a substantial number of the tenants.

All the foreigners who had resided in Easterhouse had been forcibly repatriated back to their or their descendents' countries of origin, but there was little the authorities could do about the other undesirables. More treatment centres had been opened to try and cure the addicts of their problems, and Society now looked upon the bearing of a child outside of wedlock as harshly as it had done in the 1950s, but the funds were not available to finance all of King Rupert's commendable projects. An underclass still existed in Glasgow, as it did in so many other cities.

"Stacey Connolly? Now, let me see," the elderly woman said, rubbing her hirsute chin in thought, "wasn't she the lassie they found floating in the Clyde?"

"Yes, that's right. She used to stay in the flat on the second floor. Did she know her?" Veronica enquired, involuntarily holding her breath.

"Stacey? Oh, yes, her and me were good neighbours, until we fell out one week. My oldest son had come back to stay with me for a while, and he used to wind her up something chronic by playing his music at seven o'clock in the morning. Stacey worked until the early hours, see. After all that trouble I asked the council to move me. They found me this flat instead."

Veronica whooped with delight.

The woman looked startled. "What was she to you, dear?"

"Stacey was my *mother*. Look," she stuttered, "can I come in for a moment? I've been trailing around this block for an hour now. Just as I was about to give up hope-" She could not finish her sentence as a wave of emotion flooded over her.

"Are you all right, pet? Of course, you can come in. You'll have to excuse the mess though. My cleaner's not been today yet."

Veronica gingerly picked her way through the detritus scattered on the floor of the one-bedroomed flat. *I reckon the cleaner's not been for a month, let alone a day*, she thought.

"Make yourself comfortable, dear."

Veronica sat herself down on the cleanest part of the battered sofa, and tried not to stare at the mess. Her home was always spotless. When Maggie and Caroline had both been working a Mrs Brown had popped in every morning to vacuum and polish.

"So, how can I help you, pet? Stacey's been gone a long time now, and my memory's not what it was. Did you lose contact with your mother, or something? Why have you come here after all these years? Are you one of those undercover police officers, although I must admit they don't usually come wrapped in such *sexy* packaging as yourself?" She leered toothlessly at her visitor, and crudely rubbed her crotch.

Veronica detected a note of caution in the woman's voice beneath her obvious lust which was understandable, when a complete stranger turned up on one's doorstep unannounced, however *sexy* she might be.

She reminded Veronica of the old crone that had accosted her at the Records Office, although that one had not flashed her sexuality so overtly as this octogenarian. *Fair is foul, and foul is fair*, she thought to herself. *Hell's bells, I'm becoming as bad as Jimmy!*

"I'm not from the police," Veronica stated, *although I am milking one for information*, she mused to herself.

"I was adopted. I never knew my mother. I did meet her sister though the other day. She gave me Stacey's address."

"So, what do you want to know, dear?" she reiterated. "I'd tell a pretty girl like yourself anything. I don't suppose you're into women though, are you?"

Veronica blushed. "Well, I am bisexual, but I think you are just a wee bit too old for me."

"What a shame," the woman muttered.

Veronica was starting to feel rather uncomfortable, claustrophobic even. She needed to escape this old crone's lechery.

"I just want to find out what happened to her, but I suppose if you had fallen out with her you wouldn't know."

"I remember the police sniffing around here after they had found her body, but like I said to them I haven't the foggiest idea what happened to the poor mite. You look like her though, with those green eyes of yours, and that lovely blonde hair." She reached across to Veronica and tried to finger the strands.

"I'm sorry that I have wasted your time. Look, I have to go." Veronica could feel the perspiration trickle down her back. Then she remembered her aunt telling her that Stacey had found a way to *clear her debts*. A flash of inspiration came to her.

"This might be a strange question, but were there any *loan sharks* operating in this area back then?"

It was the woman's turn to blush. "Aye, there was one chap. Quite nasty, he was. I only ever knew him as John. He still stays in the block. Number 203 is his flat. Why do you want to know something like that?"

Veronica suddenly felt a breeze of cold air on her face. She glanced through the door into the woman's bedroom. She guessed its filthy window was the only one in the flat. It was firmly shut, as was the front door.

"It doesn't matter. Look, I do have to go. You've been really helpful. Thank you."

In a stride or two she was at the door which was thankfully unlocked. As she let herself out Veronica heard the woman cackle, "What about a kiss then for my troubles?"

Veronica shivered and made her way back up to the third floor. She paused for a minute or two as she was climbing the rough stone steps, consciously aware that she may well have been placing her feet in exactly the same spot as her mother had done many years before. She twisted round and gazed out over the city.

Central Station was directly in front of her, its famous glass-walled bridge carrying the platforms over Argyle Street. She recalled Maggie telling her once that its nickname was *Heilanman's Umbrella*, because for several years people who had come to Glasgow to find work following the Highland clearances had met there at the weekends. Admiring its distinctive Venetian-style windows and its gold lettering, she smiled to herself.

This was certainly a day to evoke old ghosts.

Once more she found herself rapping on a door. *If I ever want a change of career, then no doubt Jimmy would readily offer me a job with the Force*, she thought to herself. I must have knocked on almost every door in this tenement block. Her stomach grumbled again. Right, let's just have a word with this *John*, see if he ever loaned any money to my mother, then I shall call it a day, she decided.

"Yes, what do you want?" the man asked, rubbing his eyes. "Can't a fellow have a wee snooze after his lunch without being disturbed?"

Veronica guessed that he was in his mid-sixties. Dressed casually in a pair of jogging pants and a polo shirt, it was obvious that life had treated him rather more kindly than the woman two flights down.

"I'm sorry to have woken you but, is your name John?"

"What if it is? What's it to you?" he asked gruffly, blocking the entire doorway with his corpulent frame.

It was obvious to Veronica that if she suggested to this man that they had a wee chat inside, he would probably tell her where to go, in no uncertain terms. It was best just to make her enquiry brief, and to the point.

"I know that you used to be a doorstep lender many years back-"

The man shrugged his shoulders and raised one

eyebrow as if to say, *So what?*

"Do you remember a woman in her forties by the name of Stacey Connolly? She stayed on the second floor."

The man looked thoughtful for a moment, yawning with his mouth wide open. Veronica caught a whiff of his halitosis, a nausea-inducing mixture of bad teeth, cigarettes and beer.

"You her daughter, are you?"

Veronica felt lightheaded. "Well, yes, in fact I am, but how did you know that?"

"Spitting image, love. I do remember your mother. She was a good lass, always paid me on time, never late with her payments. Mind you, she liked nice things, so she kept borrowing too."

Veronica smiled. *Perhaps her feminine charms were having a pacifying effect on this one too.*

"She all right, is she?" the man asked, his voice taking on a more pleasant tone.

Something inside Veronica's head warned her to tread carefully with this big fellow. "Unfortunately, my mother passed away recently. I was going through her things, and came across a scrap of paper with your name and address on it. I just wondered who *John* was, that was all," she said.

Wow, I am good. Perhaps I should have gone to drama school after all, and not bothered with the hotel trade, if my improvisation skills are anything to go by.

The man reddened. "Ach, that was real nice of you, but

truth be told I haven't seen your mother for many years. I suppose I did have a soft spot for her back then. Most of my customers just gave me a lot of grief, but your Mum always had a pleasant smile for me. More often than not she would invite me in for a cup of tea. Treated me with respect, she did, not like the rest of them."

Veronica's legs were starting to ache, but she dared not interrupt the man. She felt another waft of cool air pass across her, although there was no wind that day. She waited for him to continue. He seemed keen to talk. Perhaps he's just lonely, she concluded.

"I got into business with a mate of mine who made porn films back then. Your mother told me that she was *on the game*." He hesitated. "You knew that, right?"

Veronica nodded.

"I felt sorry for her, see. I couldn't afford to waive what she owed me, but I knew from our little chats that she wanted to find a more respectable job."

He shuffled his feet and took a deep breath. "Well, rightly or wrongly, I suggested that she took part in a film. The money she earnt would have been enough to clear her debts, and give her a bit of hope for the future, like. That was the last I saw of her. I just assumed that she had moved to new pastures. I knocked on her door one day, but couldn't get a reply. If it had been anyone else I'd have chased it up with her landlord, she still owed me the money, see, but soft-hearted fool as I was I just thought to myself, good old Stacey, she's escaped this dump, good luck to her."

Veronica felt yet another shiver pass through her. God hope that I've not caught a chill, she thought.

"What was your business partner's name? You know, the chap who made the porn films?"

Without thinking, the man answered, "Mike Jones, his name was. Why do you ask?"

That name's familiar, Veronica mused. "It doesn't matter. It's been nice meeting you, John," she said in a rush, hurrying away from the flat.

It was only when she was sinking her teeth at long last into her bagel, whilst waiting at Central Station for her train back to Stirling that she remembered who *Mike Jones* was. She fished inside her rucksack for her purse. From its side pocket she pulled out a piece of paper torn from one of the Highland Hotel's writing pads. *Mr. Michael Jones*, it said.

TWENTY-FOUR

"My Stacey making dirty movies? I can't believe that. It was bad enough that she earned her living by selling herself on the street. To then discover that my only sister had produced a child and, now I've got *this* to contend with. Bloody hell!" Lisa exclaimed ten days later on hearing her niece's news.

****

Veronica's mind had been whirling ever since she had found out about her mother's activities two weeks previously. They had been short-staffed at work and she had felt obliged to accept the hotel manager's offer of overtime, not on reception but on the portering side.

It had felt strange working alongside somebody other than Miss Riley, but considering all that was going on in her life at the present time, quite a relief really. The last thing she needed right now was to embark on a new relationship. She had a funny feeling that the reception manageress would not be satisfied with a one-or-two night stand. Knowing her luck, the woman would fall hopelessly in love with her. Extricating herself out of that one would be really difficult, possibly even putting her job at risk.

In four months' time she was to start shadowing the

general manager. This represented the next phase of her training to become a fully-fledged hotel manageress. Thankfully, the Stirling hotel did not require her to do a stint as a chamber maid, as the Royal Highland would have done. She really had not relished the idea of spending her day cleaning one lavatory after another. She did not even do that at home. She was looking forward to learning how to actually run the hotel, to discover all *the tricks of the trade*, so to speak.

Veronica still held a burning ambition to build her own hotel empire one day, but to realise her dreams she needed more than experience. What she required was a sponsor, someone who believed in her abilities, and more importantly a person who would be prepared to plough a wad of cash into her new venture.

Veronica loved her home country, and despite the promise of more opportunities down south she fully intended to open her first four-star hotel in Scotland. *If I can't find a property to buy, I sure as hell will have one built.* The plan was to have a chain of top class establishments across several continents, by the time she was thirty. There was no way that she was going to jeopardise her career over a doomed love affair.

Women were great for satisfying her rampant sex drive, but it was Terry whom she loved. He had stolen her heart years before, and Veronica knew that one day on returning home he would be there waiting to sweep her into his arms. Part of her knew that this was just a foolish romantic dream, did she expect him to come riding over the Skye Bridge on a white charger like some medieval knight, but as far as Veronica was concerned there was only one person in a lifetime who was destined to be your soul mate, and for her that was Terry. She felt pretty guilty about having slept with Jimmy on three occasions, but until she had discovered for certain what had actually caused the sudden demise of her mother she needed to feed him the occasional titbit to keep him compliant.

Veronica had decided one afternoon whilst lugging a guest's suitcase up to his room that she needed an ally to continue her search. She had contemplated asking Jimmy to accompany her, but Mr. Jones may well have recognised the detective from the newspapers. DS Jack's face had appeared several times in the national press following the closure of some big case or other. The last thing she wanted was to make the fellow feel uneasy. In reality Veronica had little idea of how her meeting with the pornographer would unfold. The plan was to simply ask him what had happened on the day her mother had taken part in one of his films, and *play it by ear* from that point. It looked like her improvisation skills would prove useful once again.

Veronica did not really have any close friends, not somebody who she would feel comfortable involving in her plans anyway. That evening whilst enjoying her customary soak in the bath it had suddenly dawned on her who her perfect companion would be. *Auntie Lisa! Why didn't I think of her before? She is after all my mother's sister, and already she feels like my best friend.*

Things had calmed down at home. Maggie had questioned her about her trip to Hope Street on her return to Stirling, and had seemed satisfied with the brief résumé of her day. She had told her that today she would be traveling to Edinburgh to see her aunt again, but nothing more.

All right, just take care, love, was all that she had said that morning, kissing her daughter on the cheek. Perhaps Caroline had had a word with her.

"I'm really sorry, Lisa but it may be a clue to her disappearance, and eventual fate."

The two of them were once again sat on the sofa in the older woman's apartment, but this time there were cups of tea between them, rather than a bottle of whiskey.

Veronica had telephoned her aunt the week before, and Lisa had responded warmly to Veronica's suggestion that she pop round to see her again that weekend. On greeting her at the door, Veronica informed her that they were going out for the afternoon. Lisa had assumed that this meant a spot of retail therapy. It was obvious to her that her niece had an impeccable taste in clothes, she looked elegant even in just a pair of denim jeans and a top, and she relished the idea of touring the shops arm-in-arm. Her delusion had become apparent rather abruptly though once they had begun talking. Their destination was not some designer boutique, but the West End of Glasgow.

"So, tell me again why we are going all the way over to the Great Western Road this afternoon?"

Veronica sighed and glanced at her watch. "Look, it's almost twelve o'clock. We need to get a move on if we are to be back by dark. I'll explain it again to you on the train," she said, trying desperately to keep her exasperation out of her voice.

"Do I need to take anything with me then?" her aunt asked in a resigned tone.

"No, just make sure that you've got your head screwed on tightly! I don't know what the matter is with you today. You were more with it when I left you last time, and that was after you had consumed several drams of whiskey!"

Lisa affected an air of mock indignation. "You just watch your mouth, girl and remember who I am. Your dear mother might not be around to take you in hand, but as your aunt I am entitled to a bit of respect. Now come, let's get out of here, we've a train to catch," she said, pushing her niece out of the door. The two of them giggled together, more like best friends than newly discovered relatives.

The two of them emerged from Hyndland railway station, blinking in the sunshine. The weather had looked a little inclement earlier in the day, but thankfully the clouds had mostly cleared, leaving just a few wispy ones to pattern the blue sky. They had caught the *Edinburgh Waverley to Glasgow Queen Street Shuttle,* and then changed trains.

Lisa had a vague feeling of excitement bubbling within her. After Veronica had given her an almost moment-by-moment account of her day touring the Hope Street flats she was now, in a strange way rather looking forward to meeting this Mr. Jones.

She had taken on board her niece's logic. Considering that Stacey was already working as a prostitute, it was hardly an enormous leap into the pornography industry. It seemed likely that this man whose flat they were to visit could indeed be the missing link to her sister's tragic death. Of course, neither of them knew at this moment whether he had been directly involved, but Lisa had a strong suspicion that he was. What puzzled her the most was how come the police at the time had not come up with such a clue, as her niece had revealed on one single visit to the place where Stacey had stayed. She was sure that their afternoon would prove to be most productive, as long as this *Mike Jones* was at home of course.

"98 Great Western Road," Veronica stated. "This must

be it."

The two of them looked up at the biscuit coloured
facade. A pair of polished black marble columns
accentuated the entrance to the block of apartments. The
whole place reeked of wealth.

Veronica thought back to the Hope Street flats, and felt
a tear escape from her right eye. She very rarely cried,
but to think of the squalor that those poor people stayed
in compared to the obvious luxury of these residents
moved her. It was unlikely that she would have felt
much sympathy for the Society's drop-outs if it had not
been for the fact that her late mother had resided there,
but still. One thing she did know was that making sex
movies certainly paid!

Lisa rang the bell but there was no reply. Veronica
pushed the heavy door open, affording them free
passage into the lobby. One of the residents must have
forgotten to pull it closed behind them, she thought,
sending up a silent prayer to the ornate ceiling. The
whole place seemed to be deserted. Everybody must be
having a long lie-in, it was the weekend after all, she
concluded.

An almost silent elevator took them up to the fourth
floor, and then Veronica unexpectedly gripped her aunt's
hand. Now that they were actually standing outside of
the man's door a peculiar feeling of fear permeated
through the young woman.

Casually dressed in black jeans and a red T-shirt, Mike

peered through the spy hole, and involuntarily gulped on recognising the young lady from the hotel. *What in the Devil's name did she want*, he thought to himself.

****

Ever since he had confessed his past misdemeanors to his son Mike had become just a tad paranoid. It seemed that it was easier to live with the knowledge of one's crimes if nobody else knew about them, but once somebody else shared your dark secrets, then that was when the trouble begun.

Mike did not believe that his son felt any remorse for what he had done, and similarly neither did he. The loss of the nine lives were he admitted rather sad, but a necessity. The snuff movies had made a lot of money for the business, and was it their fault if some people got their kicks from watching a woman die whilst having sex? At least they met their Maker with a smile on their face! No, it was not guilt that threatened to addle Mike's mind, but the fear of being found out.

Christopher was safe. The double jeopardy law had been reintroduced two years ago which meant that a person could not be tried twice for the same crime. It did not matter whether the defendant had been convicted or acquitted. The King had ruled that *it was an essential element of protection of the liberty of the subject*. Good old Rupert, thought Mike.

It had been about sixteen years since Mike had watched his final victim gasp her last breath. After her body had been found he really thought that his number was up, but the months had rolled by, and had become years. According to the papers the girl's sister had eventually been traced, and her body had been placed six feet under the ground, instead of twelve feet under the water.

Stuart, the fellow who had literally sliced into his co-workers had succumbed to lung cancer ten years previously, he had smoked like a chimney so it was not exactly a shock to his nearest and dearest, so similar to his son's trial it would potentially be just the former boss of Naughty But Nice in the dock. Christopher had never revealed the name of his co-conspirator.

****

Veronica looked at her aunt who nodded her approval. She rapped hard on the door of the flat. It looked like a new coat of paint had been just applied, so shiny was its lustre.

The cogs of Mike's mind started spinning. *Should he open the door and find out what she wanted? Had there been some problem with his credit card at the hotel? Why would the management send out one of their lowly receptionists, on a Saturday of all days? Wouldn't they have just rung him? No*, he decided, *it can't be that, so what?*

Another hammering interrupted his thoughts. *Bloody hell, she'll be damaging the paintwork next.* Only last week he had hired a contractor to give the whole flat a new lick of emulsion, inside and out. Mike could still smell its cloying, but not altogether unpleasant odour.

He peered once more through the spy hole. It was like looking at one's reflection in one of those *crazy mirrors* at a fairground. The image was not quite what it seemed. On the third rap, more urgent and insistent than the last, he gave in.

Deciding that he had better err on the side of caution, he unlocked the door and pushed it open just a few inches, the security chain still insitu.

"Can I help you, miss?" he asked the young woman politely.

Veronica signed with relief. It had been a risky gamble dragging her aunt all this way, not knowing if Mr. Jones would be at home, or not. She enquired as to his identity.

"That's a strange thing to ask, miss, seeing as I was a guest at your hotel. Was there a problem with my card? Fancy you coming all this way just to sort that out," Mike gabbled nervously.

Veronica observed that beads of perspiration were forming both on the man's forehead adjacent to his hairline, and on his top lip where there was evidence of a slight shaving rash. She felt confused. *What the hell was he on about?* The last thing on her mind right now was work. Then it dawned on her.

"Oh, no. This has got nothing to do with your hotel stay. I processed the payment myself. It went through just fine. No, I'm here on personal business. I've brought my aunt too."

The girl's words did not make Mike feel any better, but he stayed in a very respectable place, and whatever the reason for the receptionist's visit he did not want his neighbours overhearing. He straightened his arms at his sides and balled his fists, pounding the sides of his legs just above the knees. He silently chastised himself for being such a wimp.

Slowly sliding the chain back and opening the door fully, he said, "Well, you had better come in then."

Lisa wrinkled her nose as the all pervading smell assailed her nostrils. Beneath the paint she detected the faint aroma of cigarettes, and some expensive aftershave. Letting her eyes drift around the living room of the apartment, she thought, whatever else Mr. Jones proves to be, he has certainly got good taste. His choice of furniture and decor were uncannily similar to her own. He obviously favoured traditional pieces over the more modern style. Then she turned her attention to the man himself.

Like Veronica's jeans, his were designer, and although she guessed he was of a similar age to herself he looked good on it. Lisa always reckoned that the advancing

years sat better on a man's face than they did on a
woman's. His skin was deeply lined, but offset by a tan
more likely to have been acquired on a sun-drenched
tropical beach, than in an artificial way. He wore his T-
shirt tight, and the muscles of his chest were defined by
the material. His biceps bulged where his hirsute arms
meet his clothing. So what if his stomach rided over the
top of his waistband a little, nobody was perfect.

*Bloody hell, in a different time and place I could quite
fancy you*, she thought, blushing gently. It had been over
a year since Lisa had enjoyed the attentions of a
gentleman, romantically, or in a more carnal sense. It
was a bloody good job that her niece was with her, or
else who knows what might have happened.

Veronica stared at the man. *So, you directed my Mum
in a dirty film, eh?*

Deep down, she was not sure what she thought about
her mother being a porn actress. She made out to
Maggie that she did not give a damn that she was the
daughter of a prostitute, but in reality it did bother her.
Veronica was as open-minded about sex as the next
person, probably more so, but she would never pay
somebody to make love to her, or sell her body to the
highest bidder. Akin to her sympathies for the druggies
in Hope Street her opinion of prostitution was only
modified by her mother's connection to the trade.
Despite his obvious good looks and his regular use of
the gym Veronica took an instant dislike to the man who

was currently suggesting to them that they made themselves comfortable.

"So, what can I do for you, two ladies?" Mike asked, trying desperately to maintain an outwardly calm appearance regardless of the churning in his bowels.

"We have been lead to believe that you used to make pornographic films. Is that right?" Veronica said.

"Maybe I did," Mike replied vaguely. "What about it? I retired from all that years ago."

"And very nicely too," Veronica muttered under her breath. Out loud, she said, "My mother, Stacey Connolly worked for you once, I believe. Do you remember her?"

The beads of wetness on Mike's face coalesced into a dribble, and despite his liberal application of deodorant that morning he became aware that two damp patches were forming under his axillae. He remembered Stacey all right. He could almost hear the mechanisms in his brain whirling.

Despite working out at his local gymnasium twice a week Mike suffered from hypertension, and at this moment he swore that he could feel his blood pressure soaring. His doctor had told him that it was due to his unhealthy diet. *What was the point*, he had told him sternly on his last visit, *of exercising regularly if when he got home he tucked into a huge plate of deep fried haggis and chips?* He did have a point.

Should I deny knowing her at all or-, he mentally

interrupted himself. No, hang on a minute, it was sixteen years ago, and even back then there was nothing *illegal* about making a porn movie. What he couldn't figure out was the connection between any of his old employees and the two people presently sat opposite him.

"Yes, the *lady* you speak of did work for me once, but what I don't understand is why you two are here at all. From the look of you, I would hazard a guess that neither of you have ever watched a porn film, so why in the Devil's name would you be interested in one of its participants?" Mike shrugged his shoulders nonchalantly, making his muscles quiver. Lisa almost swooned.

Veronica too was wrestling with her thoughts. *How much should she reveal to this man? Ach, what the hell, honesty was always the best policy!*

"Stacey was my mother, and this lady here," she waved her hand at Lisa who smiled warmly, "is her sister."

Bloody hell, Mike thought, his bowels demanding the most urgent of attention. This time it seemed that his paranoia was justified. "Will you excuse me for a moment please, ladies, I must just pop to the little boys' room." He disappeared at a great rate of knots behind one of the doors leading from the lounge.

"Well, what do you think?" Veronica asked her aunt. "I have a feeling that our Mr. Jones is holding something back from us."

She felt a waft of cold air tickle her face. The door of one of the bedrooms was ajar, the autumnal sun streaming onto the double bed. A breeze was gently blowing the pale blue curtains, but this was the first time that Veronica had felt the air stirring in the room that they were sitting in.

Lisa visibly shook herself. She was imagining herself and the mysterious Mr. Jones tumbling about on the sofa which he had just vacated. There was a dreamy look in her eyes.

"Sorry, dear, did you say something?"

Veronica recognised the undisguised lust in her aunt's eyes. After all she had invoked the very same response in many women, but there was no fear of incest here. Her daft companion had fallen for the very man who had directed her sister in a dirty film. Great, that is all I need, she thought.

"Never mind, it doesn't matter."

TWENTY-FIVE

A moment later the door to the bathroom was opened. A distasteful smell of excrement mingling with some flowery air freshener fought for supremacy with the paint aroma.

"Sorry about that. Just a call of nature. Now, where were we?" Mike said.

Feeling decidedly alone, Veronica decided to be blunt. The smells in the apartment were making her feel sick, and she needed to extricate her aunt before she said, or did something which she might live to regret.

"Mr. Jones, look, I'll cut to the chase. I need to know what actually happened on that day."

Mike raised his eyebrows in mock surprise. "Are you sure, young lady? We are talking about a *porn* film here, and anyway it was a long time ago. I'm not sure that I can recall all the details."

Veronica grimaced. Being addressed as *a young lady* was her pet hate. She found it very patronising. It was not quite as bad as being referred to as *a girl*, but almost.

"Despite my youth, I am quite worldly, so don't worry about offending me. Please just tell me what happened."

Again Mike felt *all at sea*. If he did not relate the going-ons during that fateful day the girl would badger him, probably come back until she knew the truth.

Okay, he decided, *if she's so keen to know just what a whore her mother was, then I'll tell her*. All he had to do was conclude by stating firmly that after the film was *in the can* he had paid her dear mother for her services, and that was the last that he had seen of the woman.

Lisa was gazing at him in overt adoration. *Bloody hell, it looks like the aunt fancies me!* He was flattered, well, kind of. He preferred his bed mates to be young and nubile.

When he came to think of it, rather like his interrogator in appearance, but any feelings of sexual attraction had been squashed the moment it became obvious that she was one of those assertive intelligent types. He couldn't stand clever women. He took a deep breath and began.

"Your mother was up to her neck in debt. Did you know that?" he asked Veronica.

The younger woman nodded in affirmation and urged him to continue.

"The movie was aimed at the bisexual market. I always wrote my own scripts back then. Quite good, they were too," Mike boasted.

"So, what actually was my mother's part in the production? Like I said before, don't spare my blushes."

Mike smiled, warming to his part. Unfortunately, the reliving of the old memories was having a disturbing effect on his crotch. He favoured tight jeans, so if he was not careful any second now *Auntie Lisa* would be on top of him like a shot. He quickly grabbed one of the cushions from the sofa, leant back rather than perching on the edge and placed it over the offending area.

"Okay, well, there were parts for three actors. Two women and a man."

"And my mother was one of these *actors*, right?"

"That is correct. As I said before it was all a long time ago, but from what I can remember the two women made love on the bed, you know kissing and fondling each other's bits. The standard lesbian stuff."

Veronica nodded once again. Perhaps unlike many people her age, she felt totally comfortable about the thought of her parents making out. Whether it made a difference that her folks were both women, she was not sure.

Even now she could vividly bring to mind the sight of Caroline sporting a strap-on, the obscene thing waving about at her crotch. The incident had occurred not long after Veronica had joined the Montgomery household, so she must have been about four at the time. Waking scared after dreaming about some monster hiding under the bed, the standard stuff of childish nightmares, she had gone running as fast as her little legs would carry her into her new Mummies' bedroom.

Fully intent on leaping onto their bed into a pair of loving arms, instead she had come face-to-face with Caroline. *Maybe that was why she never used sex toys in her lovemaking!*

"Okay, and then what happened? What part did the man play?"

Mike shifted his position. He was feeling really uncomfortable. It felt like his penis was swelling by the second. If only he had selected a pair of jogging bottoms from his chest of drawers that morning instead of the jeans hanging in his wardrobe. The temptation to discreetly slip one of his hands beneath the cushion, and release his throbbing member from its fly was beginning to dominate his mind. *Concentrate, man*, he told himself. *Otherwise you'll let out something rather more deadly than an erect willy!*

Lisa was in a trance. She barely heard Mike's words. She knew that her niece would fill her in later, and through her lustful gaze she could see that she was in full control of the situation. This was the first time in her life that she had felt so instant an attraction to somebody.

After seeing her sister's body lying on its lead bed, Lisa had thrown herself into her work to blot out her grief. There had been little time for meeting new people outside of the contact centre. The last thing that she had wanted to do of an evening was to go out and socialise. Once she had showered, cooked herself a meal and unwound for an hour or two in front of the television, it was bedtime.

She desperately wanted the the man sat across from her, but Veronica would never forgive her if she messed up this meeting with him. Her only option was to sit tight, keep her mouth shut, and dream. Lisa thanked God that a woman's arousal state was undetectable. If she had been a fellow her trousers would have been bulging by now.

"Well, the man stood at the side of the set, stroking his penis as he watched the two women making out," Mike explained.

He felt a sensation, not unlike an electric current surge through his crotch. He decided some decisive action was required.

"Look, I'm sorry but would you excuse me again for a moment?"

He returned to his original position a few minutes later, now wearing a pair of jogging bottoms.

The two women looked at him strangely.

"New jeans, a tad too tight. Now where were we?" he said, in way of explanation.

Mike had been tempted to sort himself out in the privacy of his bedroom, but instead he had just changed his clothes. At least the soft jersey material did not hug his crotch like the jeans had. He was fully erect now, his penis looking like a tent pole in his groin. With the cushion safely back in place, he continued his recollection.

Sue Campbell

"Oh, yes. The man took over the proceedings. Stacey gave him *a little head*. I take it you understand what I mean by that?"

Veronica acknowledged that she did. The older woman just stared at him.

"Then he took her, in a *doggy fashion*. He thrust into her like a wild animal and then-"

Mike slammed his mouth shut so quickly that he felt his teeth smash together. Close to orgasm, he had almost revealed the fatal stage of the production without even realising what he was saying. He felt his erection diminish, fear taking the place of arousal.

Veronica had been listening intently. She shivered at the sudden cessation of Mike's words. Something *had* happened on that day, not that her mother taking part in a porn movie wasn't enough, but there had been something else.

The man sat opposite her looked petrified, his previously animated face blushed with the telling of his story was now pale. Veronica had literally seen the blood drain from his features.

Without further thought, she leapt out of her chair and threw herself at the man. She could feel the blood thumping in her ears. Adrenaline was surging through her body.

"What happened then? What did the man do to my mother?" she shouted at him.

She felt strangely calm inside, although from outward

appearances she resembled a wild animal.

Mike pushed the girl off him. "Nothing happened. What the hell has got into you?"

Veronica was not entirely sure what had possessed her, but she now knew for certain that something dreadful had taken place that day. She had had her suspicions all along in her sub-conscious that Mr. Jones may well have been the last person to see her mother alive.

Throwing herself back onto the man, she grabbed him by the throat with both her hands and screamed at him, her mouth just an inch from his ear, "What happened next?"

The sudden loss of oxygen to his brain caused Mike to feel giddy and lightheaded. He was also aware that his erection had painfully been resurrected.

Veronica pushed herself off of the man. "Bloody hell, you've got a hard-on!"

Mike spluttered and placed his hands on his throat, gulping in mouthfuls of fresh air. The cushion previously covering his crotch had fallen onto the floor during their tussle. He looked down at himself. There was indeed something obscene poking from his groin. He could recall reading somewhere a while back about *erotic asphyxiation*, the condition where a deliberate restriction of oxygen to the brain caused sexual arousal.

Suddenly Mike knew that his time was up. He felt resigned to his fate. The girl now dripping disgust into his eyes like burning acid had somehow figured it out.

Okay, so she didn't know exactly how her mother had met her end, but she sure as hell knew that he had been heavily involved. One way or another he would end up confessing his part in Stacey's demise. *Why prolong the agony?* He stared at her perched on the edge of her chair.

"Okay, I'll tell you, but then I shall have to kill you!"
Bloody hell, that sounded clichéd, like some line from a low budget movie, he thought.

Still feeling a little lightheaded, he said, "The production that your whore of a mother was involved in was a *snuff movie*, so if you're so clever work that one out!"

Veronica knew what a snuff movie was. One of the women that she had picked up last month had had very strange tastes, and had suggested to her that perhaps they could watch such a film together. *Christ*, she thought, *it could well have been one of the ones this bastard made!*

After her date had explained what the genre actually was Veronica had had to rush to the bathroom where she had vomited up her supper. Shame really, because she was about to suggest to the woman that they met up again. It was rare for Veronica to progress pass a one night stand.

In a fit of rage, she once again threw herself at the man, her hands automatically reaching for his throat.

"You bastard, you killed my mother!"

She released her grip just long enough for him to confess, gasping, "The male actor cut her throat, not me."

"But you told him to, you wrote the bloody script!"

Her hands encircled his neck, squeezing tightly. All of a sudden she felt herself being pulled backwards.

"Stop it, Veronica! He's not worth it. We've got a confession out of him now."

Her niece's screaming had roused Lisa from her daydreaming. The two women fell together onto the floor.

Mike leered at them, his penis now visible. He was masturbating furiously.

"I bet your aunt would like a piece of this. She's been staring at me for hours."

Veronica disentangled herself from her relative, and launched herself at Mike. She had never known a rage like this.

The bastard has not only murdered my mother, he's insulting my aunt too!

Just as she was about to throttle him for the final time, he grasped his chest and moaned loudly. His body sank down into the sofa, his face pale and glistening with perspiration. Instead of using her hands, she placed just two fingers on his neck, and felt for his carotid pulse.

"He's dead!" she whispered in disbelief to her aunt. "For God's sake, let's get out of here!" Her tone of voice rose hysterically.

"Just a minute, let me just mess up the place a wee bit first," Lisa retorted, feeling remarkably calm considering the circumstances.

She stole the briefest of glances at the deceased. It was the sight of his angry looking member that would remain fixed in her memory for months to come. *At least the poor chap died happy, well, kind of,* she mused sardonically. Dribbles of semen were evident on its shaft which surprisingly was still erect, even in death.

She gripped her niece's shoulders and made her sit back down on the chair.

"It's going to all right, I promise."

Veronica's eyes also glanced at the body, but it was Mike's ghastly visage that held her attention.

"All right? How can things be *all right*? The man's dead, for God's sake!" Her voice sounded unusually high to her and she was finding it difficult to breath, suffocating even.

"Come on, Veronica, get a grip," Lisa urged her, kneeling at her feet. "We didn't actually kill him, anyhow. Didn't you see him clutch at his chest? I reckon he had a heart attack, or something."

"Ach, well that's all right then," the younger woman said sarcastically. "Just think about it, we've been in this flat for the last two hours, my hands have been round his neck more than once, and-"

"Don't worry, I've read enough crime novels to deal with this."

Veronica looked at her aunt with a bemused expression on her face. "I don't believe this! Here we are stuck with a body, with me facing a murder charge, and you're going on about Miss bloody Marple!"

She felt her stomach flip, and her mouth filled with vomit. She slapped her hand across her lips and ran for the bathroom, just making it to the lavatory in time.

Lisa took the opportunity to ransack the place. She upturned the coffee table that had been between them and Mr. Jones, flicked his CDs out of their racks, and just for good measure pulled out several drawers both in the lounge, and in his bedroom. She stood back to admire her handiwork.

"Looks like you've been having fun!" Veronica stated, striding over to join her aunt.

Lisa was relieved to see that some colour had returned to her niece's cheeks, and that there was a hint of a smile on her face. She had been extremely concerned about her ability to cope. She put her arms around Veronica, and placed a kiss on her forehead.

"Well, what do you reckon? Does it look convincing? Nobody saw us come in here, so what's to say a pair of burglars couldn't have done the same? Let's say they got in in the early hours, accidentally woke up *Mr. Handsome* here-"

Veronica looked once more in disbelief at her aunt.

"Ach, just ignore me, I'm a frustrated old spinster. Anyway, where was I? Oh, yes. He takes on the intruders, is doing quite well, despite their attempts to half throttle him, but he then collapses following a massive coronary. Any good?"

Veronica's heart swelled with a renewed respect and affection for her aunt. "You're brilliant, you are, do you know that? Just two things, though. What if one of the neighbours heard two women in here at lunchtime, rather than a couple of chaps in the wee hours, and what about our fingerprints? Mine must be all over the bathroom, for one thing and," she glanced once more at the body," over *him."*

"No need to concern yourself over that. This kind of place has got to have first class soundproofing and," she waved a duster at Veronica as if she was a magician performing a trick on the stage, "if you give me a minute I'll go and wipe off all the discriminating marks."

"You're unbelievable, you are!"

A flash of inspiration struck Veronica. "And once we're well away from here I shall give the police an anonymous call to inform them of the break-in. I'll make sure that I get through to a certain *DS Jack*. He owes me a favour or two."

TWENTY-SIX

Veronica smiled to herself. She was sat in one of the few remaining gay bars in Aberdeen. The reputation of the club was such that anyone vaguely straight dared not enter its hallowed portals. It had been a month now since that rather eventful Saturday, and all seemed just fine.

She had spent the night at her aunt's place after they had returned from Mr. Jones's apartment. Veronica knew that Lisa had only insisted that she delayed her return home until the following morning, in fear that so soon a confrontation with her parents would more than likely inch her mood close to the hysterical again.

As planned she had telephoned the Edinburgh police station where Jimmy worked and affecting a moderated voice, perhaps she should have entered the acting profession after all, she had informed him in the role of a posh lady that she had heard, *some rather disturbing noises emanating from one of her good neighbour's apartments in the early hours.*

Why are you calling me, madam? he had asked her. *Thank you for the information, but you really should have rung 999.*

Veronica had explained, by this time it was her aunt who was in hysterics sat as she was on a wall bordering one of the gardens on the Great Western Road, that she was *an old lady, prone to confusion.* At that point Veronica had rung off.

Two days later the incident was headline news in the national newspapers. Apparently, the *burglary* had been pined on to two local lads who had committed many similar offences. The report had revealed that Mr. Jones had indeed died of a myocardial infarction. Apparently, he had left behind a grieving son.

Jimmy had called her the following week, wanting to meet her. They had ended up spending the night together in their usual hotel in Stirling. After they had had sex, he had candidly asked her about her search for her mother's murderer, as to whether she had made any progress. Veronica had blushed, and informed him coyly that the matter had been dealt with. She affected the same accent as she had during the last time that she had rung him.

The detective, propped up on one elbow had stared down at his lover with a bemused expression on his face. On attending the crime scene he had had no idea that his *paramour* had been involved, but whilst directing the Scene of Crime Officer a most peculiar sensation had come over him. He had felt quite faint, and had excused himself to stand by one of the bedroom windows in the apartment, gulping in the welcome fresh air.

His mind filled with thoughts of Veronica. This was

most unusual. Jimmy took his career very seriously, and prided himself on his professionalism. It was true that he often thought about his mistress when he was off-duty, but during his working day he stayed focused and had a reputation for being reliable and efficient. He excused himself for the leaking of the previous information to Veronica as just being *a favour for a friend*. He really couldn't see what the harm was, the address he had given out was her aunt's after all.

This new *favour* sat with him uncomfortably. For one thing he had a strong suspicion that the deceased had played a significant role in the death of Stacey Connolly, otherwise why would Veronica have been there. He wondered if the case was somehow linked to the more recent prostitute murders.

If he had not been so infatuated with the young receptionist, or *hotel trainee manageress* as Veronica was always correcting him, then his investigations would have taken him on a completely different path. To stop his superiors scrutinising his actions he knew, whilst leaning against the window frame in the apartment that he had to charge somebody *pretty damn quick*.

The Robertson twins had come to mind. Now in their forties, they had plenty of form, and had spend most of their lives being incarcerated for some crime, or another. A further year would not make much difference to either of them. Winter was but only a few months away. They would be warmer and better fed in the nick, than huddling in their dingy flat in Hope Street.

Jimmy knew that if he had been able to close both murder cases successfully, and with perhaps more conviction then Commander Banquo would have no doubt offered him a promotion.

The CID officers in Aberdeen were still investigating the disappearance of that legal clerk from the city. Despite his many years of experience of gruesome crimes a shiver had crept up Jimmy's spine on hearing about the surgical screw assumed to have come from the woman's body, being delivered to the desk sergeant.

As it was he had to be satisfied with pleasing the woman he loved. He had tried to draw her out the following morning as they were laying in bed together, but she had just slid down his body and taken his first erection of the day into her mouth.

Only later had she whispered to him seconds before he ejaculated deep inside her, *My mother can now rest in peace. Mike Jones orchestrated her demise.*

Sex always made Veronica more eloquent in her speech.

Veronica took a sip of her gin and tonic, and sighed deeply, savouring its peculiar flavour infused as it was with essences of rose petal and cucumber, as well as the more traditional juniper. She felt at peace with herself. She took a moment to reflect on recent events.

It was a shame in a way that the man who had actually murdered her mother had died of natural causes years ago, but at least by hastening the death of the *organ grinder* she had exacted her revenge, and now Stacey's ghost was finally laid to rest.

Bedding the detective once in a while was certainly paying off. Veronica knew that without his careful handling of the situation she would currently be on remand facing a convoluted trial and its consequences, rather than enjoying a long weekend in the *granite city.*

****

Thanks to her aunt's ministrations by the time Veronica had turned her key in the front door of her parents' house in Stirling the day after Mr. Jones had died, she felt calm and comfortable with all that she had seen, and done.

Maggie and Caroline would never know about the events of the previous twenty-four hours. They had yet to meet her aunt, but Lisa had telephoned them the night before to reassure them that their daughter was okay, that she had just missed the last train back home. Very little was said on Veronica's return. Life essentially just carried on as it was before.

A line from one of the books which she had studied for her English Higher had come to Veronica's mind as she had laid in bed a week later. Like the Indians in Wilkie

Collins's The Moonstone she had *the patience of a cat and the ferocity of a tiger*, or so her aunt had informed her.

Veronica had checked her e-mails whilst she was in the throes of packing her bag for her Aberdeen trip. Terry was inviting himself over to Stirling with an *estimated time of arrival of sometime before Christmas*. He apologised profusely for his tardiness on the communication front. Veronica had sent him dozens of messages, but she had not heard from him in weeks. She suspected that he was furiously wrestling with his conscience once again.

On opening his latest e-mail, and reading his enthusiastic words Veronica had whooped for joy, and literally punched the air with a sense of relief. It always surprised her that she had kept the affection between them alive for so many years.

"I love you, I love you, Terry," she shouted.

Caroline had come bounding up the stairs. Worry was etched on her face. Veronica reassured her that she was just fine.

"Terry's coming to see us soon!" she exclaimed, her features glowing with happiness.

"You've waited longer for him, love, than I did for Maggie."

They hugged and on leaving the room she added blushing, "I reckon you're as besotted with him as I was, and indeed still am, with her."

Veronica laughed in joyful affirmation, and began typing her reply.

Do come as soon as you can, darling, it began. *I cannot wait to throw my arms around you.*

Whether it was thoughts of what she wanted to do to her beloved Terry, or just the need to pay homage to her rampant sex drive that drove Veronica to seek out a woman on her first night in Aberdeen was open to debate.

Miss Riley's attentions at work were becoming rather feverish. Veronica had caught her on several occasions with the unmistakeable look of lust in her eyes. They had shared another passionate moment when the reception area was for once devoid of guests.

Later the older woman had grabbed her unexpectedly as Veronica had been filing some invoices in the office, which was tucked away from prying eyes. Miss Riley had shoved her up against one of the cupboards, and kissed her fervently, her tongue flicking into Veronica's mouth like a snake's. With their bodies clamped together, Veronica had responded with her usual enthusiasm, feeling the familiar ache of arousal deep between her legs.

Then her boss had whispered fatally, *I love you.*

Veronica had panicked. *I'm sorry, Jackie but I don't love you.*

Miss Riley had stopped grinding herself against the object of her affection, and pulled back with tears in her eyes. Not saying another word, she had swiveled on her high heels, and with as much dignity as she could muster had walked away.

After a week the atmosphere between them was still strained. Gone were the knowing glances and the friendly banter. Miss Riley was now totally professional with the trainee manager. Truth be told, the older woman felt more embarrassed and angry with herself than anything else. *Why, oh, why had she uttered those three words?*

Veronica had hastily booked a couple of annual leave days to coincide with her next weekend off. She needed a break to allow the proverbial dust to settle between her and the lovestruck manageress. Her interest in Scotland's third most populous city had been sparked off by one or two of the hotel guests who had extolled its fine selection of shops, and its long sandy coastline. Never having visited Aberdeen, she decided to make the most of her time off and discover its delights for herself.

After an exhausting second day trailing around the various shopping malls Veronica had returned to her hotel. The room was only costing her twenty pounds per night, as it was part of the chain which she worked for. The Aberdeen hotel had been awarded a Michelin star for its outstanding cuisine, an increasingly sore point for her boss back in Stirling. *Jealousy is a most unattractive trait in a manager*, she would often chide him.

Veronica had deposited her not insubstantial collection of bags wearily by the window, and peeled off her clothes. She ran herself a hot bath, and let out a protracted breath as she lowered her tired limbs into the foamy water.

I need a woman, she thought to herself. What with work and everything Veronica's period of abstinence had been longer than usual. Of course she still masturbated once or twice a week, but it was not the same as taking her pleasures with a warm breathing body in her arms.

She felt really bad about Miss Riley, and truth be told she rather fancied the sixty year woman with her curly blonde hair and slightly plump figure, but her heart would not allow her to fall in love with anyone else. Perhaps the two of them could go out for a drink together on her return to work, sit down like mature rational adults and reach a compromise that would suit them both. As long as Jackie was not under any illusions that they would be exchanging marriage vows any time soon!

No, what Veronica needed was a night of uncomplicated sex with a hot Aberdeenshire lady. Somebody older than herself preferable, who could hold a decent conversation before they ripped each other's clothes off. Veronica usually took the dominant role, but she preferred her women to be slightly butch. She was not looking for some sort of *drag king,* or any one too overpowering, but despite her assertiveness Veronica enjoyed her femininity. She had read on some Internet site that her tastes were perhaps a little out of the ordinary, but it took all sorts to make the world. It would be interesting to see what gems the *silver city* could offer her.

She lay back in the bath and ran her hands over her slippery body. Glancing at the clock on the wall, *how thoughtful of the management to hang one in here*, she thought, Veronica let her mind wander.

Her lover was kissing her slowly from her throat down to her navel, making her skin tingle with erotic pleasure. Then she moved lower, flicking her tongue between her legs. Veronica's hand slid down to where those imaginary lips where now creating jolts of electricity.

Almost subconsciously, she massaged her clitoris and ever so slowly let her finger drift inside, feeling the ridges of her vaginal wall. In her mind's eye she had rolled her lover over so that now she was uppermost, her long legs stretched out between the woman's thighs. Veronica kissed her deeply on her full lips and then began to suck on her nipples. Now rubbing her own clitoris urgently as she felt her orgasm building, her thoughts turned to Terry.

She was still *on top,* but now her vagina was filled

with a hard throbbing penis. She raised and lowered herself rhythmically, ensuring that her *G-spot* could be stimulated to the utmost. Then her mind was just filled with her beloved's face as she felt herself take off into orbit. She placed a finger into her vagina, and delighted in its contractions. The intense sensation seemed to come in waves until, what seemed like minutes later it felt like she was gently falling back to earth.

TWENTY-SEVEN

"Hello! Can I join you?" the buxom brunette enquired, making Veronica jump.

Their eyes met, and they smiled at each other.

The sign outside of the club said, *Oh Henry's*, but the place now went by the name of *Bar Indigo*. It was situated on Adelphi just off Union Street in the centre of the city. Veronica was sat in the lounge area on one of their comfy dark brown sofas, and she indicated to her visitor that she should take the seat opposite her.

"My name's Kathy. What's yours?" she asked politely.

Veronica guessed that the not unattractive woman was in her early forties. She was dressed in white slacks with a navy blouse. She could detect a faint whiff of cigarette smoke about her person as she sat down, placing her drink on the table between them.

"I'm Veronica. Nice to make your acquaintance." She half stood up and stretched out her right hand to shake the woman's.

Kathy had spotted Veronica as soon as she had walked confidently into the bar half an hour earlier. She had waited to see if the stunning young lady was waiting for a companion, or just out as she was to socialise and perhaps pick up someone to warm her bed for the night. She had seemed to be deep in thought.

It had been almost three months now since Kathy had disposed of Angie's body in her back garden in Laggan. Quite why she had fished out that surgical screw from the back of her kitchen drawer, and sent it to the Aberdeen police was still a puzzle to her. She now regarded it as a *moment of madness*.

The only vague logic which she could assign to it was the need to inform Angie's mother that her daughter was indeed dead and not just missing, but that did not really make any sense. The other pieces of metalwork which Kathy had found at the bottom of the old oil drum in which she had dissolved the body, several more screws of varying lengths and an angle blade plate, were still lying amongst her clean tea towels.

She did not feel at all guilty about ending the life of a promising career woman, any more than she did about killing the three prostitutes. Ever since her husband had walked out on her all those years ago Kathy's opinion of the human race had taken a dramatic downward turn.

You pour all your love and your very soul into a relationship, then the bastard lets you down, so sod them, sod the lot of them, was her motto.

She supposed involving herself in the snuff movies had hardened her heart, and mind even further. Human life to Kathy was not exactly worthless, after all she still had her wee daughter whom she tried to see once a month, but was it not worth sacrificing if taking that life gave one such a great deal of pleasure?

The urge to feel that extraordinary high again was becoming a desperate obsession. She had tried to suppress it by working overtime at the supermarket in Inverness, but that just tired her out physically. She needed to achieve that adrenaline rush again so badly, and there was only one way to do that.

She gazed lustfully at the girl sat across from her, imagining her hands around her neck. She could feel the moisture and heat building between her thighs. This was her first time in Bar Indigo. She felt comfortable although the music playing from the loudspeakers was not exactly to her taste. The drinks were inexpensive, and although the clientele were mainly male she could spy half a dozen female couples dotted about. Feeling rather like a golden eagle assessing its prey, Kathy proceeded to *chat up* her intended.

Thirty minutes later she suggested to Veronica that they could perhaps retire to her hotel to *get to know each other a little better*. Kathy could not believe her good fortune. Apparently, Veronica was only in Aberdeen for the weekend, so nobody would miss her locally.

Finding out that her adopted parents were a lesbian couple was an added bonus. It meant that her young date was completely comfortable with the whole same-sex thing, although it had been rather disappointing to discover that due to a certain incident as a child

Veronica now had a loathing of all sex toys. That was a pity. Kathy had been looking forward to thrusting into the little beauty.

Also she had a feeling that this one might not be so submissive as her usual quarry. It was obvious that she could hold her own, and was nobody's fool. Still all things considered, Kathy reckoned it was going to be *one hell of a night.*

The only problem was how to deal with the outcome. By careful questioning she knew that it was unlikely that Veronica would agree to visit her in Laggan. It was a long way from Stirling, after all.

She had excused herself ten minutes later with the promise of returning after her *nicotine fix.* Standing outside in the alley in which the bar was located Kathy had taken a deep drag from her cigarette, and *put her thinking cap on.*

She was staying in a large hotel a mere ten minutes walk away. After checking in yesterday and settling into her room, considering the price of a two nights stay it was a good job that she had done all those extra hours sat behind her till, Kathy had taken a wee wander around. She had simply marveled at the old fashionedness of the laundry chute on discovering it, but now it could prove to be the solution to her predicament.

All she needed to do was wrap the body in a sheet, and drag it a hundred yards to the service door. Then she would slide it down the chute and collect her *package* two floors down. She would make some excuse when they returned to the hotel about having to move her car. The vehicle would then be in position for her to load Veronica into its boot in the early hours before the housekeeping staff came on duty. Back in Laggan there was already a bag of sodium hydroxide waiting for them in the outbuilding.

Veronica felt her usual excitement. Kathy had transpired to be a most interesting companion, although how much truth was in her stories was rather difficult to accurately judge. She had readily accepted her suggestion that they spend the night at her hotel. It would be more discreet than going back to the Barcelo one. Apparently, her date was a single mother, and she worked all hours to provide for the two of them. The recount of her life had quite touched Veronica. It had been rather a sad tale, and would account for the worry lines etched into her face.

They seemed to share similar sexual tastes as well. The only thing that had really bothered her was Kathy's vagueness over where she stayed. *The Cairngorm National Park,* was all that she would say, and for the briefest of moments there had been a degree of tension between the two of them.

Kathy took her hand whilst they were walking back to the hotel. Veronica steered them into a dark alley they were passing, and trapped her body between hers and the wall. She kissed her passionately with pent up emotion. Kathy responded by forcing her voluptuous thigh between Veronica's legs, rubbing her crotch suggestively. The younger woman moaned as she felt the buttons on her flies being urgently undone. In a few seconds Kathy's fingers had gained access to her most secret of places, and were thrusting up inside her.

"Oh, my God, I'm coming," Veronica gasped.

Twenty minutes later Kathy pushed open the door of her room.

"I *want* you!" Veronica whispered into her ear, as they fall backwards onto the double bed. Just in time Kathy remembered her car.

"I want you too, darling," she purred, "but first I need to do something. I'll only be five minutes."

"Bloody hell, I suppose you need another cigarette. I guess you didn't have much time on the way here."

Kathy sniffed her fingers and smiled. "I can do much better than that. Five minutes and I'll be back. Why don't you take a shower or something?"

Veronica looked slightly offended. After all she had only bathed six hours ago. "Do I smell or something then?"

Kathy simply shook her head, and disappeared into the corridor.

Veronica shrugged and clambered off the bed. She

could not be bothered with a shower, but her teeth could do with a clean. She had had a packet of crisps at the club and a few olives. In her hurry to go *out on the town* the notion of having supper had completely escaped her.

Never mind, she thought, spying a room service menu on the dresser. It looked like they served food all night so perhaps the two of them could feast on prawn and mayonnaise sandwiches, followed by a baked strawberry cheesecake, after they had satisfied their sexual appetites.

Veronica started as the door was flung open. She had been flicking through the latest copy of *Diva*. Maggie bought it occasionally from the newsagent in Stirling. *How to make your girlfriend melt*, it stated on the front cover.

Kathy came over to her and smiled, the aroma of cigarettes most evident on her breath. She lifted Veronica up as if she was a feather, and they rolled together onto the bed. Dipping a finger once more into the younger woman's vagina she commented, "I reckon you're well past your *melting* point!"

Veronica was in the throes of her second orgasm when she felt a tightening around her neck. *What the hell-*, she thought, but blacked out before she could finish the sentence.

Kathy climaxed just as Veronica lost consciousness. She felt *fantastic!* That long wait had certainly been worth it. She felt for her lover's carotid pulse. Nothing.

Working methodically she climbed off the bed and dressed quickly. Underwear seemed superfluous. Stripping the duvet off, she untucked the bottom sheet, and wrapped Veronica tightly in it.

Her mind flashed back to the last girl who had undergone a similar fate, but of course Christopher had been there then. Similarly, she placed a red bright lipstick kiss on her latest conquest's thigh.

"Silly me," she laughed out loud. She had quite forgotten about Angie.

Suddenly she stopped what she was doing, and glanced at the body wrapped from head to foot in its shroud. She could have sworn that it had moaned! Kathy prodded the body in its ribs and listened intently. *Nothing.*

"Your mind's playing tricks on you, you silly sausage," she muttered to herself.

Twenty minutes later she was sat behind the wheel of her car. Thankfully, the service car park seemed to be deserted. *These recent events would not have been out of place in some black comedy*, she mused, a smile playing around her lips. On reflection it had been rather fun!

Veronica had slid nicely down the chute, and then Kathy had followed her headfirst. It had reminded her of an adventure park in Edinburgh that her mother had taken her to as a child, although this time she had had to bite her lip to stop her whoop of joy disturbing the other hotel guests. It was a good job that her date had looked after herself in life otherwise lifting her into the boot would have been even more perspiration-inducing than it had been.

"Okay, let's get back to Laggan," she stated to her reflection in the rear view mirror.

The receptionist had looked at her a little strangely when she had insisted on paying for her two nights stay in advance, instead of at checkout. The last thing she needed was the hotel chasing her for an unpaid bill. All things considered, everything had gone very well.

Veronica gradually regained consciousness, her heart racing and her mind filled with panic. *Where the hell am I?*

It felt like her body was *folded up*, there was a burning pain in her legs. She was in complete darkness, save for a dim chink of light in front of her. Her prison smelt of dog and petrol. Her whole body was wrapped up tightly, in something. Then she became aware that she was moving in a forwardly direction.

Bloody hell, I'm in the boot of a car! she thought.

The last thing she could recall was having sex, but who had she been with? Come on, think, she berated herself. It had been a woman. She had picked her up at that club in Aberdeen. Then what had happened? She couldn't remember.

Suddenly she had an urgent need to urinate. She tried to move her stiff limbs, and slowly felt the material loosen. She managed to unfree one of her hands. She pushed the fabric off her face and head.

The vehicle, Veronica assumed that was what she was incarcerated in, came to an abrupt stop. Frantically, she pushed upwards, and the light from the full moon illuminated the interior. The sheet, for that was what it appeared to be, was still wrapped around her torso. If she did not free herself within the next few seconds it was going to become very wet!

Taking a deep breath, she managed to roll herself out of the boot. She yelped as her body hit the ground. The driver's door was open, but there was no sign of her kidnapper.

Her bladder emptied itself. Pushing the sodden sheet from her body, Veronica crawled into the undergrowth with tears in her eyes. She felt a cool breeze, and her mind kicked into action. She vaguely recalled that there was something with her in the boot.

"My bag!" she exclaimed, rolling herself back towards the car.

They appeared to be at the edge of a wood. Veronica somehow managed to both grab her bag, and slam shut the lid of the boot. She crawled into some kind of ditch and only then realised that she was completely naked. She retrieved the sheet, even wet and smelly it was better than nothing, and from her hiding place she watched the car.

A familiar figure came into view. *Yes, that was the woman she had slept with last night.* Without even glancing at the boot, the brunette disappeared from view and the engine kicked into life. Shivering, Veronica sighed heavily and reached with a thumping heart inside her bag.

"Thank God!" she muttered, scrolling through her list of contacts. She casually noted that it was four o'clock in the morning.

A sleepy voice answered her call in a low whisper. "Hello, is that you, Veronica? Are you all right? It's the middle of the night!"

"Jimmy, I'm so sorry to wake you up, but I'm in a spot of bother."

The detective glanced over at his wife snoring noisily beside him.

"Just a second," he said into the handset.

With his heart racing, he walked into the en-suite bathroom, and closed the door behind him.

"Where are you, love? What's happened?" he said with concern, and tenderness in his voice.

There was no reply, although the line still appeared to be active. *Bloody hell*, Jimmy thought. *What do I do now?* "Veronica, can you hear me, love?" he said urgently. He listened intently. Nothing, although he could detect a noise in the background. Then he realised what the faint sound was. *An owl was screeching!*

He stood in his pyjamas in middle of the room for a few seconds, and then theatrically slapped his forehead with the palm of his hand.

"*GSM localization*! I can find out where she is by tracking her mobile phone," he exclaimed to his reflection in the mirror above the hand basin. She was obviously outside, *somewhere.*

Mrs Jack woke up, disturbed by her husband rising from their bed. "Him and his bloody waterworks. If that man doesn't get his damn prostate sorted out soon, I'll-," she muttered.

Jimmy came back into the bedroom, rubbing his eyes. "Sorry to have disturbed you, love. It's work. I've got to pop down to the station for a few hours."

"Not again!" his wife retorted, turning her back to him and pulling the covers tightly around her. "You and that bloody job. Roll on the day you retire!"

"And be here with you all day, not bloody likely!"Jimmy snapped, but Mrs Jack was dead to the world again.

TWENTY-EIGHT

Six months later there was a huge crowd gathered in the central courtyard of Buckingham Palace. If you stood underneath one of the archways, and looked towards the London residence of King Rupert and his consort they appeared as a sea of people, but instead of hearing the crashing of waves on the shore one could detect an insistent but low-toned hum.

Most of them were staring transfixed at a wooden structure whose solid legs were planted firmly on the red tarmac. These supported a large platform above which a type of gantry had been built. Although from a distance it was difficult to make out, a section of the board had been cut out, divided into two and then replaced so that it formed a trapdoor with two flaps.

From the scaffold a noose could be seen, gently blowing in the spring breeze. A *Hangman's Knot* had been fashioned at its end, its thirteen coils a credit to the executioner who had prepared the gallows earlier that morning. The monarch had ruled that the original type of ligature should be replaced. The current one tended to break the neck, rather than strangle the prisoner.

Steps led up to the platform. They were slick with the recent rainfall, but now the clouds were clearing and the sun was throwing its shadows upon the ground. A whiff of onions could be detected in the air from the opportunistic fast food vans parked up in The Mall.

Amongst the throng there was a contingency of eight people from Scotland. They were sat on a pair of tartan rugs, looking rather conspicuous. The three gentlemen and five ladies had arrived shortly before six o'clock after taking an early breakfast at the Ritz Hotel, where they had checked in the previous afternoon. Conveniently it was situated just five hundred yards from the Palace.

It was with a certain degree of excitement that the party had boarded their aeroplane at Edinburgh airport the previous day. The ladies would have then been quite happy to have taken the *Gatwick Express* to Victoria, and used the Underground to reach Green Park station, but Grant would have none of it. He had been embarrassed enough that they had had to take a scheduled flight, there was no way his dear friends and family were going to have to bear the rough and tumble of the public transport system.

The Ritz's Phantom Rolls-Royce, a rather newer model to leave the company's Goodwood factory than the surgeon's own classic Silver Ghost was waiting for them as they had exited the terminal. From the expression on Veronica's face Grant thought she was going to explode with delight, but his stern glare had reminded her that a certain decorum was expected in public.

Ironically, this trip down to England reminded Grant of his Investiture when he had been knighted for Services to Medicine, but this time he was not alone. As the chauffeur had driven them through the streets of London he had reflected with a glint of sarcasm that here they all were to gawp at someone being executed, but for his big day not one of them had been bothered to accompany him. His bad humour had quickly dissipated though as they drawn up in front of the famous five-star hotel. Even from the lobby its opulence, grandeur and beauty were obvious, and quite breathtaking.

Perhaps as a means of compensating for his previous visit to London Grant had booked his party into two of the Ritz's finest suites. The *Prince of Wales* and the *Berkeley* both boasted two double bedrooms, with en-suite bathrooms. With marble lobbies and elegant reception rooms, these were as far removed from standard hotel bedrooms, as fish fingers were from caviar.

Maggie and Caroline were sharing one of the suites with Grant and Duncan, in the other Clare and Lyn were keeping a discreet eye on Veronica and her mysterious boyfriend, Jimmy. Veronica had insisted on bringing along the detective, seeing that he had been the one who had come rushing to her side after Kathy had tried to murder her.

Jimmy had informed his wife that he felt obliged to attend the execution. He was after all the police officer who had finally brought the murderer to justice. Mrs Jack had scoffed, and slapped his face, leaving a crimson hand print on his left cheek. Quite why she had felt the need to inflict that particular punishment on her long-suffering spouse was not open for discussion. As far as she was aware her husband was staying with a chap that he had met at the Police Federation Conference the year before. She had not bothered to question him further.

Caroline had stood in the middle of the spacious sitting room in the Berkeley Suite with her mouth open. For once she was quite speechless. It felt like she had stepped back in time to the Edwardian period. There were antiques everywhere. A rectangular table with gold gilded legs had particularly caught her eye. She ran her hand over its marble top, delighting in the coolness of the stone.

Grant had wandered in from his and Duncan's bedroom, their unpacking now complete, and laughed out loud. "Am I to understand that you approve of my choice of accommodation then?" he asked her, his eyes twinkling merrily.

"Grant, what can I say? This must have cost you an absolute fortune!" she exclaimed, sinking down onto the dove grey three-seater sofa, and stretching out her legs.

Maggie came into the room. "Have you seen that bathroom? It's got gold taps, and a tub big enough for three."

She pointed to the table that her wife had been so in awe of. "The floor in there is made of solid marble too. That's why I've been so long, I've been down on my hands and knees, admiring it!"

Grant offered his paw-like hand to Caroline and pulled her up onto her feet. He took Maggie's hand too.

Duncan had crept up on the three of them discreetly. He hugged his husband from behind. "I love the very bones of all of you, but this bear of a man takes some beating!" He fondly grabbed Grant's bottom.

For a split second the surgeon considered scrapping his plans for the afternoon, and whisking his beloved off to bed, he was aware of a stirring in his groin, but ever the honourable host he remarked instead, "Come on you three, let's see where my darling sister has got to. I have booked tables for us all in the Palm Court. *Afternoon tea is about to be served!*"

Duncan squealed and threw his arms around him. "Wow, only the other day I was reading about that curious predilection of the English. Will there be those fancy little teapots, and everything?"

Grant guffawed. "I expect so, but please don't be so *camp*, darling. What will our *Mr. Detective* think of you?"

Duncan feigned an air of indignation. "Well, dear, I think our DS Jack is as bent as the rest of us!"

Maggie's expression changed from one of bemusement, to that of shock and worry. "But, he's going out with our Veronica, and he's married to a woman. I think you must be mistaken, Duncan. Jimmy's not gay. No way!"

"Well, it takes one to know one, dear, as they say. Just mark my words. Anyway, your daughter's bisexual, so perhaps they're ideally suited," Duncan concluded.

He minced back to his bedroom to don a jacket and tie, preventing any further discussion of the matter. It was only at breakfast that gentleman were permitted to observe a less formal dress code whilst staying at the Ritz.

The beautiful apartment-style penthouse took up most of the top floor of the hotel. Occupying almost two thousand square feet of floor space, the Prince of Wales suite contained both a drawing and a dining room, as well as a butler's kitchen.

Clare, unlike her brother had succumbed to temptation, and was currently being made love to her by her wife in the master bedroom with its delicate period woodwork, not that either of them had yet found the time to admire the fine decor.

Veronica was stood by the window looking out over Green Park. Mature lime and London Plane trees divided the immaculately kept lawns. The grass was festooned by thousands of bright yellow daffodils. She started as Jimmy came to stand by her side.

Taking her hand in his, he quoted a few lines from one

of his favourite poems.
"A host, of golden daffodils,
Beside the lake, beneath the trees,
Fluttering and dancing in the breeze."
Veronica smiled at him and sighed deeply.
"Are you all right love?" he asked her tenderly.
Jimmy still could not believe that he was actually staying in one of the country's most prestigious hotels, with the woman he loved. The events of that day six months ago would forever remain in his mind.

The desk sergeant had been rather surprised to see him at five o'clock in the morning, but had sensibly not enquired as to the detective's intentions. Using the station's tracking device he had located the spot from which Veronica had made her call. Apparently, she was on the outskirts of a village called Tomintoul in the Cairngorm National Park, between Braemar and Grantown-on-Spey on the A939. For a moment or two Jimmy had considered making a call to the local officer, but quickly decided for the sake of discretion it would be best if he made the trip up to the Highlands himself. On discovering that it was ninety miles between Edinburgh and Tomintoul he reckoned he could be with Veronica in about an hour and a half.

Hell, anything could happen in that time, he thought, his mind whirling. Trying his utmost not to panic, he called Veronica's mobile number.

"Hello, is that you, Jimmy?" a faint voice asked him.
Letting out a repressed sigh of relief, he said, "Yes, it's me, your knight in shining armour."

Veronica had managed to crawl out of the ditch after she had regained consciousness for the second time that day. She found herself in a field of Aberdeen Angus cattle. Feeling rather lightheaded, she had started to shiver.

Her plan to order something off the room menu had never come to fruition. Considering the circumstances her thoughts were remarkably calm and collected, although it scared her something rotten to think how close to death she had come. The events of the last few hours seemed like some ghastly nightmare, from which she had thankfully woken up, but only just. *Trust her to choose some mad woman to satisfy her carnal desires!*

She knew full well that stronger emotions would come into play later, ones of anger and recrimination, but for now it was a matter of survival. She was cold, hungry and rather damp, both from her own excretions, and the soggy conditions of the ditch. From what she could tell she had no obvious injuries, although her throat burned, both inside and out. She really could not remember what had happened to her. She could recall being in the throes of an orgasm and then waking up in the boot of the car, but that was about it.

Maybe I can stand up, she thought.

Across the grassland there was a farmhouse. Smoke was gently rising from its chimney. *There is no way that Veronica Montgomery is going to perish in some God damn field*, she thought. If I can only get over there, perhaps the occupants will offer me some food and clean clothes. She considered ringing Jimmy again, but decided to wait until she was safely inside somewhere.

Once Kathy had discovered that her boot was empty no doubt she would retrace her tracks, and come back to search for her. In her state of mind there was no telling what she would do. The gods had saved her once from a fateful end. It was unlikely that they would do it again. Looking up at the autumnal sky heavy with rain clouds, Veronica staggered to her feet, wrapping the sodden sheet around her, and proceeded to make her torturous way to the house.

"My, my, what do we have here?" the old woman asked her on opening the door.

Veronica smiled weakly and then passed out, collapsing on the doorstep. She came to slowly, and for a few seconds thought she was back at the hotel. "No, leave me alone!" she shouted, believing that it was Kathy stood there, looking down on her.

"Hush, hush, child, you're safe now," the farmer's mother explained.

Then Veronica remembered. Looking around her, she did feel *safe*. She was lying on a sofa, and a huge fire was crackling in the grate opposite her. The sheet was gone, and instead the softest of dressing gowns was wrapped around her body. She blushed, realising that her *Samaritan* must have undressed her.

As if reading her thoughts, the woman said, "Don't worry, dear. I have brought up three bairns of my own. You don't have anything that I haven't seen before. I kept the sheet. If you've been attacked, then the police might need it for evidence."

Veronica looked in renewed admiration at her rescuer. She reckoned that she must have been in her eighties, and there was even less flesh on her bones than she had on her own slender frame.

Pushing herself up into a sitting position, she said, "Thank you, but how did you manage to-?"

The old woman interrupted, "Drag you in here, you mean?"

Veronica nodded.

"Don't you be worrying your pretty self about that. I'm stronger than I look. I stay here with my son and his wife, but they're away for the weekend, so it's just you and me, dear," she cackled, reminding Veronica of the old crone whom she had met in Hope Street.

Bloody hell, not again, thought Veronica. *This one might have raised three children, but she sure as hell liked the fairer sex too.* Never mind, at least she was warm and dry. She glanced around for her bag.

The woman passed it to her as if conjuring it up out of

thin air. Grinning, she asked, "Is this what you are looking for, dear?"

Looking relieved, Veronica replied, "Yes, thank you. If your house hadn't been here I don't know what I would have done. I would have surely perished out there."

The woman touched her hand tenderly.

"I need to call a friend of mine. He'll come and pick me up, I'm sure, but he stays in Edinburgh. What is this place called, so that I can tell him where I am?"

"This be Tomintoul, love. I have some beef stew in the fridge. My daughter-in-law made it for us all before they set off for Glasgow on Friday night. My other son's in the hospital down there, see, and the two of them have gone to visit him. The stew's two days old, but I'm sure it will be just fine if I warm it up in the microwave. It looks like you could do with a decent meal, although I don't suppose it will be your usual breakfast fare. I'm sure that I could find something upstairs that will fit you too. You don't want to be greeting your friend wrapped in a dressing gown."

Veronica was close to tears. *Thank God for the kindness of strangers*, she thought. Smiling warmly at the woman, she expressed her appreciation.

"No bother, my child, you are most welcome," she said breathlessly, bending over to place a kiss on Veronica's forehead.

TWENTY-NINE

Just as Veronica was tucking enthusiastically into the stew, her mobile rang. Jimmy was relieved to discover that his beloved was safe. He assured her that within two hours they would be on their way back to Stirling.

The old woman was now sat on the sofa watching her visitor enjoying her food. It was nice to have a wee bit of company for a change. Of course, her son and daughter-in-law were usually around, but they were always so busy looking after the farm, and catching up with the domestic chores.

The girl reminded her of Karen, her first love. She had been tall, slender and blonde too. Back then it was not acceptable to either one's family or Society in general to be a lesbian, so their affair had been conducted with the utmost discretion. They had both been rather naive. Karen had ended up falling in love with some chap from the neighbouring village, leaving her friend heartbroken. Eventually they had both married local men, but the old woman, as she was now, never forgot the delights of sapphic love.

She took female lovers regularly throughout her married life. Her husband had never suspected. He had been the most traditional of men. A blacksmith by trade, he had been content enough to come home to a steaming plate of food on the table, and have all his needs attended to around the house. He had hardly noticed that his wife lay there impassively during their weekly bouts of lovemaking.

Jimmy kept to his word. By seven o'clock, dressed in warm but rather baggy clothes Veronica was sat in the passenger seat of his Rover with the heating system full on. The detective soon realised that asking his mistress further questions about her ordeal was pretty pointless. She had described her assailant to him, but she could not remember much about the events of the previous night. He carefully placed the soiled sheet in a plastic evidence bag. Despite its condition he suspected that there would be at least incriminating fingerprints on it. Within half an hour Veronica was sound asleep.

After an hour Jimmy turned off the A9 and parked the car in the entrance of a farmer's field. He imagined Veronica had escaped from her confines in a similar place. It was no good, he just could not concentrate on his driving. Even from Veronica's vague recollections, he suspected that this *Kathy* person had killed before.

She had told him that the woman had seemed rather nervous when they had arrived at the hotel, and that she had left her alone for twenty minutes or so on the pretence of needing a cigarette, even though the room had boasted a balcony where she could have acquired her nicotine fix. Veronica had related that on her return her lover had had a *wild look* in her eyes, but that she had dismissed it as an indication of her sexual arousal.

I do inspire lustful thoughts in people, both men and women, Veronica had said to him, placing a hand flirtatiously over his crotch. His penis had jumped at her touch.

I know, he had replied, *but there will be plenty of time for that later. Let's just get you back home to your parents.*

They had chatted for a few more minutes, Veronica describing the moment when she had felt her neck being squeezed, then she had smiled dreamily at him and fallen asleep, but not before reciting the car's registration number. Amazingly, she had memorised it after rolling out of the boot.

Good girl, Jimmy had remarked, we *'ll make a copper out of you yet!*

Looking out over the fields with his penis in his hand, the golden urine splattering onto the grass Jimmy, using all the skills which he had acquired over the years, tried to arrange the facts into some semblance of order. He still could not quite believe that Veronica had had the forethought to commit to memory the details of the vehicle's plate. All that studying for her Highers must have honed her encoding and retrieval skills to perfection. He supposed remembering a short sequence of figures and letters was nothing compared to absorbing all those works of literature, but still he felt very proud of the young lassie. It would prove to be a vital clue in tracking Kathy down. The DVLA were always most happy to co-operative with the police.

As to what actually had happened last night after Veronica had lost consciousness, a rookie detective could have figured out. There were marks on her neck, indicative of an attempted strangulation, and she had awoken to find herself wrapped in a sheet like a body prepared for the morgue. Despite the case being well out of his usual patch Jimmy was determined to deal with this investigation himself, discreetly if necessary. He tucked himself away and clambered back into the car. Veronica stirred. *It's all right, love. We're nearly home*, he said, leaning over to kiss her forehead.

****

"Sorry to disturb you, madam," Jimmy flashed his identification card at the buxom brunette in her early forties who opened the door of the isolated cottage in Laggan, "but are you Kathy Williamson?"

The woman blinked at him as if she had just woken up from a deep sleep. *Bloody hell, the police*, she thought. *I can hardly make a run for it, can I, so just play it cool*, she told herself. *Just deny who you are*, another voice was telling her in her head.

"No, that's not me. I don't know of anyone who goes by that name either."

The detective sighed. This was not going to be as easy as he thought. The woman's features matched Veronica's description of her down to the smallest of details. The photographs held on her police file proved that this was without doubt Kathy Williamson. *No, this is the one, all right!*

Just forty-eight hours ago he had safely deposited Veronica with her adopted mother in Stirling, and true to his word he had located the house of the car owner. There was no way that he could have faced going home to his wife, his mind was too restless for that, so he had slept in his car for two nights outside of the station, and eaten his breakfast and supper in the police canteen.

In the privacy of his office he had found out a lot of information about Mrs Williamson. She had been charged with criminal damage several years ago over some neighbourly dispute. Apparently, she had had an argument with the chap who stayed next door to her. Cursing at him out in their adjoining gardens, in frustration she had shoved the fence which divided the two properties. The wood had splintered on one of the posts. According to the deeds, the structure belonged to the neighbour and he had reported her to the police. On appearing in the Justice of the Peace court, Kathy had pleaded *not guilty*. On hearing all the evidence the stipendiary magistrate had favoured the prosecution. Kathy had received a thousand pound fine, and was ordered to pay the legal costs. On being arrested her fingerprints and mouth swabs had been taken.

Much to Jimmy's relief and delight the forensic laboratory had informed him that the sheet although devoid of prints, perhaps the suspect had worn gloves, had contained within its folds traces of vaginal secretions from two sources. One of these proved to be an exact match for Mrs Williamson's DNA records. *Bingo!* Jimmy had thought.

Before depositing Veronica at home he had taken her to the station in Edinburgh where she had made a statement. That along with the marks on her neck which he had photographed himself in the privacy of the interview room was sufficient evidence to charge the woman with attempted murder, but Jimmy was all too aware that his personal involvement with the victim would cast a shadow over the whole case. He made a decision to make further covert investigations. After all he still suspected Veronica's lover had attacked women before, didn't he?

****

"I'm sorry, love but I don't believe you. Do you mind if I come in?"

Before the woman had a chance to answer Jimmy pushed her aside and found himself in the kitchen of the cottage. The detective picked up the envelopes of unopened mail on the table. *"Mrs K. Williamson,"* he read out loud in an arrogant tone. "Do you mind if I take a look around?"

"Excuse me, you've no right to barge in here without a warrant," Kathy stated forcefully.

"So sorry!" Jimmy retorted sarcastically. Ignoring the woman, he started turning out her kitchen drawers.

Kathy felt the energy drain from her. This was it, there was no way that she could remove the mementos before the detective found them.

"So, what do we have here?"

Jimmy knelt down on the stone floor, making sure he faced the woman and examined the orthopaedic screws and plate. "If I'm not mistaken a similar one to these was posted to the police station in Aberdeen. Ever heard of a lady called *Angela James*, have we?"

The woman just stared at him.

Jimmy stood up. "Kathy Williamson, I am arresting you for the murder of Angela James, and the attempted murder of Veronica Montgomery. You do not have to say anything, but it may harm your defence, if you fail to mention when questioned, something which you may later rely on in court. Anything you do say, may be given in evidence. Do you understand?"

A voice inside Kathy's head whispered to her, *Tell him about the three prossies. Clear your conscience. You may as well swing for them all!*

"I understand," she said to the detective, "but I want to confess to three other murders as well."

****

Veronica leaned against the detective as they were stood by the window overlooking Green Park.

"Yes, I'm okay," she reassured him. "I was just thinking about how we got to this point. I shall be glad when tomorrow is out of the way. I can't wait to get home and pick up my life again."

Jimmy smiled at her. "I trust that *life* has room for me in it. I don't think your family quite know what to make of me."

Veronica hugged the detective. "Of course there is, you silly sausage but you're married, Jimmy. We can never be together properly. Let's just make the most of our time together here in London, away from prying eyes."

The detective who was to be promoted to an Inspector on his return to work could not really argue with that. He knew that he could never leave his wife, however much he wanted to.

"Do we have time for a quick fumble now? All those moans and groans from the master bedroom are turning me on something chronic!" he asked mischievously.

Veronica laughed. She had waited patiently for Terry to make an appearance last Christmas, but all she had received was excuses by e-mail. The man now stood in front of her might in theory be unavailable but he loved her, and most importantly he was physically in her life, not on the other side of a computer screen. She doubted whether she would ever love him but one thing was certain, she was definitely staying away from *women* for awhile.

" Uncle Grant expects us to meet him downstairs in half an hour and we haven't even unpacked yet, but hey, why not!"

Forty-five minutes later Grant knocked on the door of the suite. Clare opened the door, panting slightly. Jimmy appeared out of the guest bedroom in a similarly disheveled state.

"Bloody hell, it's like a brothel in here." He raised his voice. "Will the four of you please get yourselves dressed into something fitting for the establishment at which we are currently staying, and come down to the Palm Court restaurant immediately. Afternoon tea is being served, but it won't be if you don't get a move on!"

"Yes, Grant!" they all chimed in perfect unison.

****

The crowd roared as the open-topped horse drawn carriage swept into the courtyard of Buckingham Palace. More befitting to the eighteenth century than the twenty-first, the accused was helped down from her seat. She turned her back to them, and stared at the monarch resplendent in his maroon tunic sat up on his dais, with Prince Stephen by his side.

Grant's mobile buzzed, indicating a text had come in. His sister frowned at him. "Sorry," he mouthed at her.

Hello, Sexy, it said, *I'm watching you! There's no forgetting those frolics in the stables. Maybe one day we might make a repeat performance!*

The surgeon lifted his binoculars to his eyes in the pretence of watching Veronica's assailant mount the gallows. Instead his gaze focused on the King's consort. Grant reddened. This was the first time that he had heard a word from the prince since their liaison at Holyrood. He suddenly gripped his husband's hand who was sat next to him and whispered, "I love you" in his ear. If Fate had dealt him a different hand it would be him up on that platform having the noose secured firmly around his neck. Nowadays treason was awarded the same punishment as murder.

Maggie put her arm around her daughter's shoulders. Veronica had recently related to her what had happened in Aberdeen that fateful weekend after Jimmy had dropped her off. The two of them had had a good cry together, and more tears had flowed as Maggie had learnt what had occurred in Tomintoul.

Two months later Jimmy had paid them an unexpected visit. *This is an official one*, he had said, winking at

Veronica. Caroline had been there too, and he had related to them his full findings.

Apparently, the son of the man who had ordered the execution of Veronica's birth mother had been responsible for the three recent deaths under similar circumstances, despite the verdict of the jury at his trial. Veronica had overseen the father's demise in his apartment in Glasgow. Kathy Williamson whose execution they were now witnessing had not only tried to kill Veronica, but had actually taken the life of the legal clerk in Aberdeen, and been the one in the pornography films in which the three women had met their grisly ends. *She had actually strangulated her co-workers!* Jimmy had calmly informed them that the making of so-called *snuff movies* was now big business.

Caroline had arranged an impromptu dinner party and Maggie had done her best, ably assisted by her daughter to explain to her best friend and his husband all that the detective had told them. Clare, Grant's sister and her wife had been there too. Over the post-prandial coffee the eight of them had agreed to make the trip down to London to see Mrs Williamson receive her just reward.

****

"It's all over now," Maggie whispered to her daughter as the trapdoor opened, and Kathy's body dropped through the aperture. After what seemed like hours, but was only a minute or two the executioner placed his fingers on her neck, feeling for the carotid pulse. His nod to first the King, and then to the crowd indicated that she was dead. A huge cheer went up from the people.

Veronica felt a cool breeze on her face. She thought back to what she had discovered on reading her late mother's diaries only the week before. She now knew who her father was. She felt even closer to Maggie than usual.

Her mobile sounded as if reading her thoughts, but it was not her aunt. Terry's words filled her with as much excitement, and a sense of foreboding as to when she had learnt the true identity of her father.

"Let's get back to the hotel," she suggested to her family. "I have some news which I must share with you all.

"Just for a second the image of the old photograph which Maggie kept in her bedside drawer at home appeared in front of Veronica's eyes. She shivered. Their second night in London would change each one of their lives forever.